Praise for the novels of

JASON PINTER

"gripping" James Patterson

"excellent" Lee Child

"stunning" Jeffery Deaver

"first-rate" Tess Gerritsen

"brilliantly executed" Jeff Abbott

"remarkable" Steve Berry

"fast and furious" Simon Kernick

"top-notch" Michael Palmer

"cracking" *Daily Mirror*

"chilling" *Sunday Tribune*

"twisting" *New Mystery Reader Magazine*

"explosive" *Shots*

*Also available by **Jason Pinter***

THE MARK
THE GUILTY

Coming in 2010
THE FURY

THE
STOLEN

JASON
PINTER

Published in Great Britain 2009.
MIRA Books, Eton House, 18-24 Paradise Road,
Richmond, Surrey, TW9 1SR

© Jason Pinter 2008

ISBN 978 0 7783 0301 5

58-0709

Printed and bound in Spain
by Litografia Rosés S.A., Barcelona

To my sister,
who taught me the meaning of friendship.

To my father,
who taught me the meaning of generosity.

To my mother,
who taught me the meaning of strength.

ACKNOWLEDGEMENTS

The first thanks go to my beautiful wife, Susan, who more so than on any of my previous books humbled me with her patience and understanding. After many coffee-fuelled late-nighters and supportive pep talks, this book is as much yours as it is mine.

Joe Veltre, who has proved time and time again that the best business relationships are also great friendships. Thank you for both. Thanks also to Diane Bartoli and Sara Wolski, who are always gracious with their time.

Adam Wilson. Thanks for always being there in a pinch, and answering even the silliest questions faster than humanly possible. I'll stump you soon, I promise…

Donna Hayes, Dianne Moggy, Margaret O'Neill Marbury, Heather Foy, Maureen Stead, Ana Luxton, Jayne Hoogenberk, Ken Foy, Michelle Renaud, Don Lucey, Andi Richman, Katherine Orr, Craig Swinwood, Loriana Sacilotto and Stacy Widdrington. The best is yet to come. Thank you, thank you, thank you all.

I also owe a debt to George Witte, Sally Richardson, Andy Martin, Kylah McNeill, Keith Kahla and Kelley Ragland. I'm sorry our time together was cut short, but every day was a real treat. I'm lucky to have spent so much time working with people who know how to publish the right way.

Susan Schwartzman. After knowing you for just two weeks, I was in awe. By the time this book comes out, I can only imagine what you'll have accomplished.

Bonnie and Joe, Maggie Griffin and Terry Lucas. I still have a lot to learn about this crazy thing called writing, but when you've had friends like these, everything seems possible.

Linda McFall. Three down, and hopefully many, many more to go. If I feel spoiled, it's your fault for being such a terrific editor. Thanks also for your help on understanding the (often frightening) mind of the American toddler. Thank you again, ad infinitum.

To the booksellers and librarians who have made it possible for people to read my stuff.

To everyone who's read one of my books, thanks for giving me the greatest job in the world. You keeping reading 'em, I'll keep writing 'em.

And to reporters around the world who risk so much to write about good, evil and everything in between, Henry Parker offers a sincere thank-you. He wouldn't be here without your inspiration.

Dear Reader,

It is said that the most painful experience a parent can endure is losing a child. The pain and anguish must be simply incalculable. But what happens when a child presumed gone forever returns suddenly with no explanation, no injuries and no recollection of where they've been?

In *The Stolen*, Henry Parker must face perhaps the most difficult, and most personal, story of his young career. Because when he investigates the sudden reappearance of ten-year-old Daniel Linwood, Henry soon realises that despite the jubilation of Daniel's parents, something far more sinister is beginning to take shape. And as Henry fights to uncover the truth, caught in the balance are a family, a community and several people who will stop at nothing to make sure those questions stay unanswered, and that Henry is silenced – permanently.

I hope as you read *The Stolen*, you might ask yourself the same question that drives Henry to find the truth: how far would you go to protect your loved ones?

Enjoy *The Stolen*...

Jason Pinter

Prologue

"Finished."

I saved the document and eased back in my chair. My body had grown accustomed to long days and nights spent in its discomfort. The last few months, I had arrived home nearly every night with a sore tailbone or stiff back, wondering if the supplies department would turn a blind eye and let me expense a newer model. Eventually I forgot about it. Then one day, I noticed I hadn't thought about the aches and pains in a long time. They were a part of me now.

The past three days and nights had sped by in a blur of keystrokes, Chinese food containers and discarded coffee cups. I was on the kind of crash deadline that a year ago would have had me sweating rivulets, but now barely raised my pulse. The fact was, without those deadlines to keep me focused, the pains might not have ebbed away.

Saving the file, I looked outside my window over Rockefeller Plaza. The view had changed—bright morning into gauzy summer afternoon, fading into the kind of New York night where the constant bright lights disguised any sense of time.

Until recently, the night always heralded the end of my

workday. I would file my story with Evelyn Waterstone, the *Gazette*'s Metro editor, pack up my things, throw some goodbyes to my night-shift colleagues and one or two guys at the sports desk who were putting together the box scores, and head home to meet Amanda. Good conversation, a hot shower, maybe a movie or a show we'd recorded, they'd all be waiting. Then I'd fall asleep with a whisper of her hair across my face.

Amanda.

We met two years ago. Our introduction wasn't exactly the setup for your average romantic comedy. Our paths crossed while I was on the run after being falsely accused of murder. I had nobody to turn to. Nowhere to go. And just when the situation was at its bleakest, Amanda offered a hand to me, a total stranger. She saved my life. She was running from her own demons, having come from a broken home, spending her childhood recapping her life in small notebooks because she assumed everyone she met would eventually abandon her. It was this that brought us together. We were both damaged, broken, but together we were whole. She was everything I wanted in a partner. Strong, brilliant, beautiful. And she laughed at my jokes that made everyone else cringe. I repaid her by offering all the love I had to give. Had I offered merely love, it would have been more than enough. It's the other baggage I brought along that was too heavy for our relationship to bear.

Six months ago, a killer began terrorizing the city by publicly executing those he felt deserved his wrath. I was able to weave together the strands of his mysterious past and learned the horrific truth about his ancestry. During my search, the killer turned his sights not just toward me, but to those I loved.

He brutally attacked my ex, Mya Loverne, and left her fighting for her life. He broke into Amanda's office at the New York Legal Aid Society and nearly killed her. It was then, in the aftermath of those acts of violence, that I realized what I had to do. To protect those I loved, I had to turn away. I had to shield them from myself.

There was nothing more I would have wanted than to spend the rest of my life with her, playing shuffleboard and eating dinner at noon, doing whatever old couples did. It should have been easy. I mean, everyone complains about how hard it is to find someone in New York City. Once you find the right person, you hold on to them for dear life. Unfortunately I had to do the opposite.

Amanda nearly lost her life because of me, because of my work. And because being a reporter was in my blood, I shuddered to think that it was only a matter of time before those odds caught up. So I left her. In the middle of the street. And every day since I've had ample time to think about my decision.

We have not spoken in six months. My apartment, once warm with her presence, was now cold and uninviting. The stove, where we used to burn our attempts at lasagna, hadn't seen a pan in weeks. The place reeked of carelessness, abandoned by a man who felt like a stranger in his own home.

Work had always been my passion. Now it was my whole life.

Underneath my desk was a small duffel bag in which I kept a clean shirt, slacks and a pair of loafers. Every other day I would venture back to that unfamiliar home, unload the dirty laundry and pack up a clean change of clothes. Every other week the accumulation of soiled attire would be sent to the cleaners, and the cycle would start again. I would change in the men's room, always drawing a few *weren't you just wearing that?* looks from my colleagues.

I heard a noise behind me, turned to see Evelyn Waterstone striding up to my desk. Evelyn had barely given me the time of day when I first started working at the *Gazette,* but she'd warmed considerably over the past few months. Evelyn was in her late fifties, a solid tree stump of a woman who commanded attention, respect, and made everyone leap to the side when she walked by. Like many of the newspaper's top talent, Evelyn was unmarried and childless. She was also one of the best editors in the business. Somehow I'd grudgingly gained her respect. I figured as long as I kept my head down and did what I did best, it would stay that way.

"Got your story, Parker," she said, barely slowing down as she approached, then stopping abruptly before she knocked my desk over. "I swear you must have replaced your brain this year or taken basic grammar and spelling lessons. I haven't had to smack my head in frustration at your copy in almost a month. You keep it up like this, I might actually be able to cut back on the migraine medication."

"They say reading is the cure for all ills," I said.

Evelyn eyed me skeptically. "Who said that?"

"You know…they."

"Tell 'they' that they can shove their quotations up my keester. Anyway, keep up the not-so-terrible work. You're giving me more time to spend with crustaceans whose brains haven't fully grasped the '*i* before *e*' concept." Evelyn shot a glance toward Frank Rourke, the city's top sports columnist, to whom *grammar* was a term of endearment for his mother's mother.

Then Evelyn leaned forward. Sniffed. Scrunched up her nose.

"My God, Parker, you stink worse than O'Donnell the morning after St. Patrick's Day. Your pieces might be clean, but you reek like my nephew's diaper. Go home and shower, seriously, otherwise I'll tell Wallace he has a rodent infestation in the vicinity of your desk."

"I'm not that bad, am I?" I raised an arm, took a whiff, and immediately nodded in agreement. "I'm on my way."

When Evelyn left, I took the duffel out from beneath my desk, opened it. Sniffed. Closed it right up. Maybe it was best to just burn this load.

I grabbed the bag, left the office, took a cab to my apartment. I blew in the door, took a three-minute shower, and seven minutes after that I was wearing a fresh outfit with a spare packed away. Another cab brought me back to Rockefeller, where I strode into the office with a sense of pride that I knew was well undeserved. I waved to the night security team. They were too busy watching a ball game to wave back.

The newsroom was nearly empty. A quiet newsroom felt like an unnatural beast, but I'd grown used to it.

I opened my drawer, pulled out a down pillow I'd bought myself as a present. I took a fresh pillow cover from the bag, pulled it on. Buried somewhere in those drawers, beneath a mountain of papers, was a photo of Amanda. I'd taken it at a concert at Jones Beach last summer. It was raining. I was concerned the camera would be ruined. Amanda told me not to worry, that if special moments weren't worth some sort of risk, how special could they be?

Without saying another word I snapped the photo. She was right. The moment was worth far more than the risk.

Her brown hair was plastered to her cheeks, her neck. Her tank top clinging to her rain-slick body like silk. Her eyes were closed, the music pouring through her. That was my favorite photo of Amanda. It used to sit on my desk. Now I couldn't even look at it, because it only made me think of the night I ended the best thing in my life.

Then I did what I'd been doing every night for the past four months. I placed the pillow on my desk, put my head down, and slept.

1

"James, get your behind down here and finish your greens!"

Shelly's voice boomed through the house, and even though it took eight-year-old James Linwood only thirty seconds to turn off his Xbox 360 and race down the stairs, his younger sister, Tasha, was already sitting at the table, eyeing him while munching loudly on a celery stalk. When James sat down, Tasha, six years old but already a grandmaster at winning the game of sibling rivalry, stuck a green, mush-filled tongue out at her brother, who was more than happy to return the favor.

"That's enough, both of you. James, baby, I never excused you from the table. You have to *ask* to be excused." James looked at his mother and gave an exaggerated sigh, then picked up a single piece of lettuce. He took a bite, grimacing as if it had been marinating in oyster juice. "I don't know what you're looking at me for," Shelly said. "Some people actually think vegetables taste good."

Tasha nodded along with her mother, opened wide and shoved a whole stalk of celery in her mouth.

"Those people are stupid," James said, nibbling at the lettuce.

"No, if you knew what kind of vitamins and minerals veggies had, you'd know those people are quite smart," Shelly said. "Did you know LeBron James eats a double helping of carrots before every game?"

"Does not," James replied.

"Does too," said Shelly.

"Does too," said Tasha.

James gave his sister a cold glare. He tore off a piece of lettuce and chewed it with vigor, letting several shreds of green gristle fall onto the table.

Shelly watched her children eat, their eyes more concerned with her approval than their nutrition. The soft jingle of a wind chime could be heard from the back porch, as well as the noise of a television set blaring from the house next door. Mrs. Niederman's hearing had begun to go last year, and now she watched Alex Trebek at a volume that could be heard from space.

Shelly took a moment to gaze around her house. Just a few years ago, the back porch was riddled with termites, the wood rotted, the whole structure ready to collapse. She never would have let Tasha and James play on it. Randy was never very good with tools, and they simply didn't have the money to rebuild it. Not yet.

After their terrible ordeal, when their family had been fractured, the Good Samaritans of Hobbs County had reached out to help the Linwoods. Now barely a day passed where James and Tasha weren't outside shooting off water guns, dangling from the railing like a pair of spider monkeys. At least the porch had been rebuilt.

While the kids were at school, while Randy was away at work, Shelly would often find herself looking at the old photos of their house, taken when they'd first moved in years ago. She barely recognized what it had become.

The white paint was fresh, blue trim even, the mailbox upright. Nobody egged their house on Halloween, and she never had to call the police to report the teenagers who used to drive by once a week and knock the mailbox sideways with wielded baseball bats. Those kinds of things never happened anymore. There were more cops; she could feel their presence. They stopped by every so often, just to see how she and Randy were holding up. *I'm fine,* Shelly would say. *We're fine.*

The cops always turned down a cup of coffee. As though being any closer to the sorrow might somehow infect them.

James was grimacing through his last scraps of food when Shelly heard the doorbell.

"That's got to be Daddy," Shelly said. "He probably forgot his keys again this morning. James, would you let your father in?" James didn't move. "Did you hear me?"

"I'm cleaning my plate like you told me. I can't answer the door and eat at the same time." He smiled at this catch-22. Shelly sighed, though silently proud of her son's intelligence.

"Fine, you can stop eating if you let your father in. But if I hear that video game start up before you finish your social studies homework, you won't watch television until you graduate college."

James sprung up like he'd been shot from a cannon, then bolted from his chair.

Shelly smiled at her daughter. Tasha. Her beautiful, young daughter, who would grow up to be strong and vivacious like her mother had never been. Shelly felt an ache in her stomach and placed her palm on Tasha's cheek. Tasha smiled at her, that big goofy grin full of baby teeth.

"Mom?" James's voice bellowed from the hallway. "There's a kid here. Do you know anyone named Daniel?"

A napkin fell from Shelly's hand and fluttered to the floor.

"Wha…what did you say, baby?"

"Daniel. There's some kid at the door says he knows you. Wait, huh? Uh, Mom? He says…he says you're his mom."

Shelly leapt from her seat. She dashed through the house, nearly knocking over the coffee table, and sprinted into the front hallway.

The wooden frame was open to reveal the screen door. A boy was standing behind the screen, looking confused as to why he hadn't been allowed in yet. Shelly covered her mouth to prevent a scream from escaping her lips.

On the other side of the door stood a boy Shelly both knew and didn't know. He was about five foot three with a lock of dark hair that fell over his hazel eyes. His father's eyes. His limbs were gangly, full of sharp angles, as if he'd grown a great deal in a short amount of time and the flesh hadn't caught up to his bones. Everything and nothing was just like she remembered.

"Baby, oh my God…"

She gently pushed James away from the door and tore open the screen. The boy stood on the front porch with a look of slight bewilderment, a twinkle of recognition, a blurry memory slowly coming into focus. He didn't move. Instead, the boy's eyes met Shelly's as though waiting for something, and before another second passed Shelly Linwood gathered the boy up into her arms and squeezed him like there was no tomorrow, until his arms tentatively wrapped themselves around her body and held on. She remembered how he'd felt in her arms, and though heavier, he was the same child she'd held in her arms for the first six years of his life. She showered the boy's head with kisses until he pulled away slightly, an embarrassed grin on his young face.

"Oh my God," she whispered. "Oh my God, oh my God, oh my God. Baby, is it really you?" The boy shrugged, then was muffled as Shelly attempted to squeeze the life out of him again.

Shelly heard a car pull up. When the engine cut off, she looked up to see Randy's silver V70 Volvo in the driveway. The door opened, and her husband climbed out with a groan. Randy was forty-one, just ten pounds heavier than when they'd met in high school. His jawline was still visible above a slight jowl, his arms still maintaining some of the tone from his linebacker days at Hobbs High. Shelly loved to run her hands down his arms when he lay on top of her, the definition of his triceps making her shiver. It had been a year since she last felt that, but now she needed to feel him closer more than ever.

Her family.

Randy stretched his back, ran his fingers through his thinning hair, then reached back inside to grab his briefcase.

"Honey," he said, noticing the commotion on the front porch. "Please tell me there's a Michelob left in the fridge, I—"

"It's Daniel," Shelly blurted. "He's back."

Randy looked up, confused. Then when everything came into focus, his briefcase fell to the ground. He stared for a moment, shaking his head, then ran up the steps to join his wife. He placed his palm over the boy's forehead, pulled his hair back, gazing into the young, confused eyes. Then he joined his wife in the embrace.

"You people are weird," James muttered. "I don't get it. Who is he?"

"This," Randy said, turning the boy to face him, tears streaming down his face, "is your brother. His name is Daniel. Do you remember him?"

James had been just three when it all happened. Shelly didn't take it personally when Daniel looked at his sibling, bewilderment reigning over his face, a slight twinkle of memory.

"My brother?" James said. "I thought he was, like, stolen or something."

"He was," Shelly said, stroking Daniel's hair. "But thank you, *God,* somehow our boy has found his way home."

James looked at Daniel. There were no bruises on his body; no cuts or scrapes. His clothes looked new enough to still have the tags on them. Though he was so young, Shelly wondered if James remembered all those people rushing in and out of their house. Men and women with badges, other loud people with cameras and microphones. Once on an Easter egg hunt, Shelly had entered the bedroom to find James and Tasha rifling through a trunk stuffed full of newspaper clippings about Daniel's disappearance. James had asked Shelly about Daniel once, and she answered with a single tear, a trembling lip. He never asked again.

To Shelly, this was God's will. It was fate that her family be reunited.

To James Linwood, though, he couldn't understand how his brother, who'd disappeared nearly five years ago without a trace, could simply reappear like magic without a scratch on him.

2

The bar was sweltering hot, but the swirling fans made it more palatable than the thick sweater choking the New York streets. It didn't take long to learn that Augusts in New York could be brutal. My first summer in the city, I made the mistake one day of wearing a T-shirt and sweater to the office. Jack told me between my clothes and the *Gazette*'s sporadic air-conditioning, I'd lose ten pounds before the day was up. While I doubted the New York summer could get any hotter than my childhood years in Bend, Oregon, when later that night I peeled off my sweater and squeezed out the moisture, I realized East Coast summers were just as brutal as their West Coast counterparts.

I took another sip of my beer—my third of the night, and third in slightly under an hour—and casually glanced up at the baseball game. Out of the dozen or so patrons, only two or three seemed to care about the outcome. The others were nursing a drink, chatting up the bartender or, like the six people my age playing darts, far too busy reveling in their own bliss.

I'd gotten to know the bartender, Seamus. Things like that happen when you become a regular. Some nights I had trouble sleeping. This necessitated finding somewhere to go to kill time. Somewhere I could be lost in my own thoughts. That's how I stumbled upon Finnerty's. Quiet enough to lose yourself. Loud enough to drown everything out.

Most nights I was happy to imbibe among young Irish gents and apple-cheeked female bartenders. U2 and Morrissey seemed to emanate from the jukebox on an endless loop. Though I enjoyed the Irish pub, sitting in Finnerty's made me feel that much closer to the elder drinkers, sitting with bottomless glasses of whiskey, talking to the bartender because he was cheaper than a psychiatrist. All of this, by proxy, made me feel more and more like I was becoming Jack O'Donnell. In many ways being compared to Jack would be a compliment. Just not this one.

Jack O'Donnell, to put it bluntly, was my idol. He'd worked the city beat for going on forty years, and any conversation about New York journalism was incomplete without mention of the old man. Growing up, I'd gone out of my way to read every story O'Donnell wrote, not an easy task for a kid who lived three thousand miles away from New York. I had our library special-order the *Gazette* on microfiche. I would take on an extra newspaper route just so I could afford the next O'Donnell book in hardcover when it hit stores. I couldn't, or wouldn't, wait for the paperback.

A few years ago I'd arrived at the *New York Gazette* a fresh-faced newbie reporter who deigned only to shine O'Donnell's shoes. He was a journalistic institution, writing some of the most important stories of the past half century. Despite his age, Jack seemed to grow younger with every word he typed. Even though Jack's first assignment for me led to disaster—namely me being accused of murder—he was the first person at the newspaper to give me an honest shot at showing what I was worth. Both Jack and Wallace Langston, the *Gazette*'s editor-in-chief, had taken me under their wings, given me stories that I grabbed on to tenaciously and reported the hell out of. Without Jack I probably wouldn't have come to New York. Because of him I found my calling.

Like any idol, though, once you got closer you could see that some of the gold paint covered a chipped bronze interior. For all his brilliance with a pen, Jack's personal life was a disaster. Several times married and divorced. On the highway to alcoholism while seeming to hit every speed bump at sixty miles an hour. Yet, despite Jack's faults, he was the tent pole to which I aspired to in this business. As long as I could stop there.

Nights like tonight, I was content to sit on the aged bar stool and ignore everything. It was easier that way.

Then I felt a cold splash on my back, whipped around to see a tall, lithe redhead standing over my shoulder, her hand over her mouth as if she'd just seen a bad car accident.

"Oh, my gosh!" she said, grabbing a pile of napkins off the bar and mopping at my shirt where she'd spilled her drink. From the look and smell, I could tell she'd spilled a cosmopolitan. I'd say I was thankful it wasn't one of my good shirts, but the truth was I didn't own any good shirts. Just one more article of clothing with an unidentifiable stain.

"No big deal," I said, wringing as much liquid from the cloth as I could. "It's a bar. You kind of expect to be hit with a drink or two."

She smiled at me. I wondered if she thought I was funny, or if she was just relieved I wasn't the kind of asshole who would bark and shout at a girl who'd accidentally spilled a drink on him.

She was pretty. Tall, in good shape, but I could tell a lot of effort went into her appearance. Probably too much. Her jeans were tight, light blue tank top with a neckline that plunged far down enough to catch the eyes. Her cheeks and eyelids glistened with sweat on top of sweat-proof makeup. She was probably a natural beauty but simply didn't trust herself. I thought I noticed a small dark spot, a mole perhaps, by her right collarbone, but quickly realized it was a passing shadow. She was the prettiest girl I'd noticed in Finnerty's in a long while. Either that, or I just never bothered to notice.

"Here," she said, putting down the soiled napkins and reaching into her purse, "let me buy you a drink. Least I can do, right, since you're being such a gentleman? What kind of beer is that?"

I shook my head. "No need. It happens." I caught the ball game from the corner of my eye. The fans were on their feet. Looked like someone had hit a home run.

"Well, can I just buy you a drink to buy you a drink?"

I looked at her, a cautious smile. My beer was almost empty. And my wallet was running light.

"It's okay," I said after a moment. "Really, it's not necessary." She put her purse away, eyed me with a combination of skepticism and curiosity.

"Are you here with friends?" she asked.

"Nope. Just watching the game."

She glanced around the bar, watched the guys with gelled hair and long button-down shirts hanging over expensive jeans, high-fiving one another while a gaggle of girls cheered every dart throw.

"So you're just here to, what…hang out by yourself?"

"That's the idea," I said. Her smile turned demure. I felt her move closer. Her arm brushed mine, and for a moment

I felt that tingle of electricity. It had been so long. I didn't move my arm.

"That's kind of cool," she said. "Lot of guys try too hard to be all macho and stuff. It takes confidence to stay quiet."

I had to stop myself from laughing, considering I was afraid of my own apartment and came here precisely so I could avoid the braying of testosterone-drenched i-bankers.

"Trust me, it's not confidence," I said. "Just comfort."

"See, that's confident right there!" Then she extended her hand. "I'm Emily."

"Henry," I said. For a moment I waited, then shook her hand. Didn't want to be rude.

"I'm here with some old college friends who are in town for the weekend," Emily said, "but we're probably going to ditch this place soon and go somewhere else more, like, alive. I know you're happy to be by yourself—" she used finger quotation marks to accent this statement "—but it might be cool if you came with us."

Right then I could see the night laid out before me. Two paths. I could accept Emily's invitation, and presuming I played my cards right, that electric sensation of skin on skin would later become a wildfire.

Or I could sit here, sip my beer, stare at my reflection in the mirror and think about all the other paths I'd simply passed right by.

"I appreciate the offer, Emily," I said. "But I think I'll stay here for the night."

"You sure?" she said.

"Sure."

"Suit yourself." She grabbed a clean napkin from the bar, removed a tube of eyeliner from her purse and painstakingly drew something on the paper. When she was done, she smiled, handed me the napkin and walked away.

Her phone number was written in black, smudgy ink. Emily offered one last wave as she went through the door, pausing for a moment to give me one last chance to reconsider. I raised the rest of my beer to her. She shrugged and left. Then I let the napkin fall to the floor.

I downed the last of my beer. Seamus took a pair of empty pitchers down off the bar and came over to me.

"Another?" he said.

I looked at my glass, felt the buzz swirling in my head and decided against it.

"That's it for me tonight." He took my glass and went to serve a man shaking his glass for a refill. I stood up, steadying myself as the blood swam to my head. When my equilibrium settled, I left the bar.

I checked my phone. Four missed calls, beginning at 11:00 p.m. They were all from the same prefix, which I recognized as the *Gazette*. I checked my watch. Late job-related calls were no longer a nuisance; they were a part of my life. Perhaps that's why I turned down another beer. Somehow I had a feeling I'd have to return someone's call while relatively sober.

I walked down to the corner and bought a pack of Certs, slipping one in my mouth to try to remove the beer aftertaste. Then I dialed the *Gazette*. Wallace Langston, editor-in-chief, picked up his private line on the first ring.

"Henry, Christ, where the hell've you been?"

"It's a Friday night. You don't pay me enough to have a 24/7 retainer."

"Okay, you don't want to answer your phone, I have half a newsroom of reporters who'd drop their off days faster than a hot iron for what I'm about to tell you, so let me know if this is an inconvenient time."

"What if I said it was?"

"I'd say two things," Wallace said. "First, you're a liar. It sounds like you're standing on the street, which means you can't be that busy. Second, I'd say I don't give a crap because if you turn down this assignment, I can find another reporter who'll grab it faster than you can hang up."

"Sounds like a hot one," I said. "So maybe I'm interested."

"*Hot* isn't the word," Wallace said. "Scorching. Actually no, forget that. The only appropriate word is *exclusive*."

"Oh, yeah? What kind of exclusive?"

"You hear about this Daniel Linwood case up in Hobbs County?"

Immediately my buzz wore off. "Kid who was kidnapped five years ago and suddenly reappeared on his parents' doorstep, right?"

"So you follow the news. Glad to know we pay you for something. Daniel Linwood was five years old when he disappeared from his parents' home in Hobbs County, New York. That was five years ago. One moment he's playing outside, then all of a sudden he's just gone. No witnesses, nobody saw or heard anything. His disappearance shakes the Hobbs County community to its roots. There's a media frenzy, politicians come out of the woodwork to show their support, but the cops come up empty. Then last night, Daniel shows up at his parents' house like he's been at the movies. Not a scratch on him. And get this—the kid has as much memory of the past five years as I have of my first marriage. He doesn't remember where he's been, who took him or how he even got home. Half the known world is waging war to talk to Daniel and his parents and get the story, but up until now it's been radio silence."

"Until now?" I said.

"Until you," Wallace said. "I've been calling the Linwoods for twenty-four hours nonstop."

"I bet they appreciate that," I said snidely.

"Shut up, Parker, or I'll smack that booze right off your breath."

"You don't know I've been drinking," I said, regretfully slurring the last word.

"I've worked with Jack O'Donnell for more than twenty years. You can't fool a professional bullshit detector. Anyway, tonight I get a call from Shelly Linwood out of nowhere. She says she's ready to talk. And before I can say another word, she says she and Daniel will talk to you, and only you."

"Me?" I said. "Why?"

Wallace said, "Shelly knows she can't keep silent forever, that at some point she and Daniel will need to speak to the press. So she said when he does speak to someone, she wants it to be to a reporter he won't be intimidated by. Someone who doesn't remind him of his parents. She wants Daniel to talk to someone he can trust, whom she can look in the eye and know he won't exploit her son. Between all of that, I offered you. And she accepted."

"Holy crap, are you serious?" I said. "This is a major story, Wallace. We're going to make a lot of reporters pretty jealous."

"And I'm going to revel in it," Wallace said. "This is your story now, Parker. Daniel Linwood has probably been through a kind of hell you and I can't even imagine, and his parents have spent almost five years assuming their oldest son was dead. Be gentle. Daniel is ten years old, and we still don't know the full psychological damage he's suffered. If you press the wrong button, touch the wrong nerve, he and Shelly will clam up fast. And the *Dispatch* will be on top of this as fast as Paulina Cole can get up to Hobbs County."

"I'd die before Paulina scoops us," I said.

"Don't make it come to that, Henry. The Linwoods are expecting you tomorrow at two. Get there at noon, spend a few hours checking out the neighborhood for local color. But if Daniel wants to talk to you at one-forty-five, two-fifteen or three o'clock in the morning, you'll have your tape recorder ready to go."

"You got it."

"That means going home right now and sobering up."

"I'm on my way." This included a hot shower, a fresh set of clothes, suit and tie. I prayed these were all at the ready, otherwise an all-night Laundromat would soon be graced by my clothes' aromatic presence.

"Call me before you leave tomorrow," Wallace said. "And I mean that. *Call me.* I don't want to come into the office tomorrow and see you asleep and drooling on your keyboard. You have a home. Go there."

I said nothing. Telling Wallace that my apartment didn't feel like a home was neither his business nor concern. All he cared about, and rightfully so, was this story. I'd been granted leeway the past few years most young reporters never got. Many in my position would have been shown the door, either landing in the safety net of a small-town paper or spewing angry blogs about the dumbing-down of American media. I had no desire to do either, and preferred to help from the inside. Big-time news was in my blood. A while ago Jack O'Donnell had told me that to truly become a legend in your field, you had to lead a life with one purpose. You had to devote yourself to your calling.

Splitting your passions between that and other pursuits—hobbies, family—would only make each endeavor suffer. The past few months I'd whittled down my extracurriculars to nothing. All for stories like this.

"You'll hear from me first thing tomorrow morning," I said. "And, Wallace?"

"Yeah, kid?"

"Thanks for the opportunity."

"Don't thank me, thank Shelly Linwood. I'm not the only one counting on you to do the right thing."

The call ended. I stood there in the warm night, the sounds of the bar and the street fading away. This night held nothing else for me, but tomorrow presented a golden opportunity. So many circumstances surrounding Daniel Linwood's disappearance were a mystery, and because the boy himself couldn't remember, I wondered how much, if any of it, would ever come to light. I wondered if never getting that closure would bother the Linwood family. Or if they were just thankful to have their son back.

I put the phone in my pocket, went to the corner and hailed a cab back to my apartment. For a moment I wondered if, like Daniel Linwood, I was returning to a place both strangely familiar, yet terribly foreign at the same time.

3

The Lincoln Town Car pulled up at 10:00 a.m. on the dot, shiny and black and idling in front of my apartment as inconspicuous as a black rhinoceros. I'd heeded Wallace's advice and gone home, sleeping in my own bed for the first time in weeks. I stripped the sheets, used a few clean towels in their place, and got my winks under an old sleeping bag.

I woke up at eight-thirty, figured it'd be plenty of time, but it took forty-five minutes to clean the crud out of my coffee machine and brew a new pot, so by the time the driver buzzed my cell phone I was tucking my shirt in, making sure my suit jacket was devoid of any lint. Unfortunately I missed the open fly until we'd merged off the West Side Highway onto I-87 North. My driver was a Greek fellow named Stavros. Stavros was big, bald and had a pair of snake-eyed dice tattooed on the back of his neck that just peeked out over the headrest.

I sipped my Thermos of coffee, grimaced and double-checked my briefcase. Pens, paper, tape recorder, business cards, digital camera in case I had a chance to take some shots of the neighborhood surrounding the Linwood residence in Hobbs County. Perhaps we'd use them in the article, give the reader a sense of local color recorded words could not.

Hobbs County was located about thirty miles north of New York City, nestled in between Tarrytown and the snuggly, wealthy confines of Chappaqua. Just a few years ago Hobbs County was an ingrown toenail between the two other towns, but recently a tremendous influx of state funds and pricey renovations had things moving in the right direction. Good thing, too, because statistically, Hobbs County had crime rates that would have made Detroit and Baltimore shake their heads.

According to the FBI Report of Offenses Known to Law Enforcement, the year before Daniel Linwood disappeared, Tarrytown, with 11,466 residents, had zero reported murders, zero rapes, one case of arson (a seventeen-year-old girl setting fire to her ex-boyfriend's baseball card collection), zero kidnappings and ten car thefts. Each of these numbers were microscopic compared to the national average.

That same year, Hobbs County, with 10,372 residents, had sixteen reported murders, five rapes, nine cases of arson, twenty-two car thefts and two kidnappings. If Hobbs County had the population of New York City, it would be on pace for more than twelve thousand murders a year.

Hobbs County was literally killing itself.

One of those two reported kidnappings was Daniel Linwood. The other was a nine-year-old girl whose body was later found in a drainage ditch. Since then, those crime rates had dropped like a rock. This past year, Hobbs had four murders. One rape. Eleven car thefts. And no kidnappings. There was still a lot of work to be done, but something had lit a fire under Hobbs County. It was righting itself.

And then Daniel Linwood reappeared, hopefully speeding the cleansing process even more.

The rebuilding had naturally raised property values, and between the drop in crime and influx of new money, Hobbs County found itself awash with wealthy carpetbaggers interested in the refurbished schools, reseeded parks and investment opportunities. Five years ago you could have bought a three-bedroom house for less than two hundred and fifty thousand dollars. Today, if you scoured the real estate pages and found one for less than three quarters of a million, you'd be an idiot not to snap it up.

While there was no getting back Daniel Linwood's lost years, his family could at least be thankful he had come back to a town far safer than the one he'd left.

"Only been to Hobbs once," Stavros piped in from the front seat. "Few years ago. Pro football player going to visit his aunt just diagnosed with Hodgkins. She lived in the same house for thirty years, give or take. Guy told me he'd tried to buy her a new place, get her out of the life, but you know how old folks are. Rather die at the roots than reach for a vine. You know, even if the client's only booked for a one-way trip, I'll usually offer to hang around in case they decide they need a ride back to wherever. Hobbs, though, man, you could offer me double the rate and I would have jetted faster than one of them Kenyan marathon runners. Not the kind of place you want to be sitting in a car alone at night. Or anytime, really."

I eyed those dice tattoos. Wondered what it took to scare a man who wasn't afraid to get ink shot into his neck with a needle.

"I hear the town is different now," I said. "A lot's changed in five years."

"New coat of paint, same cracked wood underneath," Stavros said. "You don't start from the ground up, poison's still gonna be there. Anyway, you're booked for a return trip, right? I'm sure you'll be fine, long as you're finished before the sun goes down. The dealers and hoods come out thinking you're the po-lice."

"I really think you're wrong," I said, my voice trying to convince me more than Stavros. "Anyway, when we get there, I don't think you'll have to worry too much about being alone. If I know the press, they'll be camped out at this house like ants at a picnic."

"That so? Where exactly you headed?"

"Interview," I said. "A kid."

"Not that kid who got kidnapped. Daniel something, right?"

"Daniel Linwood, yeah."

"Hot damn, I've been reading about that! Awful stuff. I mean great he came back, but I got a six-year-old and I'd just about tear the earth apart if she ever went missing. Those poor parents. Can't even imagine."

"Better you don't."

We merged onto 287, then headed north on Route 9, driving past a wide white billboard announcing our entry into the town limits.

Hobbs County was covered in lush green foliage, the summer sun shining golden through the thick leaves. Trees bracketed sleepy homes, supported by elegant marble columns. I lowered the window and could hear running water from a nearby stream. This was New York, but not the big city you read about in newspapers. It was the kind of place where you bought homemade preserves and knew everybody's name. Over the past few years, though, the names got wealthier, the jams more expensive. Shelly

Linwood didn't work. I wondered how the Linwoods were able to afford the newfound royalty of Hobbs County. And whether Daniel had come back to any sort of recognizable life.

We wound our way to Eaglemont Terrace, threading down Main Street. All the stores were open, Hobbs residents walking small, freshly groomed dogs while carrying bags from the town's boutique shops. Lots of cell phones and BlackBerries. Pretty much the same ratio of technology to people as NYC.

It was just before noon. I had two hours before the interview was scheduled to begin. As we turned onto Woodthrush Court, I made out a row of cars and vans clogging the street, metal lodged in an artery. The main cluster looked to be centered around one house, no doubt the Linwood residence. I didn't want to make any sort of grand entrance, and once the other reporters saw me, they wouldn't leave me alone. They knew I had the exclusive, and they wouldn't make my job any easier.

"Do me a favor, stop here," I said to Stavros. The Greek man obliged, eased on the brakes until we were stopped a few blocks down from the mess.

"You want to hang out here? I can put the radio on, even got a few CDs in the glove. You like The Police?"

"Eh. Sting never really did it for me. Just want to walk around the neighborhood for a few minutes. Get a sense of the place."

"Your time," Stavros said. "Tell you something, it might have been a few years ago and my memory's as soft as my dick, but this sure ain't the same town I drove through a while back."

"Hold that thought," I said to Stavros, unbuckling my seat belt. "The last one, not the one about your...never mind. I have your cell number, so I'll just call when I'm ready to leave, right? You'll be here?"

"Faster 'n instant coffee."

"Glad to hear that, thanks."

I grabbed my briefcase, stepped out of the car. It was a sunny day, high seventies, a light breeze rattling leaves and lowering the humidity. I breathed in the fresh air, wished I could find it in the city outside of Central Park. It was strange to be in a town where you could see the horizon miles away. Unobstructed views over houses just a story or two tall.

While what I said to Stavros was partly true, about wanting to stay incognito to the press as long as possible, I also didn't want to give the wrong impression to the Linwoods themselves. I didn't want to roll up in a Lincoln with a driver, step out of the backseat like some dignitary. If I was going to talk to Daniel Linwood, it was going to be on his level. With all the attention he'd be facing over the coming weeks, his family didn't need to feel like they were being talked down to.

I walked to the opposite side of the street, slow enough to avoid arousing suspicion, fast enough that residents wouldn't think a solicitor was creeping around in their front yards.

When I was just a block away, still unnoticed, I stepped into the pathway between two clapboard houses and sat down on a stone bench. I gathered my notes, made sure the tape recorder had fresh batteries. And then I sat and watched the beehive.

The reporters camped outside the Linwood home were standing on the grass, their vans having left tire tracks in yards all across the street. No doubt the locals would complain to the city council about this, but with a story this big there was no stopping the boulder from rolling downhill.

Since the night Daniel came back, the only comment from the Linwood home had been "no comment." Today that would change.

I sketched brief descriptions of the homes, the climate, the scene in front of me. Enough to give Hobbs County some color. I snapped a few pictures of the houses, even took a few of the press corps just for kicks. Then I waited.

At one-forty I stood up, stretched and started to walk over. My heart was beating fast, and I wiped my palms on the inside of my jacket. One of the tricks of the trade Jack taught me. Most people wipe their hands on their pants, and that does nothing but make your source think they're being interviewed by a guy who can't jiggle out the last few drops of piss. Inside the jacket, nobody could see you were hiding the Hoover Dam in your armpits. Good thing Jack was a classy guy.

I was hoping to enter the Linwood residence as quickly as possible. I didn't want to answer any questions, or see my face on any newscasts. I'd had enough of that.

Silently I crept toward the house, when all of a sudden a gravelly voice said, "Look who crawled out of the sewer," and I knew I had a better chance of finding a winning lottery ticket in my hamper than staying incognito.

One by one the heads turned. Clean-shaven newsmen with three-hundred-dollar haircuts, women wearing makeup so thick it could have been a layer of skin. They all looked at me with sneers reserved for subjects they were used to interviewing in solitary confinement. A piece of gum snapped, then landed on my shoe. I flicked it off, kept walking without looking to see who was guilty. Never let them see you angry.

I nudged my way through the crowd without making eye contact with anyone. I recognized a male reporter from the *New York Dispatch,* somewhat surprised to see that Paulina Cole hadn't taken on the story herself. Paulina Cole was the *Dispatch*'s top columnist, a post she took after leaving the *Gazette.* We'd actually worked next to each other for several months, but now there was as much love between us as Hillary and Monica.

You'd never picture the devil as a five-foot-six woman with platinum-blond hair, impeccable skin tone and a take-no-prisoners, ball-busting attitude that could have made the toughest Viet Cong piss his pants. At first I admired Paulina. The newsroom had very much been an old boys' club during her climb, and she'd had to endure a lot and work fantastically hard to get where she was. But then she showed her true colors. She showed that one thing's for certain in the media: throwing someone under the bus can make quite a lucrative career.

After publicly criticizing me in print, Paulina later ran a story focusing on the sordid family affairs of my ex-girlfriend. It was this story that led to Mya being brutally attacked and nearly killed. I'd spent many hours at Mya's hospital bed, beside her at physical therapy, comforting her mother, who was widowed at the hands of the same killer who nearly took her daughter's life. Though Paulina had fewer friends than O. J. Simpson, her notoriety was entirely part of the game. Brazen, provocative, pushing every hot button as though her life depended on it. Rumor had it Ted Allen, the *Dispatch*'s editor-in-chief, gave her a five-figure expense account to dress the part, as well. If perception was reality, Paulina Cole was the grand bitch goddess of the news.

I heard audible whispers as I walked up to the Linwood

porch. *Punk. Asshole. Little shit.* I'd taken a beating both in the press and from other reporters since my first few months at the *Gazette,* and as much as the words stung, sadly, I'd grown used to them.

Screw them.

The Linwood house was a small, Victorian-style dwelling, with jigsaw trim and spindles. It was three stories high, the top floor with a small square window, most likely an attic rarely used. Two unadorned columns were mounted on the front porch, the marble clean. The paint job was an off-white, and looked recently refreshed. I could see a small swing set around the back, a shovel and pail sitting abandoned. Surprised a reporter hadn't snagged it yet. I stepped up to the porch and took a breath, preparing to ring the doorbell.

Just then the front door swung open, nearly knocking me on my ass, and a caravan of steely-postured suited men and women came pouring out. The first few were all hefty men wearing identical pants and blazers. They wore single wire earpieces, transparent tubing with Star ear-mold devices. They didn't wear sunglasses, but the bulges in their jacket pockets said they would be in a matter of seconds.

I stepped aside. The men paid me no attention, stopping at the bottom of the porch, hands clasped behind them. When I turned back to knock, I found myself in front of a tall, lean man in his early fifties. He had wavy gray hair, a sharp, equine nose and the slightest onset of crow's-feet. He wore a smart navy suit and a brilliant smile. I recognized him instantly but tried to hide my surprise. He was talking to somebody inside I couldn't see, but when he turned around, the look on his face confirmed that he recognized me, as well. I swallowed hard.

The man cocked his head, flashed that smile again and put his hand out.

"Henry Parker, right? *New York Gazette?*"

"Yes, yes, sir." I was flattered that he'd heard of me. Either that, or he knew why I was here.

"Pleasure to meet you, Henry. Gray Talbot."

"Pleasure to meet you, too, Senator."

Talbot smiled again. "Walk with me for a moment, won't you, Henry?" It was phrased like the kind of question you couldn't refuse.

I half nodded, then suddenly Talbot's arm was around me, leading me down the steps. His grip was just strong enough to let me know I didn't have a choice, light enough to let onlookers know this would be a friendly chat. Everything about the man spoke volumes of an effortless confidence, a confidence that had captured the hearts and minds of New Yorkers desperate for a politician who deep down wasn't *quite* a politician.

Gray Talbot was currently in his fourth term as a Democratic New York State senator. In his four elections, he'd averaged sixty-two percent of the vote, and it was assumed Talbot would hold that seat until he either retired, died or decided he preferred a larger, whiter house. Talbot was currently the third-highest-ranking Democrat in the senate, behind the senate majority leader and senate majority whip. As the current majority chairman on the United States Committee on Banking, Housing, and Urban Affairs, Talbot was one of the most outspoken proponents of lowering the federal interest rate. "A home for every American who wants one" was his slogan. He was often photographed with his trademark plaything, a Rubik's Cube, constantly fiddling and working out solutions. He was quoted as saying the game kept his mind limber. Every cube he'd ever completed was kept in his home. Rumor was he needed a bookcase to house them all.

In the previous election, three years after Daniel Linwood's disappearance, Gray Talbot had outdone himself, garnering an unheard of seventy-three percent of the popular vote. And now that man had his arm around me. Talbot wasn't visiting Daniel Linwood for a simple photoop. The stakes were much higher. Daniel's reappearance wasn't merely a human-interest story, it was important enough that one of the most powerful men in the country made it his business. Yet as we walked, there were no staged photo-ops. No handshakes. No teary hugs with Shelly Linwood. Gray Talbot, as far as I could tell, was here because he *wanted* to be.

And he was the kind of man who, if he felt like it, could squash reporters with his pinkie finger.

As Talbot led me across the lawn, I could hear groans of protest as his bodyguards held the throng of reporters back. When we were out of earshot, Talbot took his arm from my shoulder and said, "I'm glad Wallace chose you to report on Daniel. Shelly and Randy think they can trust you. I'm inclined to believe them."

"Then can trust me, sir, I promise that."

"Good." Talbot turned slightly as the angry catcalls grew louder. "Ignore the parasites," he said. "They're jealous, that's all. Any one of them would trade their press badge to be where you are and do what you've done in such a short amount of time."

I felt a tingle down my side where a bullet had shattered my rib and punctured my lung just a few years ago, and wondered if that was really true.

"You know I used to live in a place just like this," Talbot said, his eyes searching the tree line as though looking for a familiar sign. "Not like it is now, the way it was back when Daniel disappeared. The kind of town where you woke up every day assuming a crash position, trying just to hold on to a sliver of hope. My biggest dream growing up was to just get the hell out and make something of myself before the evil swallowed me whole. The strongest men and women aren't the ones born with everything, Henry, they're the ones who are born with nothing but fight like hell to get it. I know how hard you've fought. And I know you'll understand what this family has gone through. To lose a child? To assume your child is dead, that you've outlived your firstborn? I can't even imagine it. So be respectful. Daniel will never get back those years, and his parents will never fully repair that hole in their hearts. If their boy's story is given the respect and honesty it deserves, well, that might go a little way toward helping. I know you have a responsibility to your job. But your job is also to mend fences when you can. This is not a tabloid story. This is not a family to be exploited. So don't you dare treat them like one."

"I wouldn't dare," I said.

"I know that, Henry." Talbot stopped, turned around, made a brief gesture, and the bodyguards began walking over. A limousine pulled up, a chauffeur getting out to open the door for the senator. He shook my hand one last time, then said, "You're a fine young man and a terrific reporter. Hopefully Daniel Linwood will have the chance to grow up and find his calling just the same."

Then he got in and was gone.

I turned back to the house, tried to figure out what to make of the encounter. Gray Talbot was known to be a humanitarian, and his troubled background only solidified his resolve to help those in need. The Linwoods obviously fit that bill, and he was more than happy to put more weight on my story. To make sure I didn't color outside the lines. Not that I planned to, but there's a difference between moral obligation and having a politician flat-out tell you.

I walked back to the Linwoods' house. This time the other reporters were silent. I rang the doorbell, and barely a moment passed before it opened to reveal a woman wearing an apron. She had curly brown hair pulled back in a ponytail, a look of both joy and exhaustion in her face. The apron was covered with stains of various colors. She smiled. Her eyes were bloodshot and weary, but happy.

"Henry, right?"

"That's right. Mrs. Linwood?"

"Please, call me Shelly. Come in. Daniel will be so happy to meet you. From what Senator Talbot told me, you two actually have a lot in common."

4

Shelly led me through the foyer and into what looked like their family room. A thirty-eight-inch television sat on a wooden stand; toys and video-game cartridges were spread about haphazardly. The couches and chairs were all dark fabric and wood, the kind you buy when you expect stains to make regular appearances.

"I was going to clean up for the senator, but…you know…" Shelly said, slightly embarrassed at the mess.

"You want Daniel to get used to living in a normal home," I said.

"Best for him to get used to a real home again," Shelly said, nodding.

A man entered the room. He looked weary but happy. He was a slightly paunchy man with a receding hairline and deep bags under his eyes.

"You must be Henry," he said, offering his hand. "Randall Linwood."

"Mr. Linwood," I said. "Thanks so much for having me. I'm grateful for you letting me into your home."

"Thank you, Mr. Parker. With so many vultures circling us since Daniel's return, it's good to have someone we feel we can trust handling the story. Shelly and I have done our homework on you and your newspaper. I think we're all in good hands."

"You are, sir. I ask for nothing but the truth, and I give nothing but my word." Shelly smiled at this, flicked at her eye as though wiping away a nonexistent tear.

"Anyway, I have to get back to the office. I wanted to be here to meet the senator, but if I miss any more time, Daniel'll have to eat Spaghetti O's for the next few weeks. Pleasure to meet you, Henry."

"Likewise, sir."

When Randy Linwood left, I heard a brief scuffle come from another room. Looking through the doorway, I saw two pairs of eyes peering at me from between the slats on a staircase. Just as quickly as they appeared, the legs they were attached to ran back up the stairs, whispers following.

"James and Tasha," Shelly said, brushing a strand of hair from her face, the red still there. "They're not really sure how to deal with all of this. We're so happy, but all this…attention, it's not what they're used to. They deal with it in their own way."

"I can't imagine going through what you've been through. But I have to say, Mrs. Linwood, you're handling it well."

"I'd say thank you, but it's not on purpose."

"Have the police been helpful?"

"Oh, my, incredibly so. I actually thought it'd be much worse, but they've barely spent more than half an hour here since Danny came back. In fact, when the senator came, that's the first time I saw more than two of them at the same time." I found that strange, but allowed Shelly to continue. She paused for a moment, said softly, "We're just so glad to have Daniel back. It's like, a wave crashing over you when you're ready to burst into flame. I can't explain it. All I know is I love him now more than I ever did."

Without thinking, my hand went to my briefcase and I started to unlatch it. My eyes snapped back to Shelly, a sheepish grin on my face.

"I'm sorry," I said. "I'd kind of like to keep the tape recorder running, if you don't mind. Things like that, what you just said, they'd add a lot to the story. I don't want the piece to be just about Daniel and how his return has affected him, but what it's meant to your family. How it affects you, your husband, your other children." Shelly smiled, nodded once. I took out the recorder, raised my eyebrows, clicked it on.

"Are you recording now?" she asked.

"I am."

"So this will go in your interview?"

I laughed. "Not everything. Not what you just said, only if it relates to Daniel and your family."

"Can you print swear words?" she asked.

"Uh…no."

"Okay, I curse sometimes and I don't want Daniel to get embarrassed by his potty-mouthed mother."

I smiled at her.

Behind Shelly, I noticed a row of photographs lining a gray shelf. Inside the frames were pictures of the Linwood family. Most of the photos had just four people in them. Shelly, Randy, James and Tasha. Two pictures had been placed in front of the others. One was of all five Linwoods: Randy, Shelly, Tasha, James and Daniel. It looked like a photo from a Christmas card, all five bundled in warm sweaters, posed on a couch with smiles as big as they could muster.

"The last photo we took as a family," Shelly said. "Tasha was only a year old."

"It's beautiful," I said. Then I looked at the photo next to it.

The picture was of their daughter, Tasha, when she was just a child, maybe one or two years old. Tasha wasn't facing the camera. Her head and body were turned away, short blond hair caught in the wind. There was nothing particularly photogenic about the pic, nothing that seemed extraordinary.

"Tasha's birthday," Shelly was quick to point out. "There was a leak in the basement. We lost so many photo albums. This is the only one we could save. Not the best shot, but it's what's in it that matters. She's just so carefree."

I smiled back at her. "Should we get Daniel?"

Shelly bit her lip, then relaxed. "Have a seat. I'll be right back."

I sat down on the couch. An oak coffee table separated me from a chair where I assumed Daniel would sit. The couch was dark brown, microfiber, half a dozen stains of varying color and size spattered about. A silver robot peeked out from beside the television set, and a few stray doll hairs were tucked between the cushions. The Linwoods' living room was well worn, well used. The photos on the mantel didn't look like they were placed there for Senator Talbot. I could tell from the dust patterns and slightly faded wood surrounding them that they were barely ever moved. That photo of Tasha, though, captivated my interest. It just seemed so out of place.

I placed the tape recorder on the coffee table; better to keep it in plain sight than unnerve Daniel by taking it out after he'd settled down. I breathed easy. Waited.

I heard Shelly say, "Come on, sweetheart," and into the room stepped a young boy. He was a little over five feet tall, with dark, tousled hair and hazel eyes. Those eyes appeared less curious than slightly fearful, as though he was being led through a curtain into somewhere unknown. His cheeks bore a few freckles that surely got him teased as a kid, but in ten years would make him look cute, even handsome. His limbs were gangly, face thin. I remembered my growth spurt at about the same age, thinking I'd end up being eight feet tall and starting at center for the Lakers. Of course neither happened. For a moment I believed Daniel's tentativeness was directed toward me, but then I realized that there was a gap of nearly five years in this boy's memory. He wasn't just feeling me out, but his whole life.

Shelly kept her hands on his shoulders, gentle but muscles tensed, as though he could topple over at any moment and shatter. Daniel's only hesitation was in his gait, otherwise he looked like a regular boy, ready to lose himself in too much homework, too many video games, and the dreams of years he had yet to know.

"Hey, Daniel," I said, standing up slightly, trying to make him relax. "I'm Henry. It's nice to meet you."

"Danny," he said. "Just Danny." No hesitation there. I saw a frown glimmer across Shelly's face, but she said nothing.

"Danny," I said. "Well, Danny, thanks for letting me talk to you." His nod said he wasn't quite as happy as me.

He smiled tentatively, sat down in a wicker-backed chair across the table from me. "Could I have a soda?" he said to Shelly. She was up and heading to the kitchen before the question was finished. When she'd disappeared, he looked at the tape recorder. "Is that thing on?"

"Yeah, it is. See that red light?" He nodded. "That means it's on."

"So it's recording what I'm saying right now?"

"That's right."

"Okay. Shit." I looked up at him. Danny had a mischievous grin on his face, slightly red with embarrassment. "Sorry, just wanted to, you know…"

"Yeah, I know."

"That won't be in your story, will it?"

"Nah. I'll keep the uncensored version for my personal files."

Shelly came back in carrying a tray with a glass of soda, another glass of water and a plate of assorted vegetables. Danny and I shared a smirk. Then I noticed what else was on the tray: a gauze pad, a bottle of what appeared to be rubbing alcohol, a cylindrical tube the size of a pen and a vial.

Shelly noticed me looking at this and said, "Daniel, sorry, *Danny* has diabetes. I thought it'd be good to give him his insulin before you got started."

"Fine with me," I said. "Danny?"

He nodded. Shelly said, "We did your arm this morning, right? Let's go with your leg."

Danny rolled up his right pant leg, exposing his calf. Shelly inserted the vial into the pen until it clicked. Then she unscrewed the cap from the rubbing alcohol, tipping just enough onto the gauze pad to wet it. She rubbed the pad on Danny's calf until it shone. Then she took the pen, pressed it against his skin and depressed the plunge. Danny winced slightly.

Shelly removed the pen, wiped down Danny's leg with a towel, then took the materials back into the kitchen. Danny rolled down his pant leg as Shelly returned.

"Sucks," he said. "Dr. Petrovsky says I have to take it three times a day."

"Petrovsky?" I said.

"Dmitri Petrovsky. He's Daniel's pediatrician," Shelly answered.

I nodded. "You should listen to your doctor. This medicine helps to keep you healthy," I told Danny.

"Still sucks."

"Do you mind if I stay during the, the interview?" she asked.

"Not at all. If it makes Danny more comfortable, I'd prefer it."

"Honey," she said, "do you mind if Mommy stays?"

"No, I don't mind if *Mommy* stays." "Mommy" came out with a slightly sarcastic bent. I smiled. I kind of liked Danny Linwood.

Shelly, satisfied, nestled into a love seat, holding a lace throw pillow on her lap.

"So, Danny," I said, "how are things going here? Are you having a hard time adjusting?" He shrugged. "I need a little more than that, buddy."

"It's okay, I guess. I'm supposed to start school in two weeks, but I don't really want to."

"Why not?"

"I don't know anybody. They're all going to think I'm some sort of freak."

"They do know you, Daniel," Shelly interrupted. "You started out in grade school with most of them. Like Cliffy Willis, remember Cliffy? Or Ashley Whitney?"

I listened.

"No, *Mommy,* I don't remember Cliffy. Or Ashley. I don't remember anyone."

"Mrs. Linwood?" I said. She looked at me. Nodded. Got it. She held the pillow tighter.

"Danny, tell me about the day you came home. You came to this house, knocked on the door." Danny nodded. "Can you tell me what happened right before that?"

Danny shifted in his chair. "I remember lying down,

then suddenly waking up. I was on the ground, like I'd fallen asleep or something. I recognized where I was."

"And where was that?"

"Doubleday Field," Danny said. "I played peewee baseball there."

"What position?"

"Third base."

"Like A-Rod," I said.

"No, he's a shortstop for the Rangers."

I was about to disagree, when I remembered that in Danny's mind, he was correct. The year Danny disappeared, Rodriguez hadn't yet become a Yankee, hadn't yet changed positions. I wondered how much else of Danny Linwood's world had changed unbeknownst to him.

"What happened then?"

"I remember hearing a siren. Like a police car or an ambulance. And then I just started walking home."

"You knew how to get home?"

"Yeah, I used to walk home every day with…" Danny searched for the rest of his sentence.

"Cliffy Willis and his mother," Shelly offered quietly. Danny looked at her angrily, then the reaction slipped away.

"Where did you walk?" I asked.

"Home," he said. "Past the corner store and that brick wall with the graffiti of the boy that got shot a long time ago. I got scared for a second when I saw the police car pull up at the field I just left, but I didn't think I did anything wrong so I just went home."

"Were you hurt?"

"No. Maybe a little tired, s'all. The doctors said they found something in my system, dia-something."

"Diazepam," I said. "It's a drug used to sedate. The police report said it was administered a few hours before you woke up. When you woke up, that's when it wore off." I said this as much to Shelly as Daniel. "I'm sorry, keep going."

"So, anyway, I walked home, knocked on the door. James opened it. I knew it was James, but he was, like, three feet taller than I remembered. And all of a sudden everyone is squishing the life out of me. Mom, Dad, Tasha, my brothers." I saw Shelly smile, the pillow gripped tight in her arms.

"Brothers?" I said.

"James," he said, "my brother."

"Right," I continued. "Do you know how long you were gone?"

"Mom says almost five years."

"Does it feel like you've been gone a long time?"

"Not really," Danny said. "I mean, it's hard when I, like, go to do something and can't do it. Like there used to be a radiator in my room where I could turn up the heat, but now we have these electronic-control things. And I don't recognize anything on TV, which sucks. All of a sudden my brothers and sister are, like, old." I felt a strange mental tugging sensation. Something Danny had said triggered it, but I couldn't quite put my finger on it.

"Danny, I know the police have probably asked you these questions already, but did you have any enemies at school? On the team? Someone you were scared of?" He shook his head vehemently.

"I remember breaking up with my girlfriend once and she got mad and cried, that's it."

"You had a girlfriend?" Shelly said. "When was this?"

"Mom, come on," he said.

"What, you can tell the whole world but you can't tell me?"

Danny looked at me, his eyes pleading. I smiled at him. Six-year-old Danny Linwood with a girlfriend. I wondered if she'd missed him, or even understood what had happened.

"Mrs. Linwood. Shelly," I said, looking at Danny from the corner of my eye. "I need to be able to talk to your son with his full concentration. I know this is hard and you have a lot to catch up on with Danny, but I need this to do my job."

"Your job." She sneered. "My job is my son."

"I know that. All I want to do is tell the truth about your boy. Trust me, I don't want to upset your family at all."

"Mom…" Danny said softly. This was likely the first chance Danny had had to talk about what happened, and it seemed to even be a bit cathartic for him.

"You're right. I'm sorry. Henry, please."

"Thank you," I said politely. "Danny, what was the last thing you remember before you woke up on that field?"

"I remember being at baseball practice," he said. "I don't know if that's the last thing that happened. But I remember Mike Bursaw got hit in the knee by a line drive and was crying, and Coach was going to send him to the nurse but Mike wouldn't let him. And I remember watching the Yankees on TV and my dad saying Jason Giambi couldn't get a hit to save his life, which is weird because he used to be so good. I mean, I had his poster on my wall, and every night I'd tell it to go three-for-four with a home run. I noticed the poster wasn't on my wall anymore. My dad said he took it down but didn't tell me why."

I didn't have the heart to bring up the fact that Jason Giambi had admitted using steroids, and his deteriorating performance was likely the result of his body breaking down. Danny Linwood was going to have enough problems reentering society; tearing down his boyhood heroes would happen eventually. Yet I understood his father's hesitance to wield the sledgehammer.

"Do you remember feeling pain?" I asked.

"No."

"Do you remember a face, someone unfamiliar, something frightening you?"

"Not really."

"Do you remember anything about the past few years? Sights? Sounds? Memories?"

Daniel sat there for a few moments. He seemed almost to be in pain, searching his thoughts as hard as he could for something, straining to find what wasn't there.

"A room," he said. "Like mine, but…I don't know."

"How like yours?"

"I think there were toys, but I don't know."

"Okay…what was the first thing you thought when your mom came out the door that day? The day you came back?"

"I remember being kind of confused. She didn't hug me like that when I came back from school or practice usually, so I kind of knew something was different. I was a little scared, like something might have happened to James or Tasha or my brothers. When my dad got home and started crying, that's when I started crying, too. Like maybe I was sick and didn't know it or something. All those TV shows where someone gets sick and then everyone is really nice to them, it's usually because they're going to die." Again I got that feeling. There was more to what Danny Linwood was saying than even he knew.

I noticed Shelly Linwood's lip trembling. She was aching to say something, gather her son up and hold him. My heart hurt for her.

"How did you find out what actually happened?"

"I still don't know what happened," Danny said, anger rising.

"I didn't mean…Who told you that you'd been gone?"

"My mom," he said, looking at Shelly. "She took me in here, sat me down where you're sitting. James and Tasha and my dad were with her. Then Mom told me."

"What did you think when she told you?"

"I didn't believe her," he said. "I thought it was, like, April Fools' or something."

"How did you realize she was telling the truth?"

"My dad showed me the Derek Jeter baseball rookie card he bought me for my birthday a while ago. He told me to look at the back. He said he'd bought the card the year I was born, 1996, Derek Jeter's rookie year. Jeter was twenty-two. Then he showed me a brand-new Jeter card. From this year. And on the back of that card, Jeter was thirty-three."

"How did you feel?"

"Scared. Upset. I mean, he'd been my favorite player and I didn't get to watch him grow up."

"What did you think about what your parents told you?" I clarified.

"Really scared," Danny said. "I cried, I think, because I didn't know what else to do. But I didn't really know why. I mean, I didn't feel sick, I wasn't hurt, it's not like I missed anyone, it was just…like, weird. Like you know when you wake up from a nap and you're not really sure what time it is?"

I nodded. The past few months of my life could have been accurately described that way.

"Do you think it'll be hard going back to school? Starting your life again? Just being a kid?"

Danny chewed his lip, looked at his mother. I could tell it was killing her to stay quiet, but she also knew her son needed to heal. And talking would help that process.

"I don't feel different. And I probably won't until I go back and, like, see people. Or like today when I want to watch a show but don't recognize anything that's on. I don't even really recognize myself, if that makes sense."

"In what way don't you recognize yourself?"

"Just, ways."

"Like what?"

He eyed his mother, a look of worry on his face. "I don't know if I can say with my mom here."

"Say whatever you need to, baby," Shelly added, for once chiming in at the right time.

"Well...I don't think I remember having hair down there."

I snorted a laugh without thinking. Shelly's face turned beet-red.

I said, "Moms don't usually like hearing things like that."

Danny shrugged. "She told me to say whatever I needed to."

"She sure did."

"How's your mom taking it?" I said. I looked at Shelly. She knew I needed this from him, as well.

"I don't know. Fine, I guess. I mean, she's always hugging me and kissing me. I mean, like the kids don't have enough to make fun of already, I don't want to show up at school covered in lipstick."

"She missed you is all," I said.

"Yeah, I know, but she could back off a little bit."

"I was your age once," I said. "I kind of wish my mom was more like yours."

Danny laughed. "Yeah, right," he said. "I guess she's just glad to have me back." Shelly was nodding, her face in the pillow. Danny looked somewhat at ease. I knew that likely wouldn't last long.

"My mom told me you got in trouble a while ago," Danny said. "She looked you up in the newspapers when she found out you were coming. Was she telling the truth? Were you in trouble?"

I felt the air rush from my lungs. I nodded. "Yeah, she's telling the truth."

"What did you do?"

I took a breath. "Some people thought I hurt someone," I said.

Danny looked at me, riveted.

"Did you?"

"Not on purpose," I said.

"What did it feel like?"

I thought for a moment, then said, "Probably a little like what you're going through. I felt like a stranger everywhere I went. Like nobody knew who I really was, they just saw what they read about or watched on TV."

"That's what'll happen to me, right? People will think I'm some freak weirdo when they don't even know who I am."

"They'll think that for a little while. Then it's up to you to prove them wrong."

"I don't see why they need me to prove anything," he said quietly. "It's not like I'm a different person or something."

I couldn't say this to Danny, but no matter what he or Shelly wanted to believe, he was a different person. Scandals resonated for a long time. Perceptions died hard.

Danny took a celery stalk, munched on it, leafy threads stuck between misaligned teeth. Shelly watched approvingly. Danny would need braces, that was for sure. No escaping that part of adolescence.

"I don't remember the house being so clean," Danny said. "And the color on the walls outside used to be gross."

"I had it repainted a few years ago," Shelly said. She turned to me. "I wanted things to be clean in case...in case my boy ever came back. I wanted him to know things would be different."

"You never lost hope, did you?" I asked.

"Never."

"Do you think things will be different?" I asked Shelly. "For Danny and your family?"

She gave me a smile, weaker than she likely thought it came off.

"Yes, they will. For the first time I truly know my babies will be safe."

Danny and I both looked at her, wondering just how she could be so certain.

5

I listened to the recording of my interview with Daniel on the ride back to the city. I tried to focus as much on Danny Linwood's cadences, his voice inflections, as what he actually said. I'd spoken to abducted children before, as well as men and women responsible for kidnapping children. The children were always withdrawn, as if a piece of their soul had been sucked out. Only they never knew why. The luckier ones, the ones that were found quicker, had withdrawn into a shallower hole. Eventually they could rejoin society, restart their lives. The ones like Daniel, who were removed for years, they weren't so lucky. It was fortunate enough they beat the tremendous odds to survive, but more than likely they'd be stuck in that hole their entire lives. They would spend as much time scrabbling for footing as they did living. With Daniel Linwood, it was as though four-plus years had simply been lopped off clean. No ragged edges to be caught on. Just a gaping hole that left barely a trace.

When Stavros dropped me at Rockefeller Plaza, I entered the *Gazette* and headed to my desk. First I would have the tape duplicated, then transcribed. I couldn't promise Daniel and Shelly that they would see my story before it ran, but I had given them my word that Daniel would be treated with respect. Right before I left, Shelly Linwood told me that Paulina Cole had been calling every fifteen minutes, begging her to reconsider giving me the exclusive. Apparently Paulina promised to set Shelly up with the *Dispatch*'s parent company, which had subsidiaries in television, film and publishing. News would be the beginning. Film deals and book deals would follow. The money would come rolling in.

According to Paulina, "The Linwoods will no longer be victims. They'll be a brand name for survival."

Shelly said their family wanted no part of it. Once my story ran, what she wanted more than anything was for her children to lead normal lives. Shockingly, Haley Joel Osment cast as Danny didn't fit in.

I sat down at my desk, checked my messages. There was one from Wallace asking me to stop by as soon as I got back. There was another from Jack O'Donnell asking if I wanted to grab a beer and a shot after work. Both sounded like great ideas.

I walked into Wallace's office, found the editor-in-chief balancing the phone in the crook of his neck while simultaneously typing on his keyboard. The receiver fell twice, and finally Wallace gave up, slamming it back in the cradle and offering a string of colorful profanities.

"You know they make earpieces for people just like you," I said.

"No way. Next thing you know I'll have a chip implanted in my cerebellum instead of a laptop. I know I can't stop technology, but I can keep it from plowing me over like a Thoroughbred. I swear, this industry was more efficient before stupid Al Gore invented the Internet."

"Hey, once the Atlantic swallows the city up, the Internet will be the least of your concerns. So what's up?"

"You talked to the Linwoods?"

"I did," I said, holding the tape recorder out for him.

"Fantastic." He looked at his watch. "How'd it go?"

"I got as much as you can expect from a ten-year-old who fell into a black hole and can't remember the last five years of his life. You get as much from looking at Shelly Linwood's face as you do hearing the story. Just heartbreaking. Strange, though. The kid disappears for almost five years, yet talks and acts like your typical ten-year-old. Nobody has any idea where Danny Linwood went, but somehow his body and mind developed like a normal adolescent boy's."

Wallace looked a minimum of disturbed by this, more distracted if anything. I had to remember that Wallace had been in this industry for longer than I'd been alive. He'd seen atrocities like this day after day, year after year. My conscience hadn't calloused over the years. Stories like this still angered me.

"That's good work, Henry. I need thirty inches for tomorrow's page one. I swear, Ted Allen over at the *Dispatch* is probably trying to bug this building as we speak to get what's on that tape."

"Shelly Linwood told me Paulina Cole all but offered her body and soul in exchange for this interview."

"Just what the world needs, another forty-year-old woman sleeping with a toddler. For the sake of Daniel's future and his sanity, he's lucky his mother picked us."

"For Danny's sake, sir."

"Danny?"

"That's what Daniel Linwood prefers to be called now. Danny."

"I'm taking it this is a new development."

"Shelly doesn't seem too keen on it."

"Makes you wonder just what happened to Daniel—Danny—during the past few years," Wallace said. "Speaking of memory lapses, have you spoken to Jack today?"

"Not in person, but he left me a message about grabbing a drink after work."

Wallace's faced showed a mixture of anger and concern. "You're going to politely decline that offer," he said.

I was about to ask why, but didn't need to. Over the past year I'd noticed a change in Jack's drinking habits. One-martini lunches had turned into three shots of Jim Beam. Drinks after work turned into drinks during work. Veins began popping up where I hadn't seen them before, the old newsman's equilibrium always seeming a little off. It was clear Jack was developing a problem. Either that, or the problem was already here and we'd just been enabling him, turning a blind eye for months.

"Anytime Jack requests your company for a drink," Wallace continued, "make it clear you don't approve and you're more than aware. A little humiliation goes a long way for a proud man. That's all we can do short of sending him to rehab."

"Would that be such a terrible thing?" I asked.

"Actually, yes. Our circulation has been flat since your reporting on William Henry Roberts last year. Paulina Cole has the *Dispatch* breathing down our necks, and Ted Allen is using every dirty trick in the book to up their numbers. Giving out more free newspapers than high schools give out condoms, dropping thousands of copies in Dumpsters and recording them as part of their circulation."

"But if the numbers are inflated," I said, "who cares?"

"Advertisers," Wallace said. "Not to mention subjects who, unlike Shelly Linwood, truly care about maximizing their publicity. If our top writer goes into the detox, it's one less leg for us to stand on, one more piece of ammo for Paulina's slime cannon."

"I'll ease off with Jack," I said. "I need to cut back on my own extracurriculars as it is."

"Glad to hear you say that, Henry. Don't think I'm unaware that you seemed to have mistakenly thought your desk came from 1-800-MATTRESS. Speaking of social lives, how's that girlfriend of yours? Amanda, right?"

I toed the floor. Looked away.

"We aren't seeing each other anymore," I said. "Haven't talked in a while, actually."

"That's a shame. Remember you talking about her from time to time. In a good way."

She was worth talking about, I wanted to say. Instead, I let my silence speak for me. It was an issue I couldn't talk about with Wallace. Or Jack. Or anyone. I wasn't fully ready to face it myself. Knowing the woman I loved was out there in the same city walking the same streets, it was enough to tear me apart if I thought about it too much. Knowing what I'd let—what I'd *forced* away.

"Not to get too parental, but you'll meet someone nice," Wallace said. "All these bylines, your name in the paper, lots of girls would probably kill to go out with a hotshot journalist."

"Yeah, nothing sexier than a guy with half a dozen cartons of half-eaten Chinese food, who makes less money than a public school teacher and doesn't own a mattress cover."

I could tell Wallace didn't find that funny. I decided to change the subject.

"Hey, know who showed up at the Linwoods' place today? Gray Talbot."

"No kidding?"

"In the flesh. Or suit."

"The savior of suburbia checking on his constituents."

"What do you mean, savior?"

"After Daniel Linwood disappeared, Gray Talbot came in and rattled the cage until someone changed the lining. Made a big stink about how the town was becoming a cesspool, how the crime rate was simply unacceptable. He got state and federal funding to rebuild Hobbs County pretty much from the ground up. Nearly doubled the police force, turned a hellhole of a town into a damn fine place to raise a family. There's still work to be done, but that place is pretty unrecognizable compared to what it was."

I thought about what Wallace said, and agreed with him. Even Stavros, the driver, had said the same thing.

"Daniel Linwood's kidnapping was a terrible thing, but the silver lining is he forced change," he continued. "That boy basically returned to a brand-new, safer home and community. That's all Gray Talbot. Rumor has it he contributed close to a million from his own coffers to aid the effort."

"I thought his suits looked nice. Guess he's got enough money for them."

"I have Gray's home phone number. It'd be great to get him on record for this story as well. He's got a lot invested in Hobbs County, both in time and money, and I'm sure he's expecting a heck of a story from you as well. You don't construct a house and then not care how it's decorated. Get to it," Wallace said. "All story, all the time. I want to see ink on your eyeballs. If I hear you had a single drink with Jack, you'll be reporting on the passing of venereal diseases in the champagne room. Show me the copy before you send it to Evelyn."

"No problem," I said.

"Then tomorrow morning, I'll send over a copy of the paper with a fruit basket to Ted Allen and Paulina Cole."

"Do me a favor, leave my name off the card,' I said. "Enough people in this town hate me."

"If they hate you it's because you're doing a good job. You're getting the scoops they want. So go make some enemies. Just make sure they're the *right* enemies."

"Operation Piss People Off to commence immediately, sir."

I gave Wallace a halfhearted salute and returned to my desk. I sent Jack a quick e-mail declining drinks.

I pushed all that aside and got to work. Punching keys. Making enemies of the right people. Something still didn't sit right with me about the interview. I needed to pinpoint it. To do justice to the story. To give justice to Danny Linwood.

6

"It's called 'declared dead in absentia,'" Amanda said. "It's when a person is presumed dead, yet there is insufficient evidence to prove such a death occurred."

Darcy Lapore chewed her gum thoughtfully. At least Amanda assumed it was thoughtful, because her brows were furrowed as if creating space for a gopher to hibernate. Regardless, she continued. Amanda Davies had been working at the New York Legal Aid Society for several years. In that time, she'd witnessed some of the most horrific cases of neglect and abuse. And she'd seen children taken from the depths of hell and given hope. Yet, as she sat there with Darcy Lapore, Amanda couldn't recall ever working on a case as bizarre as that of Daniel Linwood.

"However, if a person has either been missing for a significant amount of time—for adults it's usually seven years—or has disappeared under unusual circumstances, the death certificate can be sped up. It's a way to both give the family some closure, and to make sure they get any benefits they're entitled to, like life insurance."

"So…the Linwoods have been collecting their son's life insurance?" Darcy asked. Amanda mentally slapped her head, then for fun mentally slapped Darcy's head. Then she reminded herself that no matter how often she wanted to strangle the stupid out of the girl, she couldn't get mad at Darcy. Kind of the same way you couldn't really be upset with a puppy who peed on the rug. Though most puppies did eventually learn to hold their bladders, Amanda did wonder whether Darcy would ever really commit to the job. The girl meant well, but for some reason her ability to recall thousands of shades of lip gloss and memorize every designer from Betsey Johnson to Umbro outweighed her ability to retain legal aid information by a multiple of, oh, about a trillion. The children they worked with needed passionate advocates.

"Daniel didn't have life insurance," Amanda continued, not letting an ounce of condescension drip into her voice. While Darcy would never win employee-of-the-month— or day, or even minute—in addition to being a colleague, she'd been a better friend than most people Amanda had ever known.

Last year, when Henry ended their relationship, when Amanda had no place to sleep, Darcy opened up her home and her sofa bed without thinking twice. Darcy's husband, Nick, moaned for a millisecond, but apparently Darcy gave him a look that first night and Nick never peeped again. Amanda knew Nick brought home a salary closer to seven figures than six, so Darcy didn't need nonprofit work, or any kind of work for that matter. Nick didn't get home most nights until midnight, if not later, so if her generosity was for companionship Amanda didn't know, but she was thankful for it, nonetheless. Which meant forgiving occasional, scratch that, regular lapses in judgment.

"You know, you should have come out last night,"

Darcy said. "They gave out gift bags at the end. Each one had a tube of La Mer. I swear it's like rubbing liquid silk on your skin. And Nick's friend Spencer, remember the one I told you about? He was there, and honey, that boy can wear a Brooks Brothers."

"I'm sorry, Darce, I was tired. I'll be there next time."

"Wow," Darcy said sardonically. "If there ever is a next time, you'll have to clone yourself, like, fifty times to make up for all your excuses."

Amanda turned to her, said, "I'm sorry, it's just…it's not me. I don't get all giggly for that kind of stuff. If I'm going to meet someone, it'll happen the way it's meant to happen. Like…"

"Like a fugitive asking for a ride out of the state."

She smiled. "Yeah. Something like that."

"Well, fine. I'll tell Nick to tell Spencer to find another playmate. But, Amanda?"

"Yeah?"

"Next time you might want to come just for the moisturizer. Your dry-as-dust forehead will thank you."

Amanda shut her gaping mouth, then play-slapped Darcy. She never wanted to be rude, and surely appreciated the effort, but she wasn't a socialite, the kind of woman who spent more time getting dressed than she did sleeping. And that's what she missed most about Henry. Those nights where it was just the two of them, cuddled in sweats and T-shirts, relaxing on his couch, watching a funny movie, talking, making love, then falling asleep. Bodies intertwined as though there was no world other than theirs. And for a while, there wasn't. Then the world decided to have some fun at their expense, and dispatched a killer into their midst. And while they survived, their relationship died horribly. And now Amanda's nights were spent full of sorrow for her loss, guilt for imposing on Darcy, and desire to just move on and forget everything.

"Hey, Amanda, you see this?" Levi Gold, one of the NYLAS's partners, came into their office waving a copy of that morning's *New York Gazette*. He laid it on the table in front of Amanda and Darcy, then underlined the headline with his finger.

"I Just Want To Be a Kid"
Long thought dead, Daniel Linwood grasps for the life nearly taken from him
by Henry Parker

"That's our guy, Daniel Linwood," Levi said. Levi was a short man, yet always walked with his shoulders rolled back as though it might add an extra few inches. His balding pate was neatly combed over, his gold wedding ring always buffed to a polish. As he leaned in close, Amanda could smell a whiff of Hugo Boss. And though she'd never tell him, she'd once spied him inserting lifts into his loafers.

"Whaddaya think, we're handling this city's top legal aid case. Pretty sweet, huh? If my bonus doesn't hit four figures this year, I'll be seriously pissed."

Darcy was out of her seat ready to give Levi a hug, but Amanda couldn't stop staring at the byline. She hadn't spoken to him in months. Hadn't read the *Gazette* since they broke up. Suddenly Amanda grabbed the paper, opened it to Henry's article and began reading.

When Darcy saw the story's continuation, saw the *Gazette*'s emblem atop the margin, noticed the byline, it dawned on her.

"Oh, babe," she said. "You don't need to read this."

"I want to."

"Really, Manda…" She moved to take the paper.

"If you touch it you'll be wearing your wedding band on a stump."

Darcy withdrew, protectively holding her hand.

Amanda read the whole story in silence. When she was finished, she closed the paper and handed it back to Levi.

"Sorry for hoarding your paper."

"Don't worry about it. Least some of the newsprint rubbed off on you instead of me." Levi smiled and walked out.

"Does it still hurt?" Darcy asked. Amanda could tell along with the sympathy there was a note of curiosity in Darcy's voice. She'd never been hurt like that, never had to see an ex-lover's name in front of her. She was the kind of girl men fawned over, men who would never hurt her, because her beauty was what they craved, and they knew she could walk away in an instant. If she left, another man just like them would be waiting around the corner to scoop her up. Amanda never had that luxury. She'd always told herself once she found the right man, she would never let him go. She never wondered what it would be like if *he* left *her.* Never wondered if he was simply carrying on his life while she cried herself to sleep.

"It hurts," Amanda said. Then she turned to Darcy. "Hurts more today than usual."

"Come on," she said, standing up. "Lychee martinis at lunch today. On me. And afterward we'll work on bringing young Mr. Linwood back to life."

For once, Amanda was more than happy to indulge Darcy.

7

I arrived at my desk to find Jack O'Donnell waiting for me. Sitting in my chair, in fact. He was wearing a brown suitcoat and gray slacks with several patches sewn in. In fact, during the few years I'd gotten to know him, Jack had shown as much taste for fashion as your average wino. *Pants are pants,* he told me one night over a beer. *Just because they rip doesn't mean they stop being comfortable. You have any idea how much money I've saved over the years by giving my money to tailors instead of garment salesmen?*

The look on his face read "mildly perturbed." His posture said, "I'm sitting in your chair. So what?"

Big red veins tubed down the sides of his nose. His eyes were mildly bloodshot, and it was clear though I'd declined his drinking invitation last night, he'd hit the town with his more reliable friend Jack Daniel's, maybe met up with their buddy Jim Beam and set sail on a voyage with Captain Morgan as well.

Jack was holding a copy of that morning's edition of the *Gazette,* the front page held up and turned my way so I could see it. He slapped it with his hand and said, "Knocked it out of the park, Henry. Of course you know I plan to take full credit for this. I've already told the whole newsroom you couldn't find an acorn in a squirrel's paw without my help."

"And just when people were starting to respect me," I said. "You think this will convince Rourke to hold off making another shit bag?"

Last year, the *Gazette*'s sports editor, a rough-and-tumble jackass named Frank Rourke, decided it would be funny to leave a paper bag full of shit on my desk. Apparently this was the highlight of the week for a lot of journos. And a month later Jack forwarded me the Photoshop image of my face superimposed onto that of a dog taking a big, steaming poop. That's when I became convinced that the more literate some people are, the more puerile their sense of humor was.

"You should be proud, Henry. Big interview like that, not to mention the sensitive subject matter, you could have had all the media watchdogs all over you if you'd messed up. You want people talking about the story itself before the quality of the coverage. Best kind of press for a reporter is no press."

"That's a trick I haven't quite mastered yet," I said.

"It'll come," Jack offered. "You have the brains and the talent. Just keep doing what you were born to do and the rest will come."

"It felt good to be in there," I said.

"I bet," Jack said, and I knew he must have written a million stories like it. "Good mixture of fastballs and softballs. Nobody wanted you to give the Linwood kid the third degree, but there are a lot of unanswered questions."

"That's one thing that's strange. All those questions, and yet I'm the only one asking them."

"What do you mean?"

"This Linwood story, it's really just incredible. I mean,

this family, the Linwoods, it's like the sun has finally come out after a thousand years of darkness. Now they just want to move on with their lives, let Danny be a kid again. But nobody knows where he went, who took him, and why he can't remember a thing before the day he came back."

"So you think he'll, what, just be left alone now?" Jack said. "Uh-uh. Now's when the vultures start circling. Long-lost relatives come out of the woodwork. An uncle somewhere who claims to be Daniel's best friend even though he hasn't seen the kid in years, wants some of the money folks donated. Some cousin will write a book about how Danny wasn't such a good kid, maybe he picked his nose when he was a toddler and put gum in a girl's hair. It's sad how much money there is in the misery of others."

I had to shake my head. I knew Jack was right, but after my interview I hoped the cops would pick up the slack, ask the really tough questions. Though Danny was technically a ten-year-old boy, he'd forever be known as the one who came back. Even strangers would hesitate a second, wondering where they knew his name from. And without that closure, the questions would never cease.

"You know, it's funny," I said. "All this commotion over Daniel returning, yet the cops have no leads and nobody really seems to be digging that hard. Even Shelly Linwood herself seemed unconcerned as to why the cops weren't doing more."

"When your dog runs away, then shows up an hour later, do you really care where it went? You're just happy the thing's back."

"This isn't a dog, Jack. It's a child. Somebody took him and kept him for almost five years."

"Yeah, somebody took him. And then either they got

bored of him or he managed to get away. And the world keeps on spinning."

"That's your answer?"

"I don't need to answer," Jack said. "It's not my kid, and it's not my story."

"You don't think it's weird that Danny doesn't remember a minute of what happened? Or where he went?"

"Strange things occur every day in this world, sport. Just last Thursday I went to get a glass of iced tea, turned out the pitcher was empty. Now, I *know* I didn't finish that sucker, but did I go questioning the neighbors? Nope. I went to the store, bought another jug."

"I have no idea how this relates to an actual human being."

"It's hoopla, is what it is now," Jack said. "You wrote a great piece, Henry. Move on."

"Hoopla? They didn't outlaw that word in, like, 1800?"

"Laugh it up, tiger. A family is back together. You want to give them closure? Right now, *today,* this is the most closure they're probably ever going to get. You think people like Paulina Cole are going to stop calling? You don't think there are people out there who know the juice that can be squeezed from this family is worth money? Just because you think you have scruples, son, doesn't mean everyone else thinks that way."

"Cop cars," I said.

Jack looked puzzled. "Cop cars?"

"Danny Linwood told me that when he woke up, he heard police sirens, and that he saw a cop car pull up right where he'd been lying. I checked the newspapers and police reports from that day, and couldn't find anything about any crimes reported in the vicinity of Doubleday Field."

"Could have been a prank. Could have been a drunk wandered off before they got there. The cops could have come for any number of reasons."

"Could be, sure. But don't you think it's a heck of a coincidence that the cops are called to a scene where just a few minutes ago, a kid who went missing for five years appears out of thin air?"

Jack chewed on his lip, trying to figure out if there was a way to play it like this was no big deal. I felt a lump in my throat. This wasn't the Jack O'Donnell I'd grown up idolizing, the kind who asked questions until there were no more to ask. Who dug until he hit a vein or a nerve. This Jack seemed tired, content to be apathetic, unwilling or unable to go that extra step.

"I'm going to look into this," I said. "Somebody knows who took Danny Linwood and why." Jack didn't say a word, just shrugged his shoulders, stood up and walked away. I debated following him, then decided it wasn't worth it.

I picked up the phone and dialed the Hobbs County Police Department switchboard. I asked to be connected to whoever was investigating the Linwood abduction. Then, surprisingly, the operator hesitated.

"Hold on one moment, sir, I'm going to have to check on that." It seemed odd that despite the fact that Daniel Linwood was likely Hobbs's biggest story since, well, Danny's original disappearance, they couldn't connect me to the investigating officer right away. The operator hadn't been asked many questions.

"Sorry, sir, for the delay. Hold for Detective Lensicki."

A synthesized version of "Copacabana" came over the earpiece. It was all I could do not to slice my ears off. Finally a man answered with a curt "Yeah?"

"Detective Lensicki, Henry Parker with the *New York Gazette*. I was wondering if I could have a minute of your time."

"I know who you are, Parker. I saw you yesterday at the Linwood house. Haven't read your article in today's paper. I'll get right to it when my shift is up." He didn't sound very sincere.

"Yeah, anyway, Detective, I had a question about something Daniel Linwood told me yesterday. He said when he woke up, he heard police sirens. Now, it might have been police, it might have been an ambulance, but I couldn't find any record or report of an investigation at Doubleday Field. Could you comment on that?"

"No problem, Sherlock. There was no investigation because there was no crime. There was no report because nothing happened."

"So who called 911?"

"Excuse me?"

"I assume the police had a reason to show up at Doubleday Field with their sirens on."

"We do have routine patrols, *Mr.* Parker."

"Do you usually keep your sirens on during those routine patrols?" Lensicki stayed silent. "Listen, Officer, I'm not trying to break your balls. I just want to know why it seems like everything's back to normal now that Daniel Linwood has turned up, yet nobody's really turning over any rocks to find out where he went."

"Listen here, you little punk," Lensicki said. "You go back to your typewriter and your fancy paper. The day you tell us how to do our jobs is the day you see us coming down to your office and sticking a Bic up your ass. You want a comment about Daniel Linwood? Here you go. The investigation is ongoing. If and when we have any news to report, don't worry, we'll make sure you and the rest of the *respected* media get all the info."

"So…can I quote you on that pen-in-ass comment?"

"I got nothing else to say to you," Lensicki said. "You have any more questions you direct them to our press secretary. She's eighty-three years old and can't see out of one eye and I'm sure she'll be happy to help."

"Wow. You know, I watched *Columbo,* and always thought cops were helpful and jolly."

"Blow it out your ass, Parker."

"'Detective has strange ass fetish.' That's my headline for tomorrow. What do you think?"

Unsurprisingly, the line went dead. I felt good about myself, not just for pissing off a cop but because Lensicki's standoffishness made it clear the Hobbs County PD wasn't serving and protecting quite as strenuously as their job description called for. Somebody called 911 to alert the cops to Danny's whereabouts when he woke up, and if Lensicki wasn't interested in digging, I'd be happy to pick up his slack.

I debated calling Curt Sheffield to get his take on it. Curt was a young African-American officer with the NYPD. We'd grown close over the past few years, mainly due to our unwanted celebrity, our respect for our jobs and our admiration for a good pint. He'd been a source on numerous stories, and I was happy to repay him with a few good shout-outs for his squad. That's what was most important to Sheffield. That the job was given as much respect as possible. I was happy to help, because they needed all the help they could get.

In the aftermath of 9/11, NYPD recruit applications had dropped more than twenty-five percent. And while the police force still had approximately fourteen applications for every spot they needed to fill, a drop in overall applications meant a drop in quality of applications. That's why a cop like Curt—young, good-looking and ambitious—found himself on every recruiting poster between here and Hoboken.

Many blamed lack of recruits on the NYPD's staggeringly low starting salaries—just $25,100 during the first six months on the job, a salary that would make most janitors shake their heads. Having young men like Curt on the force showed those quality applicants that the best, the brightest and the most appealing citizens made up the NYPD. What pissed Curt off was that he was a damn good cop, yet on the street he was treated like Mickey Mouse. Kids and their parents recognized him from posters. He spent more time signing autographs than patrolling his route. I tried to get him to keep things in perspective, but unlike many cops, Curt's celebrity didn't go to his head. He wanted to stay behind the scenes. Just like a certain reporter who desired celebrity as much as he desired rickets.

I called Curt's desk, got a message saying that today was his day off. Which meant he was probably sitting on his couch watching SportsCenter and eating one of those meat-lovers pizzas that contained a little over eighteen thousand calories per slice. If I had Curt's dietary habits I'd look like Norm from *Cheers,* but the guy had the metabolism of a Thoroughbred. He could eat a cow smothered in steak sauce and not gain an ounce. Sometimes life wasn't fair.

I tried his cell phone. Curt picked up on the third ring. There was a pause between "Curt" and "Sheffield." I must have caught him in the middle of a burp.

"Hey, man, it's Henry."

"S'up, Parker?"

"Let me guess. You're on your fifth slice and third SportsCenter rerun of the day."

"Nope. Gloria's got me on a health kick. She made me some spelt toast with peanut butter, mint jelly and honey. For lunch I got a bowl of plain oatmeal with some raisins and soy milk in the fridge."

"Sounds like a delicious colon-cleansing meal."

"Yeah, it's, uh…it's really tasty." I tried to stifle a laugh. "Dude, if I don't get, like, something that used to moo in my system soon, I'm gonna start pissing soy beans."

"I do owe you a meal or two, but I'll own up later. I got a question for you. When you're investigating a disturbance, what happens if it's a false alarm? Like a burglary or break-in is reported, but when the boys in blue show up there's no evidence of anything illegal?"

"It's investigated, man. Every one. Can't say they spend a ton of time on it, but you gotta make sure it was a false alarm. God forbid it turns out you just missed a clue or someone really needed help and you left instead of lifting a finger."

"That's what I thought."

"What's this about, bro?"

"Not sure yet. I have a few questions about the Daniel Linwood disappearance that nobody's in a rush to answer."

"Kid who got kidnapped then dropped out of the sky, right?"

"That's the one."

"I feel for that family, man. Nobody deserves to go through that. My mom used to hyperventilate if I came home half an hour late from school, let alone five years. Good luck, Henry. If anyone's gonna get those answers it's you, you tunnel-visioned asshole. And hey, don't forget about your tab. Steak and a beer within the week."

"You can count on it."

I hung up and ordered a pizza to be delivered to Curt's house. I just hoped he'd finish it before Gloria got home, otherwise he wouldn't be around long enough for me to repay the rest of the tab.

There had to be more to the Linwood story. Something I'd missed, perhaps. Something in Daniel's voice, his word, his cadences.

I took the tape recorder from my desk, rewound the tape and pushed Play. I listened to the whole tape again. And when it was finished, I was pretty sure I'd discovered one pretty big question. Not to mention an explanation as to why I was confused by certain aspects of Danny's statements. One huge question had been asked by Danny Linwood himself. Only the boy didn't even know he was asking it.

8

Paulina Cole forwarded three e-mails to her assistant, James Keach, then turned off her computer and put on her Burberry trenchcoat. James had asked several times if he could leave for the day, but each time Paulina answered him by not answering him—ignoring him was her favorite form of communication—and he soon slunk back to the cubicle zoo where the other peons sat and stewed. It had become somewhat of an amusing ritual. At the end of each day Paulina would send whatever hate mail she received to James, who would make copies for three departments: Human Resources, Public Relations and the *Dispatch*'s editor-in-chief, Ted Allen. Paulina had requested the *Dispatch* print her e-mail address at the end of every column. She invited readers to write in, and in fact went home depressed on the days where she got no hate mail. Pissed-off folks tended to be more vocal than satisfied ones, so the next day she would try even harder to kneel on the public's pressure points.

She sent the e-mails to HR because it was mandated by corporate. PR wanted it in case any public figures wrote in. Ted Allen demanded it because he liked nothing more than employing a reporter who so riled up readers that they took time out of their busy (or tragically not busy) day to pen her a missive so vile that they would tell all their friends to buy the paper to *see what that bitch wrote.*

When the media reporter for the *New York Gazette* had questioned Paulina's ethics in reporting on a congressman she'd allegedly had a romantic liaison with years back, Cole responded in her column questioning the reporter's manhood. More specifically, she stated her doubt that his manhood was longer than his pencil's eraser. Both she and Ted had gotten a kick out of it, and HR needed a new folder to house all the letters she received. Naturally, the paper sold 50,000 more copies that day than the previous one, and her story was linked to by dozens of influential media Web sites. Nobody was better at riling up the bourgeoisie than Paulina Cole, and in today's America people paid good money to be pissed off.

Paulina began her career in journalism nearly two decades ago working in the Style section at a New York alternative weekly paper. Boring easily of reporting on asinine trends and mindless models, Paulina took a job on the news desk at the *New York Gazette.* Widely considered one of the city's most prestigious dailies, it was at the *Gazette* where Paulina first made a name for herself. And while her progress at the *Gazette* matched her drive, she quickly tired of the politics and backroom handshakes that were staples of the old boys' club. Wallace Langston and Jack O'Donnell were dinosaurs, analogs in a digital world. The newsroom needed a swift stiletto in the ass, but they were too busy sniffing brandy to realize the world was passing them by. And when Wallace brought in Henry Parker, then stood by him when the weasel was accused of murder, it sickened Paulina more than anything in her career had before. And she was not a woman who sickened easily.

Leaving the *Gazette* was the easiest decision she'd ever made. To her, that newspaper represented everything wrong with the current system. Old. Stale. Clueless about technology, and out of touch with the average reader. People wanted pizzazz, something to shock them, something to ignite their senses. They didn't care about politics unless there was sleaze behind the suit. Didn't care about crime unless it was a celebrity drunk behind the wheel. So Paulina was happy to dig and dish the dirt. She was happy to be hated by the highbrow, embraced by the lowbrow. But everyone had an opinion.

Once safely nestled in the bosom of the *New York Dispatch,* Paulina had made it her goal to not only boost the paper's circulation rates, but to do it at the expense of the *Gazette.* She would topple their leaders, set fire to the old guard and burn the paper to the ground. She'd laid the groundwork with her articles focusing on Henry, to the point where nearly half the city would answer "Henry Parker" when asked what was wrong with the current state of journalism.

But Henry was young. Not yet thirty, his proverbial balls had not yet dropped. Going after him was like shooting a fish in a barrel, and its ripples wouldn't travel far. To truly bring down the *Gazette,* she had to stop worrying about the epidermis, and instead dig down to its skeleton. The old guard. The reporter the paper staked its very reputation on.

Jack O'Donnell.

For years Jack O'Donnell had been the public face of the *Gazette.* He'd won countless awards, brought respectability, integrity and readership to Wallace Langston's newspaper. Yet during her tenure there, Paulina had noticed the old man begin to slip. His reporting had been shoddy, numerous quotes and sources had to be spiked by the managing editor. Not to mention the unmistakable odor that wafted from his desk, strong enough to make you fail a sobriety test just by inhaling.

It was only a matter of time before somebody took a sledgehammer to the pillar of the *Gazette,* and it was only fitting for it to be wielded by someone who'd seen the cracks up close.

Paulina turned off her office light, took the umbrella from under her desk. Her office had a beautiful view of the Manhattan skyline, twinkling lights amid the dark hues of night. The skies had opened, drenching the pavement, and the N train was several blocks away. As she strolled through the corridors of the *Dispatch,* Paulina stopped by the one office she'd asked Ted Allen to clear out for her a few months ago. A junior media reporter had been given the office, a reward for a promotion, but when Paulina informed Ted Allen what she had in mind, the young man was given a nice little cubicle by the Flavia coffeemaker.

The office was enclosed, sealed off. Exactly what she needed.

On Paulina's orders, the office had been cleared out; not even a dustball remained. Instead three rows of shelves had been installed, forming a U around the walls. What was inside the office had to be kept a secret until her story was ready. And then the bombshell would drop.

Only two people had a key: Paulina and Ted Allen himself. The key was removed from the rings of the entire janitorial staff, and Paulina only entered when she was positive there were no looming eyes peeking over her shoulder.

Tonight, she had a tremendous urge to look inside. She needed to be reminded of what all her hard work was preparing for.

Checking once more to make sure she was alone, Paulina twisted the key in the lock, opened the door and flicked on the overhead light.

What she saw inside made her glow with delight. The way the room glittered, the light reflecting on everything she'd painstakingly gathered over the past few months. And her treasure trove was growing by the day. It was only a matter of time before the contents of this room, these seemingly innocuous items, changed the face of New York journalism.

Satisfied, Paulina turned off the light, closed the door and got out her umbrella, preparing for her journey into the rain.

9

"Right here," I said to Wallace. He was holding a copy of the transcript of my interview with Daniel Linwood. I'd asked him to read it in its entirety before we spoke. So far he'd only read what was printed in the *Gazette*. There were many quotes that were cut for space, details that didn't make it into the final piece. I wanted to see if Wallace noticed what I had just minutes ago.

I hadn't noticed it upon my first few listenings. It was so subtle, yet because I was already skeptical of the whole situation, it stood out in neon lights.

"I'm not following, Henry," Wallace said. He turned off the tape recorder. "Please, placate an old man whose hearing is going. Enlighten me as to what the hell you're talking about."

"First off," I said, "Daniel mentions he heard sirens when he woke up. Yet there's no record of any complaints or investigations by the Hobbs County PD in that vicinity. And when I spoke to the detective assigned to the case, he was only slightly more helpful than your average retail clerk. And then I heard this."

I rewound to the spot in question. Then I pressed Play. When Daniel spoke that word, I stopped the tape.

"Brothers," I said. "Daniel Linwood talks about seeing his family for the first time when he got back home that day. He refers to his sister, Tasha, but then he uses the word *brothers.* As in plural. Daniel Linwood has one brother, James. There's no record of Shelly and Randall having any other sons. And then he uses the word several more times. As though he can't help it. Once is a slip of the tongue. Twice is a heck of a coincidence. Three times, like Danny says on the tape, that means something's wrong."

Wallace looked at the transcript, found what I was referring to, stared at it so intently I expected a hole to be seared through it.

"I think Daniel was referring to brothers because there was another brother in his life."

"But you just said he only has one brother, this James. I don't follow."

"I think the other brother, the plural brother, was with Danny during the years he was missing. I think whoever kidnapped Daniel Linwood had another young boy. I think even though he can't force himself to remember details of the past five years, Danny subconsciously *is* referring to it. I think whoever took him had another child, and Daniel was made to believe they were brothers. And even though James is his only biological brother, his memory still retains a stamp of some sort. A footprint of the lost years."

"Is that even medically possible?" Wallace asked skeptically.

"In 1993," I said, "medical records showed that Sang Min Lee, a thirteen-year-old Korean boy who'd been in a coma for three years, suddenly woke up and claimed to smell flowers. Sang's mother had brought fresh roses to Sang's hospital room every day for the first year of his hospitalization, then stopped when it became too expensive.

Somehow Sang's brain retained the memory of those smells, despite the fact that the boy himself wasn't even awake."

Wallace scratched his beard, put the papers down. I could tell he was thinking about this, debating whether my discovery warranted looking into, or was just a dead end that would eat up time and resources.

"Let me dig a bit," I said. "I know there's no way to tell right now, but if there is, and we can report exclusively…"

Wallace's head snapped up. I stopped speaking. He knew my engine was running, that if he unleashed the harness I'd be on this like a dog on fresh meat. I was aching to run with this story. It burned to think that nobody else seemed to care where Daniel Linwood had been for five years, why he couldn't remember anything about his disappearance or why the HCPD seemed content to vacuum it all up. I hated that if nobody stepped up, Daniel Linwood would just be another headline. A child with no past, whose future would always be clouded.

"This is awful thin," Wallace said. "You realize it might have been a slip of the tongue. A fault in the recording. My mother used to call me Beth—that was my sister's name, but she was just absentminded. There are a dozen ways to explain what Daniel said, not all of them having anything to do with some Korean boy."

"But you and I both want to know whether there's more."

I looked at Wallace, trying to will him to say it. Then he looked up at me, hands folded in front of him.

"Check it out. Report back if you find anything. And if it turns out there's another way to explain it, you stop digging *immediately*. We promised to treat the Linwood family with respect—the last thing we need is to accidentally hit a nerve that doesn't need to feel pain. There's a family at stake here, not to mention a town trying to rebuild. So use a pipe cleaner to dig instead of a pickax."

"Gentle is my middle name."

"That's a goddamned lie," Wallace said, "but I'll give you the benefit here. Good luck, Parker."

With Wallace's blessing, I went back to my desk and took out the Linwoods' phone number. I held the Post-it between my fingers and thought about the promise I'd made to Shelly. Her family had been torn apart, and it would take years before they could even hope to begin the reparations. By giving me access to their home and to their son, the Linwoods trusted me to do what was right. And I had every intent of doing just that.

First I had to make sure there wasn't a simpler explanation.

I called the Linwood house. It went right to voice mail. An automated system saying, "The person you wish to call is not available at this time. Please leave a message at the tone." I figured they'd disconnected their phone, changed their number to confuse the vultures. Only now I'd become one, too.

At the tone, I said, "Hi, Shelly, Randall, this is Henry Parker. I wanted to thank you for the other day. I did have one follow-up question, and I was wondering if one of you could give me a call back at the office. Again, this is Henry Parker at the *New York Gazette*."

Then I hung up. And sat there. Twiddling my thumbs, chewing a number two pencil, praying the wait wouldn't be long.

Perhaps the most difficult thing about being a reporter was waiting for a callback. If I was on deadline, and knew that one transforming piece of information was available yet just beyond reach, the minutes crawled by like hours. Waiting for that callback could drive you insane. I propped my feet up on the desk, stuck a pencil between my teeth and waited.

Thankfully I didn't have to worry about my sanity, because my phone rang barely a minute after I'd hung up.

"This is Parker."

"Henry, it's Shelly Linwood." She sounded apprehensive, a little concerned. She had probably assumed once my story ran I'd be out of her life.

"Shelly, thanks so much for getting back to me."

"It's no problem. We have to screen our calls, otherwise we'd never get off the line. We're probably going to have to change our number." She said this with an air of apology. She still saw me as a friend. Unlike the other vultures who wanted to pick the bones.

"I understand that. Again, I appreciate you and Daniel talking to me the other day."

"It's Danny," she said, her voice less than enthusiastic. "That's what he wants to be called now."

"Right. I remember. Anyway, Mrs. Linwood, Shelly, I was going back over the tape of the interview, and something seemed a little strange to me."

"Strange? How so?"

"When Danny is talking about reuniting with his family, he says the word *brothers*. As in more than one. And he says it several times. I know this is a silly question, but Daniel doesn't have any other siblings besides Tasha and James, right?"

"That's right." The acceptance was gone. At that moment I knew I was an outsider again.

"Any close friends he might consider a part of the family? A cousin so close he might call him a brother?"

"No."

"Has he mentioned anything to you about his abduction? Any memories that might offer a clue as to why he said that?"

"I said no, Mr. Parker." Not Henry. *Mr. Parker.* "It's just the five of us. Thank God. Now, if you'll excuse me, I have a pot roast in the oven." I checked my watch. It was eleven in the morning. Kind of early for a pot roast.

She didn't wait for me to respond, and I knew when the line went dead Shelly Linwood would no longer be returning any more of my calls. I sent off a quick e-mail to Wallace.

Shelly Linwood doesn't know where "brothers" came from. Got very defensive. Will update you on progress. H

I tapped my pencil against the desk. Wherever Danny Linwood was during those years, there was another person he'd called "brother." I was sure of it. Of course, there was a chance his mind had simply been damaged from the absence, but something in Shelly's voice and the lack of cooperation from the HCPD told me if I asked more questions, I'd find very unhappy answers. Which meant they had to be asked.

I decided to take a stab at something, then work from there.

I performed a LexisNexis search for child abductions within the past ten years, then narrowed the search to cases where the child returned alive. Sadly, there were over one thousand reported cases of child abductions in the United States during that span, and less than fifty of those thousand children had been found alive. The others had either been found dead, or never found at all.

I searched through the results looking for any simi-

larities, specifically cases, like Danny Linwood's, where
the abducted was returned to his or her home with no
memory of their time gone.

I was surprised when one hit came back. Seven years ago,
an eight-year-old girl named Michelle Oliveira disappeared
outside of Meriden, Connecticut, following a playdate at a
neighbor's house. The Oliveiras lived just four houses down
the block from their friends, a family of four named the
Lowes, which explained why she was unsupervised upon
her return home. The investigation turned up nothing but a
tassel from Michelle's hair that had been caught on a nearby
branch. After a month the search was called off. Two years
later Michelle Oliveira was declared deceased.

And three years after that, Michelle Oliveira appeared
in her parents' front yard in Meriden, in perfect health with
the exception of some vitamin deficiencies. According to
a newspaper report, Michelle had no recollection of the
intervening years.

The police had conducted numerous interviews with
Michelle, her parents and younger brother, as well as with
the Lowe family. The records had been sealed off due to
the victim's young age. The abductor or abductors were
never found. And Michelle went on with her life.

While Michelle clearly wasn't a "brother," it did make
me wonder. Meriden was just a few hours from Hobbs
County, and more important, it set a precedent for this kind
of unexplained absence and subsequent reappearance.

I needed to see those records. Fortunately I knew
someone who could help. Time to add another lunch to my
growing tab.

Curt Sheffield picked up, but it took major convincing
to get him to not hang up on me.

"Ain't no way I'm going to even touch a child abduction case, bro. Not to mention that it's in a different state, and I'd have to explain why I'm asking those kind of questions. If I tell them it's to sate some reporter's curiosity, I might as well tell them I deal crack while downloading underage porn. I'll get booted faster than you can say 'Starsky minus Hutch.'"

"So how could I get hold of those records if not through the police?" I asked, praying Curt's reach extended beyond that of his precinct.

"Only other firms who have access to those kinds of documents are the legal aid societies. They keep a database of all child-related abuse cases. I'm guessing this falls under their jurisdiction."

"Even if there was no evidence of actual abuse?"

"Just 'cause there ain't no scars on the outside don't mean they're not on the inside."

"That's deep, Curt. You write poetry, too?"

"Yeah, I'll Robert Frost your ass if you try to squeeze anything else out of me. Good luck, sorry I couldn't help more."

"Yeah, thanks for nothing."

"When can I collect on that tab?"

"I'll have my people call your people."

"Yeah, whatever. Later, Parker."

I had to get more information on Michelle Oliveira's abduction, but I wasn't going to be able to go through the police department. I sat there in silence, thinking about what Curt had said. The legal aid society.

I knew one person who worked at the legal aid society. But calling her would touch nerves much closer to my heart than Daniel Linwood.

I opened my desk drawer. I could almost sense it down there. It had been months since I'd spoken to her. But rarely a day passed when I didn't feel that ache, that gnawing in my gut that seemed to only get worse over time.

Six months ago I'd made a choice. I decided I had to give her up. I told myself at the time it was the right thing to do. A man had to put his love before himself. And since Amanda had nearly been killed twice because of me, in my mind there was no other option.

So I said goodbye to Amanda. I hadn't been truly happy in months. It didn't take a great reporter to figure out the two were directly correlated. But I still couldn't be with her.

There had been times over the past few months where I had wanted to call, where I'd gone so far as to pick up the phone and dial everything but the last number on her cell phone, nearly crying when I hung up before pushing the final key. Nights where the booze loosened up my inhibitions, and only that last vestige of clarity prevented me from calling. Like that terrible night six months ago, today there was only one choice to make.

Amanda worked for the New York Legal Aid Society. She would have access to Michelle Oliveira's records. She could help the investigation. She could provide answers.

She could also throw it back in my face.

And I would deserve it.

Maybe this was the opening I needed, I wanted. A way to tell myself it wasn't about her, even though deep down I couldn't even fool myself. Maybe it was fate. Or maybe fate was a cruel son of a bitch.

Before I had a chance to think again, I picked up the phone and dialed.

Amanda picked up on the first ring.

"Hey," I said. "It's me."

10

The girl woke up with a slight headache. Her first thought was that she'd fallen, maybe hit her head on the sidewalk or bumped into the same tree she'd rammed her bike into the other day. But she didn't remember putting on a helmet, didn't remember actually falling. And she only rode her bike when her mommy was watching. And right away she felt the terror that she was alone.

She stood up warily. Her breathing was harsh, and she felt hot tears rush to her eyes. She reached out for her bed, the couch, some familiar sign. But she found nothing. She grew desperate and called out. There was no answer.

The room was pitch-black. Had her mommy just put her to bed, accidentally left the Bratz night-light unplugged? No, there was a smell in the room, something different, something rotted. She didn't belong there. Yet when she cried, nobody came.

The girl smelled something that reminded her of her dad's breath after he came home on Sunday evenings. Mommy said he was watching the football games at the bar with his friends. His breath had that sweet smell, and her mom never let her get too close to him when he was

like that. There was a smell in the air that reminded her of
that. Reminded her to be afraid of getting too close.

After a few minutes her eyes adjusted. The room was
small, about the size of her baby brother's bedroom. There
was a small bench by the wall, and the floor was made of
wood. A slit of light shone from a crack under the door,
but other than that she couldn't see a thing.

Her throat began to choke up. She didn't know this
place. She wanted to feel her mommy's arms. Wanted to
smell her daddy's sweet breath.

Suddenly she remembered walking home from the
park, remembered feeling a hand clamp over her mouth.
She couldn't remember anything past that.

The girl let out a cry of help, then ran toward the door.
She gripped the knob and twisted as hard as she could, but
it didn't budge. She pushed and pulled and cried, but the
door stayed shut.

Finally she collapsed onto the floor and began to cry.

She wiped the snot away from her nose. She needed a
tissue. She could wipe it on her clothes, but she loved the
sundress she was wearing. Bright pink with pretty sun-
flowers. Her mom had picked it out for her at the mall, the
same day she'd bought that nice barrette in the shape of a
butterfly that mommy wore to the park.

She began to cry again. She screamed for her mother.
For her father. And nobody came.

Then she lay back down, curled into a ball, and hoped
maybe somebody could hear her through the floor.

And that's when she heard footsteps.

She sat back up. Looked at the door. Saw a shadow
briefly block out that sliver of light. She wiped her eyes
and nose. She held her breath as the doorknob turned.

Then nearly screamed when it opened. She would have screamed. If she wasn't too scared.

There was a man in the doorway. He was bald, with thinning hair and glasses that were too small for his head. He was wearing light jeans with a hole by one knee. On his hands were leather gloves. When she saw the gloves, she finally managed to scream.

The man flicked a switch on the outside of the door, and a lightbulb came on, bathing the room in harsh white. She closed her eyes, blinked through the glare, then opened them. The man was now barely a foot in front of her. He was staring at her. Not in a scary way, not like bad men on television did. In the way her daddy did when he tucked her in at night. He'd taken the gloves off. He held them out to her, then made a show of putting them in his pocket.

"Don't be scared," he said. "I would never hurt you."

The man reached out, took her chin in his hands. They were callused, rough. She was too scared to move, felt her head pounding, mucus running down her nose and onto his hand.

When he noticed the snot on his fingers, the man reached into his pocket. She closed her eyes. When she opened them, he'd taken out a handkerchief and was wiping her nose, her face.

"That's better," he said. He had a glass of water with him. He handed it to her. "Go on. Drink some."

She took it, her hand trembling. She didn't know what was in it, whether he'd poisoned it, whether he'd spit in it, but she was so thirsty she downed almost all of it in one gulp. When she was finished, he took the clean side of the handkerchief and wiped her mouth.

Then he handed her two small pills. She looked at him, looked at the pills.

"You must have a bad headache," he said. "This will make you feel better."

Then he smiled at her.

She didn't know how he knew about her headache, but if the pills would help...

"How do you feel?" he asked.

"Hurts," she moaned.

"It won't for long."

She looked at him. He was wearing a wedding ring. It was polished and it gleamed something pretty.

He stood up. Motioned for her to do the same. The girl stood up reluctantly, then smelled the aroma of pancakes coming from somewhere. Her favorite.

"Strawberry and chocolate chip. Fresh off the griddle," he said, smiling. "Let's get you fed, you can meet your new mommy and new brother, and then I'll show you to your room."

She took the man's hand, his grip gentle, and followed him out of the darkness.

11

It would have been easy to say no. For years she'd grown accustomed to disappointments, to a life that never quite went the way she planned.

The wound still hurt terribly. Doing this could rub salt in deep. And who knows? Another few weeks, few months, and the pain might have begun to die down. And given a few years, she might have never thought about him again. Things would have gone back to the way they were before the day they met.

None of that mattered, though, because when Henry called, for the first time in months his voice coming over the phone, she agreed to meet him almost immediately.

Just a few years ago, Amanda had nothing, no friends, nobody to trust but herself. Her life had been a series of half-hearted relationships, embarked upon mainly because that's what she assumed was normal. That's what she was used to. Men who were more interested in their own success than how it could be used to make others happy. She'd grown weary of that scene, and at some point, like many other girls her age, Amanda Davies had simply given up.

The irony was when she'd met Henry, the very first thing he did was lie right to her face. Looking back, she knew he'd done it to save his own life without implicating her. And while back then she contemplated literally ditching him on the side of the road, she could look back at his brazen behavior fondly.

He'd tricked her into giving him a ride out of town when he was mistakenly wanted for murder. In the end Henry was able to clear his name, yet there was a moment, that moment when he'd come clean, admitting his lie, when she could have left him on the side of the road to die. But in that moment Amanda was able to look into Henry Parker's eyes and tell one thing. This was more real than anyone she'd ever known.

Henry's eyes gave away everything. The year they knew each other, he could never hide anything. She could read his language—words and body—like nobody else. And he offered himself in a way that was both selfless and confident, and utterly consuming.

That's why when he ended their relationship, it wasn't simply another thing to forget. Being with him was the first time Amanda felt a future. She couldn't be the only one who thought that way, though, so when he decided to end it, for her own sake in his words, she didn't fight. She didn't want to be another one of those sad girls, trying to convince a guy to stay.

If she was meant to be happy, she would be. If not, that was life.

So when Henry called her out of the blue, after radio silence for nearly six months, the easy thing to do would have been to hang up. To tell him to go screw himself.

Instead she found herself sitting on a bench in Madison Square Park, waiting for him to arrive, looking at every boy that walked by, waiting to see if the months had been as cruel to him as they had to her.

The park was neutral ground. That was one condition she made him agree to. They had to meet far enough away from both their offices that they could sit, and talk, and see what was what, without any distractions.

Amanda folded her arms across her chest. The sun was bright over the trees. She sat and watched couples lounging on the green grass. The line snaking outside the Shake Shack, home of the best burgers in NYC. Her purse was splayed open slightly, and Amanda noticed the glint of her keychain. Attached to the silver loop that held her keys was a small red heart made of leather. Henry had brought it home one day. He'd attached it to the chain when she was in the shower. When she asked what it was for, he said it was because she had the keys to his heart. At first she laughed. It was a pretty cheesy gesture, something out of a bad romantic comedy, but that night they made love, and as Henry lay there, naked, staring at her, she knew that he'd meant it.

It would have been easy to throw the heart away. Looking at it now, she was glad she'd kept it.

She buttoned the purse and looked up to see Henry walking down the gated path. He stopped briefly beside the dog run to make faces at a small shih tzu that was trying to leap at him with its tiny legs. Henry was making bug-eyed faces at the dog, and Amanda couldn't help but smile. He looked up, looking for her, saw her, and Amanda saw his cheeks flush red. He quickened his pace and walked over to her bench, sat down next to her. A foot separated them. It felt like a mile and a millimeter at the same time.

"Hey," she said, offering a purposefully bland greeting.

"Hey, Amanda." He half leaned in, unsure of whether to offer a hug, a kiss or nothing. She felt a brief flash of electricity when he did it, felt slightly disappointed when he pulled back, but glad at the same time. "What's up?"

He looked good. Better that she'd hoped in some ways. Perhaps if he'd showed up thirty pounds heavier, with an unflattering beard and gut paunch, it'd be easier to move on. Yes, his eyes were bleary and red, probably from late-night deadlines, but it was still Henry. She'd gotten used to those eyes, his near-constant state of exhaustion. And despite that, every night she missed falling asleep next to him, Amanda remembered how proud it used to make her to see his name headline a terrific story. She looked at his shock of brown hair, an inch or so too long, and couldn't help but smile.

"You need a haircut," she said.

"Really?" He ran his hand through his hair. Amanda remembered doing that for him. "You think?"

"Yeah, you could use a trip to Supercuts."

"So," he said tentatively, "what's up?"

"I don't know. Work. Life. What's usually up," she replied. He nodded. She wanted to say *you called me,* but that was combative. "You know you called me." Screw it, she had to say it. Henry nodded, chewed on his thumbnail for a moment.

"Just want to start by saying I'm sorry about what happened. You know, between us. I didn't…"

"Stop," she said, her face growing warm, slight anger bubbling up. "You said your apologies a long time ago. If I wanted to hear them again, I've got a good memory and a lot of sad songs on my iPod."

"That's not why I called you," Henry said. "I just… You know, I don't really know how to start it."

"Why do you need to in the first place?" she asked. Her heart was beating fast, frustration building. She'd begun to wish she'd stayed at the office, hung up the phone, let everything heal the way maybe it was meant to. Seeing him was maddening and invigorating at the same time. And she wasn't ready to open back up.

"I need your help," Henry said. "It's not for me. It's for a kid."

"A kid?" she asked, surprised.

"Daniel Linwood, have you heard about him?"

"Of course. My office is handling the paperwork. You know, I never realized bringing someone back from the dead was as easy as filling out a bunch of paperwork. Scary to think there's enough precedent that we have the forms on file. I'm actually thinking I might do the same thing with my aunt Rose, freak the hell out of Lawrence and Harriet. That'd make a pretty neat headline. 'Girl brings dead, smelly aunt back to life, scares the hell out of her adoptive parents.'"

"It's been a while since I wrote obituaries," Henry said. "But I bet it's like riding a bike."

"Think of it as an anti-obituary."

"Now, those I don't have a lot of experience with."

"So Daniel Linwood. The boy who came back after five years. I saw your story in the paper. What do you need to know about him?"

"Well, long story short, there's a lot about his disappearance and reappearance that doesn't sit well with me. For one thing, there haven't been any suspects arrested in his kidnapping or disappearance, and from my talks with the detectives in Hobbs County they're looking as hard for him as O.J. is for the real killer."

"I'm waiting to hear what this has to do with me."

"I'm getting to that. So I interviewed Danny for that story…"

"Danny?"

"Yeah, that's what he likes to be called now. Anyway,

during the interview, he said something kind of strange. He used the word *brothers*. As in more than one. And he used it several times, even when I corrected him, like his brain was hardwired to do it. But Danny's only got one brother. It might have been a slip of the tongue, but there's also a chance he retained something from his disappearance, something about his kidnappers or where he was. Maybe he remembers somebody else, somebody his own age, being wherever he's been the past five years."

Amanda sat, listened intently. She felt the familiar rush Henry got when he was excited about a story, the same sense of pride she felt *(used to feel)* when she was proud of her man.

"I did some digging," he continued, "and it turns out a girl named Michelle Oliveira went missing several years before Danny. Similar circumstances, both children disappearing without a trace, then suddenly reappearing out of nowhere, remembering nothing about their disappearance. No suspects ever arrested. Nobody ever found out how or why she went missing."

"I think I get where this is going."

Henry nodded. "Michelle Oliveira's records are sealed," he said. Henry waited, knowing she would respond.

"But you know I have access to them at the legal aid society."

"That's right."

"That's why you called me."

Henry stayed silent, looked at Amanda, his eyes full of remorse. It was genuine. "I've been an asshole. I'm not apologizing again, we both know that's over and done with. But this is important. It's a boy's life, Amanda, and I didn't know who else I could turn to or trust. I still trust you."

"I don't know if I trust you."

"I'm not asking you to trust me. I'm asking you to help me for the sake of someone else."

Amanda was struck by the tone of his voice, the sense of coldness. But she knew it wasn't meant to hurt her. In a way it was meant to protect her.

"I'm not asking you to take me back, or anything like that. I know you don't want to. I'm asking you to help because you're the only person I know who can do this, who has access to those records. The only person who *would* do this. Something is wrong with this story, and I need to know what." He added, "For Danny Linwood's sake."

Amanda sat for a moment. A cool breeze whipped through the park. She watched a smiling couple holding hands, eating sandwiches just a few feet from them, as though their whole lives existed in this small world where problems were as light as the leaves. She thought about her life, what it was like before and after Henry. How there didn't seem to be enough of it lived.

"I can get you those records," she said. "But that's all I'll do. I'll help you with whatever information you need in regard to this Oliveira girl, but I'm not going to ask for anything in return. And I don't even want you to offer."

"I won't," he said, though the words seemed hard for him to say.

Amanda stood up. Smoothed out her skirt. Henry stood as well.

"Michelle Oliveira?" Henry nodded. Amanda clutched her purse, felt the sharp edges of her keys. "I'll call you later when I get the files. One thing, I'll only give them to you in person. I could get in deep doo-doo if my supervisor knows I'm doing this, so I'll contact you discreetly. Don't send me any e-mails, don't call or text message. I don't even want to see a carrier pigeon. You might trust me, but I sure as hell don't trust Verizon."

"That's a deal."

"Then I'll call you," she said. Amanda turned around to leave.

"Hey, Amanda," Henry said.

"Yeah?"

"It was good to see you."

"I'll call you," she said, glad the smile on her face couldn't be seen as she walked away.

12

Sometimes all you can do is wait. That's what I did back at the office while waiting to hear from Amanda. I went over the Daniel Linwood transcript half a dozen times, word by word, line by line, to make sure I hadn't missed anything else. I listened to the tape, tried to hear the cadences in his voice, catch a sense of apprehension, a feeling that he was holding back. And though I strained hard to hear it to the point where I tried to convince myself, it simply wasn't there. Daniel Linwood had laid it all out. At least the way he remembered it. Or didn't remember.

Those words stuck in my head. *Brothers.* Such a small thing, Danny himself hadn't even noticed it. When a person misspeaks, they often correct themselves. If not, they won't make the mistake again. Not Danny Linwood.

At about five o'clock, when I was beginning to think it wasn't coming, that tomorrow would be a repeat of today, I got an e-mail. The subject heading read "Marion Crane." Right away I knew who it was. It was tough to hold back a smile.

When I'd been on the run for my life a few years ago, Amanda and I had stopped at a hole-in-the-wall hotel to plan our next move. She signed the ledger using the same

name, Marion Crane. The Janet Leigh role from Hitch-
cock's *Psycho*. Marion Crane, the girl who would have
done anything, including stealing thousands of dollars,
just for a better life.

The e-mail was brief.

Battery Park City. Starbucks. Bring money to buy me a
double latte and maybe a scone if I'm feeling adven-
turous.

I wondered why the hell she had to pick Battery Park
City of all places. Battery Park was at the southernmost tip
of New York City, but was barely in New York City. I'd been
there a few times, reporting on a new housing development
that was alleged to be one of the city's first "green" buildings, but a little digging turned up that the solar panels
alleged to power thirty percent of the building's generator
were nothing more than fancy aluminum, and the developer
had pocketed a few hundred grand from snookered tenants.

Since I wasn't calling the shots, I hopped on the 4 train
and rode it to the Bowling Green stop. When I got off, I
immediately saw two Starbucks (or was it Starbuckses?
Starbucksi?) across the street from each other. I walked
into the first one, didn't see Amanda, and sheepishly left.

Battery Park had a stunning view of the Hudson River,
the grand Statue of Liberty easily visible from the shore.
Because of its proximity to the ocean, the temperature in
Battery Park was ten to fifteen degrees cooler than the rest
of Manhattan, so in August it was still a brisk sixty-five.
I was glad I'd decided to wear a sport jacket.

The second Starbucks thankfully was the right one,
though if I came up empty I didn't doubt there was another
one right around the corner, or even inside the restroom.

Amanda was sitting by a back table reading a discarded copy of the *Dispatch.* Next to her purse was a small tote bag. Inside it I could see a thick folder with stark white printouts spilling out. She saw me coming and put down the paper. I pulled out the chair to sit down, but Amanda shook her head.

"Uh-uh." I stood there, confused. "Double latte. One sugar."

"Scone?"

"Nope. Gotta watch my girlish figure."

I wanted to tell her she needed to watch her figure like Britney needed another mouth to feed, but decided against it.

I nodded, bought the drink, fixed it to her specifications, set it down on the table and sat down.

"The *Dispatch?*" I said, gesturing to the discarded paper. "Really?"

"It's for show, stupid. I'm here incognito."

"Right. So that's it? The Oliveira file?" I said, gesturing to the tote bag. She sipped her drink, nodded.

"I feel like we're investigating Watergate or something," she replied. "Passing folders under the table."

"If that were the case, I could think of a few places a little less conspicuous than Starbucks."

"That why we're in Battery Park. You think either of us knows a soul down here? Besides, I thought you loved the Woodward and Bernstein stuff."

"I do, but Robert Redford is a little too old and leathery to play me. And Dustin Hoffman's too short for you."

Amanda looked around exaggeratedly. She eyed the barista, squinted her eyes. I had no idea what in the hell she was doing. It was as if she was expecting a rogue team of FBI agents to come out of nowhere and load her in the back of a van. Sadly, it wasn't even two years ago when two FBI agents *did* break into her house and shoot someone in her bedroom.

Maybe that's what made it funnier.

She pressed her foot up against the tote bag underneath the table. Then she kicked it toward me. Then she gestured at the bag before taking a long, slow sip of her latte.

"Oh, is that for me?"

She eyed me contemptuously. "Oh, for Christ's sake, open the damn thing."

I picked up the tote and pulled out the folder. The top sheet was Michelle Oliveira's birth certificate. She was born on November 15, 1991. That would make her sixteen today. Michelle Oliveira's parents were Carlos and Jennifer Oliveira. At the time of the abduction, the family resided in Meriden, Connecticut. According to tax records, Carlos worked as a housepainter, and Jennifer had worked in a variety of temp jobs over the years. Secretary to an orthodontist. Court stenographer. Doctor's office receptionist. Telemarketer.

Together, the Oliveiras' income never exceeded thirty-four-thousand dollars a year. They had two other children, a boy, Juan, now fourteen, and a girl, Josephine, twelve. Juan was a high school freshman, Josephine was just about to begin the seventh grade. Their sister Michelle was kidnapped on March 23, 1997, not yet six years old. She returned on February 16, 2001, nearly four years later.

According to the report, Michelle had spent that afternoon at the home of Patrick and Lynette Lowe. Michelle was in grade school with their daughter Iris, and according to interviews with the Lowes, and confirmed by the Oliveiras, Michelle often went to the Lowes' home after school to play. She would often stay at the Lowes' from approximately three-thirty to six, at which time she would come home to get ready for dinner. As the Lowes lived just four houses down on the same block as the Oliveiras, the families admitted she walked home on most occasions unsupervised. On March 23 she left the Lowes' home at approximately a quarter to six. At six-fifteen Jennifer Oliveira called Lynette Lowe to ask when Michelle would be home. When Lynette Lowe informed Jennifer that Michelle had left half an hour earlier, and Josephine could not find Michelle on their block, she called the police.

The Meriden PD found no trace of Michelle Oliveira. They compared tire tracks found on Warren Street to all vehicles registered to inhabitants of the block. All vehicles checked out. Nobody had seen Michelle after she left the Lowes. No neighbor glimpsed the girl. Nobody came forward. Michelle Oliveira had simply vanished.

The next page contained her social security number, employment records, known addresses. And her parents'.

I looked at Amanda. She was absently sipping her coffee while eyeing me.

"Did you read this already?" I asked. She nodded.

I continued reading. In 2003, two years after Michelle's reappearance, the Oliveiras moved from Meriden to Westport. Westport, I knew, was a much more affluent part of Connecticut. Records indicated that the Oliveiras were able to sell their home in Meriden for nearly $800,000, nearly triple what they'd paid for it ten years earlier. That was quite a profit for a family who couldn't afford to do much refurbishing.

"What are you thinking?" Amanda asked.

"I'm thinking I'm throwing away money by renting my apartment."

"Seriously," she said. "As soon as I can afford it, I'm leaving Darcy and buying a studio."

"Good luck coming up with half a million dollars," I replied.

"No way."

"You want three hundred and fifty square feet in Manhattan? Damn right you'll need half a mil." Amanda shook her head, obviously realizing that living for free with Darcy wasn't so bad.

"One thing's for sure," I said. "The Oliveiras couldn't wait to get the heck out of Meriden after Michelle turned up."

"Can you really blame them? I mean, their daughter disappears, do you really want to hang around and subject her to those memories? Subject your other children to that? I'd want to start my life over, that's for sure."

"I guess you're right," I said "God, that has to be every parent's worst nightmare come true."

I thumbed through the papers and the rest of the police reports, paying particular attention to the reports from the day Michelle disappeared and the day she returned. The police work had been thorough. More than thirty neighbors and friends had been interviewed, as well as all of Michelle's classmates, teachers and her private music instructor, which the Oliveiras admitted cost nearly a hundred dollars a session. In the report, Carlos and Jennifer acknowledged the expense, stating their daughter was a gifted violinist and they simply wanted to give her the best chance to "make it."

"Michelle's currently enrolled at Juilliard," Amanda said. "Full scholarship."

"You don't say. I guess Michelle did make it. That's called beating the odds."

I found an interview the police had conducted with Michelle's violin teacher, a Ms. Delilah Lancaster. Ms.

Lancaster was scheduled for her weekly lesson with Michelle the evening she disappeared. At eight o'clock she showed up, unaware of the situation. According to the report, Ms. Lancaster had seen the police, got spooked, tried to run away, which led to her questioning and being a part of the police report. Delilah had confirmed their relationship, mentioning that Michelle had recently begun working through a book called *Solo Pieces for the Intermediate Violinist.* They had just begun lessons on George Frideric Handel's "Air," from the *Water Music.* She had just completed works by Vivaldi and Mendelssohn.

Four years later, when Michelle returned, the first person she asked to speak to was Delilah Lancaster. According to the Oliveiras, nobody was closer to Michelle than Delilah Lancaster. The police ran a cursory investigation into the woman on the chance they'd find some sort of impropriety. They uncovered dozens of e-mail correspondences between the two and many phone calls to and from each other's homes, but they seemed to be more of the gifted student/dedicated teacher variety. Lancaster taught Michelle Bach and Mozart and Vivaldi, fingerboards and upper bouts. She was clearly a gifted student, but nothing seemed out of the ordinary.

Carlos Oliveira remarked to the Meriden *Record-Journal* after Michelle's reappearance that socially, his daughter seemed to have withdrawn. She was unsure of herself, timid.

"She spends hours, I mean, hours a day locked in that room of hers, fiddling with the violin as if it's all she's got in the world. We try to push her to go outside, play like a normal girl, but all she cares about are those strings. She used to have so many friends. She was such a popular girl. At least she's safe now, that's what matters most."

"The music teacher," I said. "I think I'll give Ms. Delilah a ring. It seems like she was the closest person to Michelle Oliveira, and spoke to her the most after she came back. All Michelle had left was her violin. If anybody knows anything it might be the music teacher." I held up the folder. "Can I keep these?"

"Sure," Amanda said. "But I swear, Henry, my career is on the line."

"No worries. I'll take good care of this."

She looked at me, as if debating whether I could be trusted. Finally Amanda stood up. She downed the rest of her coffee, flung it at the garbage. It rattled around and fell in.

"Keep me in the loop, will you? It sickens me to think this has happened to more than one child. That it even happened to one is just…God, horrible."

"You know I will. I know what this means to you. I hope you know what it means to me. And not just from a professional perspective."

"I know." Amanda gathered her purse and began to walk out of the store.

"That's it?"

She looked at me, her eyes a mixture of hurt and confusion.

"That's it," she said. "For now, that's all I can take." Then Amanda left.

I watched her until the door had closed and Amanda had rounded the corner. It took a moment to regain focus.

I decided the next step was to call Delilah Lancaster. It was clear she and Michelle were very close, to the point where Delilah was contacted before any of Michelle's school friends. I figured there was a reason for that. If the violin was all Michelle had left, I needed to speak to the person who probably influenced her more than any.

I sat in the store for another few minutes, then gathered up the folder and left. I hoped that somewhere, Daniel Linwood and Michelle Oliveira knew two people were going to fight for them.

13

The next morning I went to Penn Station first thing and
bought a ticket on the 148 regional Amtrak en route to
Meriden, Connecticut. Delilah Lancaster was scheduled to
meet me. I'd spent the previous night going over her
comments, trying to gain a better understanding of her
relationship with Michelle Oliveira.

I took a copy of the file on Michelle Oliveira, a copy
of that morning's *Gazette* and a large iced coffee that
promptly spilled all over my linen jacket when a kind man
with a Prada briefcase elbowed me in the head. I went to
the bathroom compartment on the train to clean it, and
though I was able to avoid stepping in the unidentified
brown goop on the floor, I left with a softball-size blotch
on my chest. I debated finding Prada man and throwing
him onto the tracks, but I needed my composure. Not to
mention I needed to stay out of jail.

When the train pulled out of the station, I cracked open
the *Gazette* and read the story Jack had written for this
edition. The piece focused on the looming gentrification
of Harlem, how real estate prices were soaring, specula-
tive investors, many of them foreign, were snapping up
town houses and condos like they were Junior Mints. The

average two-bedroom had nearly doubled in price over the past decade. Foreign investors, emboldened by the weak dollar, were monopolizing the market. The prices Jack quoted quickly confirmed that if I ever desired to buy in New York rather than rent, I'd either have to win the lottery or find a sugar mama.

The reporting was solid, one of Jack's better recent efforts. Too many of his recent articles felt slapped together, rushed, pieces he forced past Evelyn and the copy editors simply because he was the man. Had the stories been written by a younger reporter who hadn't yet cut his teeth, won major awards and written a shelfful of bestsellers, many of them would have been spiked. The old man needed an intervention. The ink of the newsroom was still the blood that pumped through his veins, but he was a train slowly careening off the tracks. Without some straightening out, the impending crash would permanently derail his career.

The train took about an hour and forty-five minutes to reach Meriden. I finished the *Gazette* and spent a good twenty minutes staring at an advertisement featuring a man quizzically holding an empty bottle of water before realizing it was hawking Viagra. When the train came to a stop, I noticed a man with a friar's patch of baldness jotting down the ad's Web site before hustling off the train. One new customer.

I disembarked the train and took in the city of Meriden. I hadn't spent much time in Connecticut, only having traveled here once to interview a fast-food worker who'd witnessed a murder while on vacation in NYC. A lot of New Yorkers commuted into the city from parts of Connecticut—Greenwich being a popular hub—in large part due to the ever-booming Manhattan real estate market. For just a thirty-minute train commute, a million bucks could buy you a home or large condo as opposed to a one-bedroom with the view of fire escape.

Meriden, though, was no Greenwich.

What struck me first was that the Meriden train station resembled less of an actual station and more like a glorified bus stop. A small hut was the only building on the gravelly lot. It had boarded-up windows, graffiti sprayed layer upon layer. A ticket vending machine sat lonely outside the hut, like a relic from the 1970s. I wasn't even sure if it accepted credit cards. A dirty, bearded man sat on a bench fully asleep, his yellow windbreaker also looking as if it hadn't been removed since long before the man's last shave. He looked comfortable, and clearly wasn't waiting for the train.

The air was cool, but I had no doubt the day would grow hotter throughout the morning. I buttoned up my jacket, stuck my hands in my pockets, and waited. The surrounding buildings were low, squat, though they seemed to have an air of vigor. Fresh coats of paint. Newly cemented sidewalks, clear of footprints and cracks. It looked like a city wrenching itself toward respectability, while experiencing a few hiccups along the way.

As well as brushing up on the Oliveira case file, I also read about the demographics and income of the city of Meriden, specifically how both had changed over the years during Michelle Oliveira's disappearance. In 1997, when Michelle was abducted, more than forty percent of Meriden residents lived below the poverty line. The median income was a shade over $28,000. And more than sixty percent of residents had one or more children.

Today, the median income was more than $45,000, and was growing at a rate far larger than the national average. Plus, only nineteen percent of residents currently lived below the poverty line. Yet less than half of residents now lived with children. I wondered if Michelle's abduction had anything to do with this. Whether the horrific nature of Michelle's disappearance convinced families it simply wasn't safe to raise a family here.

From what I could tell, this was a city that seemed to want to right the wrongs of its past. A city that desperately wanted to prove it was safe for girls like Michelle. And whatever part of the city didn't want to improve, it would remain contentedly criminal. A place where a girl could be abducted, and her abductors could remain free. That part of the city would be what it always was, and whatever happened was simply God's—or the criminal's—will.

I stood outside for a moment, unsure of what to look for, until a honking car horn brought my attention to the Chrysler sitting alone in the lot. A woman was in the driver's seat. I could see her through the windshield, an uncomfortable look on her face. She didn't want to be here. I walked over, peered in through the passenger-side window.

"Delilah Lancaster?" I said.

She nodded, said, "Get in."

I obeyed. She started the engine as I buckled my seat belt. We peeled away from the station, leaving the tracks in our wake.

Her car was if not new then new*er*. A black 300 model, it had less than ten thousand miles on it, and there were no telltale signs of wear and tear on the interior. A classical station played on the radio, and I noticed Delilah's hand moving in nearly perfect rhythm, sliding gently up and down the steering-wheel cover as though she was conducting the symphony herself.

Delilah Lancaster was in her early forties. Her black hair was pulled back in a tight bun, a few errant streaks of gray shining through like silver threads. Her face had aged gracefully, the lines and striations of a woman who was comfortable in growing older. She moved delicately but with purpose, her eyes fixed on the road.

We sat in the car for several minutes, neither of us speaking. She drove past several streets of well-maintained homes. We passed by those into a less-friendly part of town that resembled the train station in its sense of abandonment. When we stopped in front of an empty building, I turned toward her to ask where we were.

"I agreed to talk to you," she said, her hands still on the wheel despite the engine being off. "But I don't want it in my house or in any place of business or pleasure. That's the agreement."

I nodded, reached into my bag for a tape recorder. She eyed it, curled her lip.

"This is also part of the agreement," I said. "You have to go on the record." She nodded. I turned the recorder on.

"You know I went through all this seven years ago," she said. "The police questioned me many times. I know I got scared that night, but all those police, I thought somebody had been killed. For a moment I thought it might have been Michelle. All I know is, one day I was Michelle Oliveira's tutor, the next day she was gone from this world, and then several years later she rose like the phoenix."

"Why did you think she might have been killed? That seems like you were jumping to a pretty terrible conclusion."

"When you've lived in this city as long as I have, you've seen young boys killed because they were targeted by rival dealers. When you've seen young girls caught in the cross fire, then you can say that I'm jumping to conclusions. I did think Michelle might have been another victim. That she'd been taken away forever."

"Well, now she's at Juilliard," I said. A slight smile crossed Delilah Lancaster's lips.

"She's the most talented individual I've ever had the pleasure of working with," Delilah said. "The moment I walked into the Oliveira home for the first time and listened to that girl play, the French bow moving in her hand like the wind, I knew it. French bows are mainly used by soloists, and most young students don't even know the difference. But Michelle, she made her father buy a French bow. Nothing else would suffice. Most young girls have posters on their walls of their favorite bands, their favorite athletes, boys they have crushes on. Do you know what Michelle Oliveira had posted on her wall?"

I said I didn't.

"You're aware that most girls that age don't have posters, or much of anything on their walls. They haven't yet begun to have crushes, and wouldn't know who Orlando Bloom was compared to Barack Obama. But Michelle, she had a poster on her wall. I don't even know where she got it, or how. But right on her wall, above her bed, was a picture of Charles IX."

I waited for an explanation. "Is that a King of England or something?"

Delilah shook her head. "Charles IX is the oldest violin in existence. It was made in 1716 by Antonio Stradivari. It is kept in pristine condition at the Ashmolean museum in Oxford. You can imagine this is not exactly a common item for a five-year-old to worship."

"Stradivari—is he related to the Stradivarius?"

"The same," she said.

"For a young child to hold such an instrument in this regard, it simply made my heart float. When she disappeared—" Delilah lowered her head, clasped her hands together "—I felt like I'd lost a kindred spirit. Someone who understood the beauty and passion of music like so few do in their lives. And to lose her at such a young age—I thought a great student had been taken. A shame in so many ways. And when Michelle came back, I thanked God for keeping one of his finest creatures on this earth."

"You really cared for Michelle, didn't you?" I asked.

Delilah looked at me. "*Still* care. I do care for her the way a teacher looks at a prized pupil, yes. But our bond went deeper than that. I cared more for Michelle than I did most of my friends and—" she sighed "—perhaps most of my family."

I looked at Delilah's hand, barren of any rings. She noticed this.

"My husband died three years ago. Pulmonary embolism. Life hits you when you never expect it. But I still have my music. That, at least, is everlasting. And one day Michelle will create a composition that will stand the test of time. That students, like she once was, will study."

Delilah looked out over her town, the barren building in front of her.

"This city has changed so much. So many people left after what happened to Michelle. I didn't blame them. I have no children, but if I did I couldn't justify raising them here. Now young families, dare I say *yuppies,* have moved into those houses. Rats joining a ship. I never thought I would see that in Meriden."

"You're against gentrification?" I asked.

"It pays my bills," she said. "And allows me more leisure time than I previously had. But Lord, if I could find one truly talented student in the bunch, it would make my year."

"Not many children like Michelle come along," I said.

"No," she agreed. "No, they don't."

"Aside from the obvious, was there anything about Michelle that was different when she came back? Did she ever mention a family member, a friend, somebody you didn't recognize?"

Delilah shook her head. "Michelle didn't have many friends. The gifted ones never do."

"Did she strike you as different in any way? After she returned?"

Delilah thought for a moment. "She became more withdrawn. Michelle was once a vibrant, popular girl, but she never fit in again. You can't explain to a young girl why people are staring at her, knowing she can't possibly understand exactly what happened. One night, a few days after she came back, I thought I saw scarring on her arm, but I decided it was just a pimple, some kind of adolescent puberty thing. It saddened me to see such a lovely girl just have her soul sucked away. But what person wouldn't after going through something like that?"

"Did she ever say anything to you that gave any clue as to where she might have been all those years?"

Delilah shook her head. Stared ahead of her. I looked at the tape recorder. Afraid this was all I was going to get from Delilah Lancaster.

Another song came on the radio, the violin strings prominent. Delilah's fingers flowed with the sound. Then they abruptly stopped.

"What?" I asked. "What is it?"

She cocked her head, looked deep in thought. "Beethoven's sonata," she said.

"Is that what's playing right now?" I asked.

"No," Delilah answered, her voice soft. There was a

tinge of fright in there that made my pulse begin to race. "Beethoven's Sonata no. 6. It's an incredibly difficult piece. It can take months, if not years, to master. Oh, God, I remember that night."

"What happened?"

"It was only the second or third lesson after she returned," Delilah said. "Michelle was so down. Depressed. I asked her to play something that made her happy. And she picked up her bow and began to play…oh, God…"

"What?" I said. "What happened?"

"The sonata. Michelle played it for me that night. I left the house cold, shivering. I didn't sleep for a week."

"Why?" I said, a shiver running down my back.

Delilah Lancaster turned toward me. "In the dozens of lessons I had with Michelle Oliveira, never once had she even attempted to play Beethoven. She had never tried to play that symphony. That sonata was not even in any of the books I purchased for her. Somehow she'd learned to play that piece in between the time she disappeared…"

"…and when she came back."

I looked at Delilah Lancaster. She was trembling, her hands gripping the wheel so hard they'd become white.

"Somebody else taught her how to play that sonata."

14

I marched into Wallace Langston's office and sat down. He was poring over a pile of loose pages. He simply looked up and stared at me.

"I don't recall that chair offering you a seat," he said. I stood back up. Without missing a beat, Wallace said, "Now you can sit down, Henry. What's up?"

I took out the tape recorder, put it on the desk in front of Wallace. "I just spent the day in Meriden talking to Michelle Oliveira's old music teacher, Delilah Lancaster. She—"

"Michelle who?" he said. I forgot for a moment that Wallace had dozens of other stories being run past him, and that even though this was hugely important to me, I needed to show him that I was right about my suspicions.

"Seven years before Daniel Linwood disappeared, a girl named Michelle Oliveira vanished from Meriden, Connecticut. For almost four years there was no trace of her. No suspects, no arrests, nada. Then, just like Danny Linwood, she shows up at her parents' doorstep without the vaguest idea what happened. No scrapes, no bruises, and police can't figure out what the hell happened or where she'd been."

Wallace slowly put down the pages. I had his full attention.

"I thought that whole 'brothers' thing was strange, but it seemed clear to me that after Daniel was kidnapped, he retained some information from his time gone. I wanted to find out if this was a common occurrence for kidnapping victims. Upon running a search, I found this Oliveira girl, who disappeared in the exact same way. Michelle was very close to her music teacher, this Delilah Lancaster, so I figured she might be able to shed some light and maybe help me understand Danny's case better. During the interview today, it turns out that in between Michelle Oliveira's disappearance and return, the girl learned an *entire new* violin sonata. Somehow she'd had access to both instruments and music books. So not only was she kidnapped, but she was kidnapped by somebody who knew her well enough to know she was a violin prodigy."

Wallace looked at me, looked at the recorder. "She played violin, this Michelle Oliveira?"

"A prodigy," I said. "She's at Juilliard now."

"There's no chance she started studying this sonata before she disappeared, and simply finished it later?"

I shook my head. "I asked Delilah that. She said they were using a workbook in which that specific sonata was not a part of the lesson. When they resumed lessons after Michelle returned, suddenly this ten-year-old has turned into Yo-Yo Ma."

"How did Lancaster explain it?"

"She couldn't," I said. "And neither could Michelle. Delilah asked her where she learned it, but Michelle didn't know."

"And Lancaster believed her?"

"Without a doubt. Like Danny Linwood, it's an imprint on her brain, the moves in her muscle memory. Unconscious. I did leave several messages for the Oliveiras but haven't heard back yet, and frankly I'm not expecting to. But something strange is happening to these kids while they're gone. Obviously somebody took them, and they're retaining a piece of memory from their time away. It's not much, but it definitively links Michelle Oliveira and Daniel Linwood. I don't know how or why, but their disappearances are connected."

"This is stunning stuff, Parker. And where did you get all this information on Oliveira?" Wallace asked.

"I… Most of it from newspapers. Lancaster was interviewed by the *Journal-Record*."

"You just happened to come upon this?"

"I dig deep," I said, thinking of Amanda, not wanting to get her into any trouble.

Just then there was a knock at Wallace's door. We both turned. Our jaws simultaneously dropped when we saw the striking figure in the doorway.

"Gray," Wallace said. I recognized the man immediately, but for the life of me couldn't imagine why he was here.

The man entered, striding up to Wallace with casual confidence.

Wallace said, "Henry, you've met…"

"Senator Talbot," I said. "We met just the other day."

Gray Talbot smiled at me. "Hello, Henry," he said. "I hope I'm not interrupting anything."

15

I stood out in the hall, trying to hear what Wallace and Gray Talbot were discussing behind closed doors. Though Wallace had told me to wait by my desk, I wasn't nearly patient enough. I felt better pacing a tread on the carpet outside of his office. I wondered what the hell Senator Talbot was doing in the *Gazette* offices. Wallace seemed surprised, and I was pretty sure Gray had stopped by totally unannounced. Generally not the behavior of most politicians who throw a press conference to announce they've voided their bowels.

I felt slightly dirty, like a journalistic Peeping Tom, straining for quick glimpses. I could only make out corners of the office—Wallace had drawn the shades. I could see Talbot pacing back and forth, his face angry. He was looking in one direction, which inferred that Wallace was sitting at his desk, most likely being defensive.

I got the distinct impression that Wallace was being read the riot act for something, I just wasn't sure what.

Finally after about twenty minutes, the door opened and Gray Talbot exited. His navy suit was unruffled, his hair unmussed, his demeanor unshaken. Whatever he'd come for today, he'd gotten it.

As he walked by he slowed up, turned to me slightly, leaned in. I could smell his light aftershave, saw a small nick by his jawbone.

"Parker," he said. "You're better than this. I haven't forgotten what we spoke about. And I hope you haven't, either."

Before I could ask what the hell he was talking about, Talbot was in the elevator.

Without waiting another second, I burst into Wallace's office. The editor-in-chief was sitting down, hands steepled, chin resting on his thumbs. He looked up at me without moving, his eyes flickering.

"Sit down, Henry." I sat.

"How did you get that information about Michelle Oliveira?" he asked. I opened my mouth to speak. "And if you lie to me you're fired."

I sighed, knew I was cornered, knew there was nothing I could do.

"I have a contact at the legal aid society. This person gave me information about the Oliveira case. The police report, and more." I kept it gender nonspecific, just in case. "The rest I did myself. Frankly I didn't really need it, it was just a shortcut—"

"Shortcuts are the death of our industry, Parker," Wallace said. "Jayson Blair took shortcuts. Stephen Glass took shortcuts. I don't expect you to want or need those. And I hope to God you yourself think you're better than them."

"It wasn't like that," I said. "I knew there was more to this Linwood story than was being reported, and I needed something to tie them together. You know there's a connection. And without those papers I might not have found it. You can call it a shortcut, I call it a story worth investigating. My source is reliable, and the papers are authentic."

"Ethics and honesty are not always independent of each other," Wallace said.

I felt my body go slack. "So what now?" I said. "What did Talbot want?"

"You forget about this story now."

I felt my body go numb. "That's ridiculous. He can't spike a story because he doesn't like my sources."

"Gray Talbot has threatened to prosecute you, and by proxy us, if any of what you've told me about Daniel Linwood or Michelle Oliveira ever runs. He knows that you obtained those files and he knows you did it illegally, without the knowledge of the LAS. Like you said, it was one rogue employee. And like a good politician he's going to hold it over our heads until we bend to his will. I know you've worked hard on this, Henry, but let it go."

I stood up. "This is bullshit," I said. "Do you really think it's the right thing to let it go? Do you honestly believe there's nothing more to find on this story?"

"We're not crusaders," Wallace said. "We're not vigilantes, or judges or heroes. You are a reporter. Nothing more or less. It's not my call to say what's right and what's wrong. But I can tell you what your job is. And as of Monday, I'll have a new assignment for you. Now go. Get rid of any files you have. Take the weekend, recharge your batteries and get ready to kick some ass next week."

"Right. Kick some ass," I said lethargically. I left Wallace's office without saying another word. I didn't know if I was going to be able to "recharge" over the weekend, but one thing was for damn sure. I wasn't getting rid of those files. And I sure as hell wasn't letting this story go.

16

I called Amanda as soon as I left the office. The call went straight to her voice mail at work. For a moment my breath caught in my throat. I prayed she hadn't been fired. Then I tried her cell phone. When she picked up, her voice sounded upbeat, familiar. Not the voice of someone whose life had taken a turn for the worse.

"Oh, thank God, are you OK?" I asked.

"Of course, why wouldn't I be? Is that asteroid finally headed for earth or something?"

"No, even worse. Gray Talbot came by our office today."

"The political dude?"

"Senator, yeah."

"What was he doing at the *Gazette?* Doesn't he get enough press?"

"That's the thing, he wasn't there about a story that had already run, he was there to make sure we didn't print anything else about Danny Linwood or Michelle Oliveira."

"That's ridiculous. Why?"

I took a breath. "He knows about the files."

There was silence. Then she spoke. "I assume you're referring to whatever files I definitely had nothing to do with."

"Those are the ones."

"Goddamn it, Henry, you promised you wouldn't say anything!"

"Amanda, I didn't, I swear. But he knew about it and threatened to either fire me or castrate Wallace if we ran any stories about Michelle Oliveira, using the information you gave me. Is it possible someone in your office knows you took the files?"

"It's possible," she said. "I had to log in to our system to print out a lot of it. But if they know I took them, why haven't I been led out by Security?"

"Same reason he came by our office. He wants this kept quiet. You get fired, the press gets hold of that, and he's got much more than Wallace Langston to worry about."

"But why is he taking such an interest in Michelle and Danny?" Amanda asked.

"I don't know," I said. "But I'll find out."

"I want to find out with you," she said. "I'll meet you at your apartment in an hour."

"Amanda," I said. "I don't think—"

"Right, don't think anything. I want to help figure out what the hell is going on. I work with kids seven days a week. Kids that have been beaten and left for dead because nobody fought for them. And now it turns out two of them are missing pieces of their lives and some stuffed shirt wants to step on it? Not on my watch."

I came this close to saying *I love you*. I didn't. But it sounded great in my head.

"I'll be at my place in an hour," I said. "See you then."

"Have a pot of coffee ready," she said. "And please, Henry. Pick up whatever dirty underwear is starting to grow spores in your hamper."

"I have a hamper?"

She hung up.

I caught a cab back home, threw every article of clothing that appeared salvageable into a garbage bag and shoved it into my closet. I was apprehensive about letting her in. Amanda hadn't set foot in my apartment in six months. Like me, Amanda had the inquisitive gene. And especially now that her ass was on the line, she was going to be a part of this until we figured out what happened to the years Michelle and Danny had lost. I just needed to make sure my nasty socks hadn't grown a life of their own in the meantime.

Once the apartment was clean enough to present, I poured a glass of water and sat on the couch, thinking about Daniel Linwood and Michelle Oliveira. It had made me sick to read about how heartbroken their families were when they disappeared, how two families could be shattered in seconds. I could only imagine the joy when they came back, as though a hole in their parents' hearts had suddenly been repaired.

I hadn't spoken to my father or mother in two years. The last time was while I was on the run. I called my father one night, holed up in a dank room, waiting for two men who would either be my saviors or my executioners. I called him for two reasons. The first was to say goodbye, in the event that I didn't make it out alive. The second was out of the hope that that bastard would give me something to keep going, a reason to live, to spite him if nothing more. He gave me that, and I lived. And we hadn't spoken since. I never desired to. I didn't wish him dead, but merely hoped he took care of my poor, absent mother the best he knew how. But I was glad to be gone from that home. I was happy to be living a life where I was the only arbiter of my triumphs or failures. Like Danny and Michelle, I'd been lost, too.

The buzzer jolted me out of my thoughts. I went to the window, looked down to see Amanda standing at the door. She looked up, saw me, gave me the finger. Classy as always. I jogged to the intercom and released the door lock, then did another once-over of the apartment to make sure no dust bunnies—or actual bunnies—were hiding from view.

In the minute I had before Amanda got to the door, I considered how to answer it. Suave, with a Rhett Butler-esque baritone in my voice? Should I leave the door un-latched, sit on the couch and try to act nonchalant? Maybe greet her with a glass of water, or wine? A plate of cheese? A half-eaten Snickers bar from my nightstand?

Then I remembered it was Amanda. She wasn't impressed by overdone gestures. She'd spent years of her life sizing people up in mere seconds, a habit brought on by her adoption after the death of her parents. She was a better judge of character than anyone I'd ever known. She could tell who was real and who wanted you to believe they were real. I'd been nothing but real during our relationship. And even though I doubted we'd ever be together again, I couldn't stop being that. She saw past it. And I didn't want her to look any further.

The doorbell rang. I cleared my throat—the least I could do was talk to her phlegm-free—and answered it. She was dressed in fitted jeans, a gray T-shirt and a thin red cardigan. Her hair spilled gently over her shoulders. It was a few seconds before I realized how much I'd missed seeing her, cataloging her beauty on a daily basis. I threw the thoughts from my head, and said, "Hey."

"Hey, yourself." She was holding two cups of coffee,

and offered me one. "I figured you'd forget to brew a pot. Milk and three hundred Splendas, right?"

I smiled. "Perfect. I was kind of hoping my teeth might jitter all night. Come on in."

She entered the apartment, looked around. "Looks good," she said. "It's been a while. I was kind of expecting a bear to attack me, or some sort of underwear monster to run across the room."

"The underwear monster doesn't come out until the sock monster goes to sleep."

"I'm going to ignore you now."

She walked around to the couch, sat down, placed her coffee on the small marble table, already ringed with many old coffee cup stains, including a few that were most likely from Amanda's cups and had never been cleaned.

"This place missed you," I said, then felt silly for saying it.

"Really? It probably has enough festering life forms hiding that it did tell you that."

"Yeah, the comforter and I, we chat sometimes."

"If cleanliness is next to godliness, I think this makes you the Antichrist."

I laughed, took a sip of the coffee. Then we sat in silence for a moment.

"So Gray Talbot," she said, thankfully breaking the tension. "What does he have to do with Michelle and Daniel?"

"I did a bit of a background check on the senator," I said. "Found a few interesting facts."

"Let me guess. This was after Wallace told you to let it be."

"Naturally. Anyway, in 2001, after Michelle Oliveira disappeared from Meriden, Gray Talbot swooped in like an avenging angel and pretty much scorched the earth. He lambasted the government of Connecticut, the social services offices, the police force, criticized them all for betraying the families that lived within their borders. He said it was a sad day when an out-of-stater had to come in because the job wasn't being done right. And Talbot saved his best blasts for then Governor John Rowland."

"Rowland," Amanda said. "That name rings a bell."

"It should. John Rowland resigned from office as governor of the state of Connecticut in 2004 due to charges of massive corruption. Mail fraud, tax fraud, he even served ten months in a federal prison."

"And this guy was running the state when Michelle disappeared?"

"Kind of like having a crack addict babysit your children. Rowland was skimming money for numerous personal projects that had nothing to do with the state. He took state money and paid for improvements to his weekend cottage, took thousands of dollars in gifts from his subcontractors. Of course, after prison he did the whole rehab-image deal, everything but appear on the cover of *People* magazine. Anyway, Talbot came in after Michelle disappeared and tore Rowland a new one for letting the state go to seed. He said the state was not protecting its youth. At the time, Meriden had the second-highest crime rate in the state, and it had gotten worse over the previous few years. Even though Talbot was a New York senator, he was quoted as saying, 'This is a matter so vital to the future of our country that it would be irresponsible to only permit coloring within state lines.'"

"So Talbot ruins Rowland, then what?"

"Talbot institutes a program called 'Not on Our Watch.' He raises millions of dollars earmarked for improving security within Meriden and other surrounding counties. More money for police recruiting, neighborhood watches, more incentives for gang members and criminals to become informants. He raises thousands of dollars for the Oliveira family, basically seals up trust funds for their other children to go to college. Within two years, the crime rate in Meriden drops like a rock. He spent years working to help the Oliveiras move on with their lives."

Amanda said, "And now this guy is knocking on Wallace's door telling him to let the city move on. It sounds to me like Talbot is a guy who worked his ass off to rebuild a community, then sees some punk reporter, no offense…"

"None taken…"

"…digging around, looking for holes in the masonry."

"Not to mention the most interesting part," I said. "Michelle Oliveira grew up in Meriden, but guess where she was born?"

"I don't know, where?"

"Hobbs County."

"Like Danny Linwood?" she said. "Holy shit, that's a hell of a coincidence."

"Or maybe not," I said. "Guess where our favorite senator also grew up?"

Amanda looked at me. She said, "No way…"

"That's right, Hobbs County for two hundred, Alex."

"So this guy has taken protecting his own to a whole new level. No wonder as a New York senator he decided to stick his nose into another state."

"What's also strange, though, is that both Meriden and Hobbs County were essentially cesspools before Michelle Oliveira and Daniel Linwood were kidnapped. Since Talbot came in, they've seen unprecedented growth and community support."

"Talbot seems to have done his job well," she said. "There are certainly enough shitty neighborhoods in New York, maybe he should take care of his own backyard for a bit."

"That's why he was at Danny Linwood's home the day I interviewed him," I said. "He is looking out for his own backyard. Literally."

"What are you thinking we should do?" she asked.

"I'm not sure," I said. "But it concerns me any time a politician does something for the alleged good of the community. It makes me wonder what the quid pro quo is."

"Well, how has Talbot's career been affected since Michelle Oliveira and Danny Linwood came back?"

"Well, he's won by a landslide every time he's run for reelection," I said. "One would assume at some point he'll want to move from the senate to the governor's mansion. All that good press can't hurt."

"You think we might be a little too cynical?" Amanda said. "I mean, this guy seems to have legitimately changed lives. Maybe even saved a few. For all the politicians that talk a big game, this guy actually gets his feet dirty. Yet he ruffles a few feathers at your office and we're ready to string him up."

"I'm not doing anything like that," I said defensively. "But I need to know why two children disappeared into thin air, reappeared years later with no memory of where they went, and nobody seems to be looking too hard into that fact. I have no idea if Gray Talbot is the greatest Samaritan of all time or Jack the Ripper in a good suit. I just want the truth. And one thing I've learned in this job is that anytime somebody tells you not to look under that rock, there's something there they don't want you to find."

"And now you're going to lift that rock. Even if it means your job."

"Even if it means *your* job," I said, looking her dead in the eye. Amanda seemed taken aback, then she took a breath and calmed down.

"Guess I should have expected that."

"I'm sorry, I—"

"Don't be sorry. I want to respect you. If you pulled punches, I wouldn't."

"Sometimes I hit harder than I need to. Against people who don't deserve it."

"Yeah…" she said, eyeing me warily. "I think it's time for me to head home."

"You're sure?" I said. "You want to grab dinner or something?"

Amanda looked at me, sadness in her eyes. "Henry, this is what it is. I'll help you all you need. I want to know everything about Danny and Michelle, too. But this is what we are, now, you and me. And this is a choice you made."

"What was your choice?" I asked.

She looked at me, her cheeks flushing red, anger in her eyes. "I didn't have one," she said. "You made my choice for me."

"I know. And I'm sorry I did that. I wish I could take it back. More than anything."

Amanda took a step closer, her eyes locked on to mine. For a moment I felt embarrassed, wanted to step back.

"Two years ago," Amanda said, "you came clean about who you were. I had a choice. I could have left you on the side of the road for the assholes who wanted you dead. Or I could help you. I made my choice. And here we are. I didn't leave you then, and I wouldn't have left you ever. You decided to make my choice for me. And since you did that, I'm not going to put myself in another situation where someone can dictate *my* future without my say-so. It's my life, Henry, and if you don't like what I do with it, you should have never gotten into my car in the first place."

I finally stepped back, felt like I'd been slapped across the face. Though I had no one to blame but myself. "So what are we, then?" I asked.

Amanda walked forward until I could smell the light perfume that she must have put on before work. Because she sure didn't wear it for me.

"We're friends," she said. "Good friends. I'll help you however I can with this. But just with this. That's my choice. So either you can deal with it or you can't, but if you can't, say something now. Otherwise don't waste my time."

"I have nothing to say. I appreciate it. So will Danny Linwood."

I sat back down. Took out the papers Amanda had given me regarding Michelle Oliveira's disappearance. I began to go through them again. Amanda stood there in the hall for a moment, then came and sat down next to me. She looked over my shoulder.

"Do you mind?" she asked. She didn't quite phrase it as a question. She knew there wasn't a chance in hell of me minding. I smiled. Told her I didn't.

Then I noticed something on Michelle's medical reports. She used a pediatrician in Hobbs County for several years before moving to Meriden. I looked at the name on the birth certificate, the signature of the man who delivered Michelle Oliveira.

"What is it?" Amanda asked.

"Michelle Oliveira was born at the Yardley Medical Center in Hobbs County," I said.

"And?"

"The doctor on this birth certificate is named Dmitri Petrovsky," I said. "The same Dmitri Petrovsky who treats Danny Linwood."

17

The girl sat on the couch, listening to the two grown-ups speak as if she wasn't even there.

"I heard her coughing last night," Elaine Reed said. It was cold inside the house. The girl watched with curiosity as Elaine held a cup of tea to her cheek. She'd heard Elaine's husband, Bob, say something about not being able to work the fireplace. Bob talked loud sometimes, and used words that Elaine got mad at him for.

Elaine was a pretty woman, only a little younger than her own mom. She had bright red hair and always wore pretty blue jewelry. When the other day the girl asked what kind it was, Elaine told her that her own daddy had brought it back from Greece. She said the rocks there were as blue as the sea itself.

Bob was shorter, with thinning dark hair and a beard that circled only his upper lip and chin. He wore glasses and didn't say much and spent most of the day reading books and newspapers. He seemed to like to argue about politicians, people he said were doing this country more harm than good. Elaine always nodded and smiled when he talked like that, but didn't really seem to have any opinions of her own in that regard.

The house was so huge, bigger than her old one, and the girl was scared to walk around alone. Not that she ever had to, since Elaine insisted on holding her hand almost everywhere she went. The girl felt strange, this woman she'd just met acting so friendly, but Elaine was nice and it meant not having to be scared. Even though she was still confused, the girl loved running up and down the lengthy hallways, laughing as Bob helped her slide down the banister. Elaine placed both of her hands around the cup, took a sip and placed it on the wooden table. Bob picked it up, frowned at her, then took a glass coaster emblazoned with a bright yellow sunflower and put the cup back down on it.

"She might just have a cold," Bob said. "Kids get colds. Not everything is a life-threatening disease."

She'd heard Elaine mention that the Reed family had lived in this house for just six months, and still hadn't quite grown used to its nooks and crannies, the way it creaked during high wind, the way the linoleum was cool in the spring and hot in the summer. Yet for all the comfort, Elaine said she still felt isolated. The days were sunny and clear, and when the windows were left open the girl could see the trees, high oaks. And the fence surrounding the property.

Bob Reed had a bit of a temper. Or as her daddy would say, his blood got up something. Bob complained that they had to drive three miles just to see a human being. And he had to fiddle with some sort of remote control to work a "stupid" motor-controlled gate that allowed access to the driveway. Not to mention some brick wall that obscured the surrounding area. Elaine would put her hand on Bob's shoulder and say, "We know why this is happening. We need to make the best of it." Bob would look at her, nod, then go off on his own.

But right now they seemed concerned. A few days ago, the girl had come down with a cold. She felt shivery and warm at the same time, and no matter how many blankets Elaine piled on top of her it never went away. When they first realized she was sick, Bob and Elaine grew pale, and this scared the girl.

"Kids cough," he said now, trying to be strong. "Look at Patrick. Hawked up a ball of phlegm every night until he turned three."

"Well, this one is six," Elaine said. "And that coughing doesn't sound right. Maybe we should take her to see someone."

"Not him," Bob said. "I don't trust that man."

"Neither do I, but we have to. He told us if we ever needed medical help, we had to see…"

"Screw that crazy, scarred-up old man," Bob said. "He doesn't have to live like this. He didn't have to change his life for some strange kid."

"Patrick," Elaine said. "Think of Patrick."

Bob sighed, put his head in his hands. "Her cold will pass," he said, reaching for the newspaper. "Can't even get the newspaper delivered because 'he' said so."

"Speaking of which," Elaine said, "I think it's time for her shot."

Bob nodded. He said, "I'll do it this time."

He stood up. Headed toward the bathroom. A minute later Bob came back carrying a plastic bag.

He opened the bag and took out a gauze pad, a syringe, a small vial and a bottle of clear liquid that smelled funny. The girl watched all this. It all seemed vaguely familiar. And though that needle looked huge, like the size of a knife, for some reason she wasn't scared.

"Did you wash your hands?" Elaine asked.

"Of course," Bob replied. He took the small vial and rolled it gently between his fingers. Next he took a cotton ball, opened the bottle of clear liquid, held the ball against the open top until it was wet, then cleaned the top of the vial with the cotton ball.

"That smells funny," the girl said. Elaine scrunched her nose and smiled.

"It does, doesn't it?"

Bob didn't smile. He just kept doing what he was doing.

Bob took the syringe and pulled the stopper back a little bit. Then he pushed the needle into the top of the vial, pressing the stopper again. A small bubble of air entered the vial. Then he turned the vial upside down, the syringe pointing at the ceiling, and pulled the stopper again until a small amount of the liquid was sucked into the syringe.

He tapped the syringe until the air bubbles had risen to the top of the needle. Then he removed the needle from the vial.

Bob turned to Elaine, still holding the needle. "Where did we give it to her this morning?"

"The abdomen," she said.

"Gotcha. Caroline, would you come here?" The girl stood up warily, then went over to Bob. "Here, sweetie, sit down next to me."

She did. Bob rolled up the sleeve of her right arm, then took the smelly cotton ball and rubbed it all over the underside of her arm. Then he blew on it gently.

"That tickles," the girl said.

"Just needs to dry a bit," Bob said. He waited a minute, then took her arm and gently squeezed her skin until a fold stuck out. Caroline winced a bit but stayed still.

"Good girl," Elaine said.

"Now close your eyes," Bob said. When she did, she felt a sting as the needle entered her skin. She felt Bob's grip tighten, then a few seconds later it eased up. She opened her eyes. The needle was on the table and Bob was swabbing her arm with another cotton ball.

"You're such a brave girl," Elaine said. Caroline smiled.

18

The rental car zipped along like only a Hyundai with a hundred-and-twenty-five thousand miles could. Now that I'd been summarily dismissed from the Daniel Linwood story by Wallace, I couldn't expect to be reimbursed for expenses anytime soon. Which meant watching my budget until I proved that it was worth potentially disrupting the lives of several families, not to mention putting my career on the line, to find out what happened to two missing children. Which meant that, for the time being, the $44.95-a-day rates of the Rent-a-Wreck of Yonkers was the only thing that could fit my ever-extended budget.

As soon as I realized that both Michelle Oliveira and Daniel Linwood not only were born in the same hospital, but were treated by the same doctor, I decided to speak to this man to see what, if anything, he could shed light on. Dr. Dmitri Petrovsky worked in the pediatrics unit at the Yardley Medical Center in Hobbs County. Amanda and I were on our way to speak to the good doctor. Like good guests we were coming uninvited.

As I drove up I-287, Amanda gripped the side door handle as though the car might split in half at any moment. Ironic, considering a few years back Amanda had driven us to St. Louis at an average speed that would make Jeff Gordon cry for mama.

I noticed her clutching the side, smirked and said, "Come on, you really think I'm going to spin out or drive us both into the Hudson? Besides, between the two of us, who do you think has racked up more points on their license?"

She glared at me. "I've never had an accident in all the time I've been driving. And I've been in a car with you, oh, a total of, like, three times. Forgive me if I don't quite trust your instincts. Not to mention my Toyota was sturdier than the Verrazano bridge."

"I have such fond memories of that car."

Though Amanda and I had now been on speaking terms for just a few days, I was surprised at how easily we fell back into old patterns, the give-and-take of conversation. I was actually uncomfortable with it. Specifically, the fact that she seemed so calm. As if she knew our banter was nothing more than that, and would never get past the surface.

Two young children, both vanishing into nothing, reappearing after years, neither with any memory of their time gone. Both having been born in the same town, to low-income families with other siblings. I had no idea exactly what we were looking for, or what I expected to find, but I hoped that Dmitri Petrovsky, having borne witness to the birth of both Michelle and Danny, could yield new information.

We arrived at Yardley Medical Center a little after nine in the morning.

We stepped out of the Hyundai. It was warm outside, the sun hot and vivid. I was wearing a pair of brown khakis and a navy-blue sport coat. Amanda was in a sweater and light blue jeans. She looked a millions times better than I did, which wasn't surprising, since I had to dig through a pile of unmentionables just to find two matching socks.

The Yardley Medical Center was a long building, twelve stories high, shaped like an L, with one taller side made of red brick, the other, shorter part windowed by steel and blue glass. We walked around to the main entrance, passing ambulatory care, and entered. The lobby was not large, but it was impeccably clean. Off to the side was a flower shop, a newsstand and a small cafeteria, and another path leading to a bank of elevators. In the middle was an information desk and security checkpoint. Half a dozen people were in line. When they finished talking to the attendant, she handed them a sticker to show Security, who let them enter the elevator bank.

We walked up to the information booth. The attendant, a heavyset black woman, said, "May I help you?"

"We're here to see Dr. Dmitri Petrovsky in Pediatrics," I said.

"Your names?"

"Henry Parker and Amanda Davies."

"Do you have identification?"

We both handed over our drivers licenses. I didn't want to announce myself as a member of the press just yet. In case Petrovsky knew anything, I didn't want to give him time to prepare.

The woman looked at our IDs, then at us, then handed them back. She scribbled our names on two orange stickers, then signed each one before peeling them off and pressing them against our shirts.

"Petrovsky, Pediatrics. Suite 1103."

We thanked her, showed the stickers to the guard and

rode the elevator to the eleventh floor. The elevator was jam-packed, and the ride took forever. Finally we got off on eleven and followed the signs to the correct suite.

The eleventh-floor hallway was painted light blue. Very soothing. When we found 1103, a door marked Pediatrics, we paused for a moment, then entered.

We found ourselves in a waiting room littered with toys and parenting magazines. Various brochures were available. There were about a dozen chairs, almost all of which were filled with mothers, fathers and their tykes. I counted three pregnant women. Some of the kids were playing, some sleeping, and at least two were bawling their eyes out. Amanda took a seat, picked up a copy of *Parenting* magazine, and nodded toward the secretary.

"Would you mind signing us in, hon?"

"My pleasure, *hon.*"

I approached the secretary, a middle-aged woman with frizzy hair and a pair of red glasses perched on her nose. "Help you?" she said.

"I'm here to see Dr. Petrovsky," I said.

"Do you have an appointment?"

"No, I'm sorry, we don't."

She swiveled to a computer, pressed a few keys, then swiveled back. "He can see you today, but not likely until eleven-thirty." She handed me a clipboard with several forms on it. "If you and your wife would please fill these out and return it back to me."

I opened my mouth to explain the whole *not wife* thing, but didn't think it was worth the time or explanation.

I took the papers and a pen, sat down next to Amanda.

"If anyone asks, you're my wife."

"'Scuse me?"

"Just go with it."

"Come on, Henry, these kind of matrimonial decisions should be made by both of us for Christ's sake."

A lady holding her infant son glared at us.

"Sorry," I said, turning to Amanda. "Honey, there are children present."

Amanda gave me a look that could have melted steel. I concentrated on filling out the forms, being as vague as possible, while leaving most responses blank.

When they were completed, I went back up to the receptionist. Handing them over, I said, "I left a lot of this blank. Frankly, there are some personal issues I'd rather discuss with Dr. Petrovsky first, if you don't mind."

The woman rolled her eyes at me, said, "Suit yourself," and took the papers. When I returned to Amanda, she was buried in a copy of *Parenting* magazine.

"Wow," Amanda said, eyebrows raised. "Did you know that the World Health Organization recommends breast-feeding your child until they're at least two years old, and sometimes until they're four?"

"Why not?" I said. "Nothing brings a mother and her child closer than reading, writing and breast-feeding."

Amanda snorted a laugh, causing the other mothers to sneer at her in unison. She went back to reading the magazine. I did a cursory search through the reading material available. Since I had no aching desire to sift through a Learning Annex pamphlet or a four-month-old issue of *Cosmopolitan,* I just sat there and waited.

Finally after a two-hour wait, the receptionist called, "Mr. and Mrs. Parker."

I looked at Amanda, her face suddenly nervous. We stood up and followed the receptionist down a wood-paneled hallway into an examination room.

"Dr. Petrovsky will be with you in just a moment."

When she left, I turned to Amanda and said, "Here we go."

"You really think this guy knows anything about Danny and Michelle?"

"That's why we're here," I said. "I just want something to prove to Wallace this story deserves looking into, regardless of what some stuffed shirt says."

We sat there waiting for fifteen minutes. I looked around the room. Nothing out of place, and because we were in a simple examining room rather than Petrovsky's office, it prevented me from snooping around his framed degrees.

Then the door opened, and a fifty-something barrel-chested man walked in. He was about five-ten with a thick gray beard and a white coat that barely concealed his protruding midsection. Beneath the beard his cheeks were slightly red. He walked with a slight limp. I guessed he'd undergone a hip or knee replacement surgery recently.

"Mr. and Mrs. Parker, I am Dr. Dmitri Petrovsky." He spoke with a thick Russian accent. I took his extended hand, as did Amanda.

"Thanks for seeing us on such short notice," I said.

"It is my pleasure. Now, if you will do me one more, please, have a seat." Amanda sat down on a small metal chair. Petrovsky laughed. "No, not there. Here."

Petrovsky approached the examining table. He reached underneath, fiddled around for a few seconds, and then pulled up a pair up stirrups which he latched into place. He then slapped the green cushion and said, "Mrs. Parker, if you please."

He put his palms together and then opened them as if he were reading a book.

Amanda's eyes went wide. "Oh, hell no. Henry, this is where I get off the train. Good luck."

"Mrs. Parker?" Petrovsky said. He turned to me. "I do not understand. This is a routine part of a first examination."

Time to come clean. Or at least cleaner.

"Dr. Petrovsky, my name is Henry Parker, and I'm a reporter with the *New York Gazette*. Now, first off, I want you to know that I'm here in the best interests of two children. All I want to do is ask you a few questions. We don't want to make any trouble, I promise. And I would appreciate your complete candor. It's vital in our investigation."

"Investigation?" Petrovsky's eyes were frightened, but I couldn't tell if it was from the surprise or something else. "Please, I do not understand. You lied to Maggie at reception?"

"Not exactly, Doctor. I just needed to speak with you. If after we talk you think my motives aren't genuine, you can do what you want. But please, just hear me out. I mean well."

Petrovsky folded his arms. I took that to mean he was listening.

"I'm investigating the disappearance of Daniel Linwood," I said. "The records show that Daniel Linwood was born in this hospital, and that you were the attending during the birth. In conjunction with Daniel Linwood, we're investigating a similar disappearance, a girl named Michelle Oliveira. Michelle also was born here, under your supervision.

"Daniel Linwood," Petrovsky said, his eyes yielding a glimmer of recognition. "The name does sound familiar, yes. What has happened that you are investigating?"

This surprised me a little. The Linwood disappearance was major news in Hobbs County. Petrovsky had worked here dating back years. Either his memory had slipped, or he was being obstinate for a reason.

"A week ago, Daniel Linwood returned to his family after being kidnapped nearly five years ago. I'm looking into who kidnapped him and why."

"But you say Daniel was found, yes? He is with his family?"

"Yes, he is."

"Then all should be happy, no?"

"Not if you want a sense of justice. And I think Daniel's disappearance is related in some way to Michelle Oliveira. You know both children were born at Yardley," I said. "And they're both from Hobbs County."

"I did not know this, and I do not know this Michelle person you speak of."

Petrovsky reached into his pocket and took out a handkerchief, mopping a few beads from his brow. He put it back in, laughed slightly, then held his hands to his stomach.

"My wife," he said. "Says I should lose about fifty pounds to stay healthy. Perhaps, she says, this is the reason I have a titanium knee. I think she may be right, but she cannot tell me *how* to lose that weight."

"Doctor," I said, "Daniel Linwood has no recollection of his missing years. I need to know what could happen to a child that could do that to their brain, to their memory. If you know anything about Daniel, or what happened, that could explain it."

"Please, Mr. Parker, I am just here to do my job. I have delivered many hundreds of children in my career, and now you ask me to remember two as if they were delivered this morning? You have lied to me, and now you expect me to answer you like a man at a cocktail party who has medical questions? If you have medical questions, I would be happy to refer you to another physician in this clinic. Or if you prefer to continue down this path, I would be happy to refer you to hospital security, who will refer you to a good lawyer. That is all I have to say. Now I suggest you leave. Right away."

The look Petrovsky gave us confirmed that he was not bluffing. I had no intention of calling his bluff. I merely thanked him for his time, apologized again for the ruse, and we left.

We exited Yardley in silence. When we got to the parking lot, Amanda said, "Goddamn, that guy knows something."

I nodded, picked up the pace and headed toward our Hyundai, hoping a strong wind hadn't caused it to blow away.

"I agree," I said. "He'd heard the name Michelle Oliveira before. And I don't buy that he didn't know about Danny Linwood." I stood in front of our car, thinking about what to do next.

"Think we should head back?" Amanda asked.

"No," I said.

"Why not?"

"I'm going to wait for him. Petrovsky. I'm going to follow him when he gets off work and see where he goes. If necessary, confront him off hospital grounds. Where there's no security, nobody but us."

Amanda sighed.

"The least you could have done was tell me that upstairs. I would have grabbed a magazine from the waiting room."

She smiled at me, and we both piled into the car, waiting for the good doctor to emerge.

19

The phone call was not unexpected, but it rattled Raymond Benjamin nonetheless. He'd been sitting in his loft, sipping a glass of pinot noir, from the Argyle wineries, 2005 vintage. There were few things that beat a glass of red and a cigarette at night. Perhaps a little Coltrane. Getting a phone call from this number ruined all of it.

He recognized the area code and extension immediately, and as soon as they appeared in the caller-ID display, Benjamin knew there was a problem. Petrovsky was only supposed to call if there was an emergency. And Benjamin made it very clear about what constituted an emergency.

He answered the phone. "Doctor," Ray said. "There'd better be a fucking good reason for this."

Raymond Benjamin listened as Dmitri Petrovsky filled him in on what had occurred at the hospital that day. He ended the conversation by saying he'd watched the two people—Henry Parker and Amanda Davies—leave the hospital. Only, when they left, they didn't drive away. In fact, they'd been sitting in their car for several hours. Petrovsky and Benjamin came to the same conclusion: they were planning to follow the doctor when he left work.

When Ray Benjamin hung up the phone, he sat there for a moment, thinking. Then he got up, tossing the rest of his glass into the sink, stubbing out his cigarette in the ashtray. He called Vince and told him to be at the garage in fifteen minutes. Ray had a lot of phone calls to make.

First he called the house. The couple took it as well as he expected. He told them they'd prepared for a day like this. And if they kept up their end of the deal, it would all be worth it. And if they didn't, he only needed to remind them of the photograph.

When everything was in motion, and Petrovsky confirmed that Parker was still at Yardley, Ray Benjamin went to the garage. Vince was waiting for him. Vincent Cann was a tall, slender man of thirty-eight. His jet-black hair was slicked back, his face clean-shaven as always. A pair of designer sunglasses sat on his face. He nodded when he saw Benjamin approaching.

"Clusterfuck, ain't it, boss?"

Ray answered by not answering at all.

They piled into the car. Ray opened his window a crack. The younger man was chewing gum, his jaws working overtime. Ray reached into his pocket and pulled out a fresh pack of Chesterfields. He depressed the electric lighter, unwrapped the pack, stuck the cig in his mouth and waited.

Vince said, "Should we get going?"

"Wait a second," the older man said. The lighter wasn't ready yet.

When the metal knob popped out, Ray took the end, pressed it to the tip and inhaled deeply. There was nothing like a good Chesterfield. When the butt was half smoked, a long finger of ash hanging off the end, Ray flicked it out the window.

"Clear your schedule for the next few days," Ray said to Vince as he pulled into traffic. "We're going to be busy cleaning this mess up, and there's not a lot of time."

20

Paulina arched her back, feeling the convulsions ripple through her body. She embraced the aches of pleasure, the slightest hint of pain as Myron Bennett raked his too-long nails down her stomach. She felt the final shudder of orgasm, the sweat dripping down her chest, waiting until everything was calm before finally becoming still. Paulina looked down. She was still wearing her bra, a slight puddle of moisture collecting in between the cups.

Gathering herself, Paulina climbed off Myron, taking one more glimpse at his naked body, his erection like a flag of surrender. The boy had a beautiful body, that's for sure, and though nobody would ever know of their tryst, it secretly thrilled her to know she'd just fucked a man thousands of women would ditch their husbands and 2.4 children for.

She located her underwear, snagged the band on her shoe, kicked it into her hands and headed for the bathroom.

"Hey," Myron called out as Paulina groped her way to the bathroom door. "I didn't come yet!"

"Nobody's watching if you want to finish yourself off," she said, closing the bathroom door. Paulina looked at herself in the mirror. Her mascara was streaked. She ran the faucet and washed it off. She looked at her breasts, felt a twinge of sadness, noticed they were sagging slightly more than she remembered. For years Paulina had taken care of her body, spending countless hours at the gym, countless dollars on every treatment under the sun. But aging happened to everyone, even women who were born to fight everything. Push-up bras did wonders to enhance her natural cleavage, but nobody could fight Father Time, especially since he had gravity on his side. She thought about having them done, wondered if it was an outpatient procedure. The last thing she needed was to be out of work a day or two, then come with them *enhanced.* Boob jobs were only worth it if no one knew you'd had one.

She could hear Myron moving about in the bedroom. She heard the sound of his zipper, laughed to herself that he was too frustrated to finish the job. Myron was a nice treat, and thankfully she'd never have to see him again. At least not in person.

In Sunday's edition of the *Dispatch,* Paulina would be running a lengthy article about Myron's decade-long affair with Mitsy Russell Henshaw, wife of billionaire venture capitalist Richard Henshaw. Richard Henshaw had been a longtime critic of the *Dispatch,* specifically the paper's editor-in-chief, Ted Allen. It was what Allen called a "have your cake and eat it, too" story. It was both a juicy bit of gossip that would sell papers, while accomplishing the goal of humiliating one of Ted's most vocal enemies. Paulina figured it only fair that if she was going to report the piece, she deserved a piece of the cake, too.

Though Myron was in his late thirties and no longer in the kind of shape that had secured him deals as an underwear model in the nineties—the abs a little softer, the arms not quite as sinewy—he was still a striking bachelor, the kind of man that would turn heads and make very wealthy women think very bad thoughts.

She had interviewed him for three hours, at the end of which Paulina offered to buy him a drink. To make things a little more personal, she said, rinse off the professional. And when they were in the comfort of a pair of martinis, she let Myron know that as long as she was putting her keyboard out, he'd be putting out, too. And so here she was, room 1250 at the W Hotel, the beauty of her exorbitant expense account allowing her the beauty of Myron Bennett.

Yet as much as she'd savored the night's pleasures and would enjoy the media circus surrounding Myron's affair, she'd be glad to get back to work on the real story that had kept her juiced the past few months. Underwear models came and went. It was a rare occasion that you could do something that *mattered.* And in just a matter of weeks, she'd be ready to bring Jack O'Donnell down like a house of cards. And with Jack, the veneer that was the *Gazette* would tumble as well. And that kind of satisfaction would last longer than any orgasm.

Cinching up her robe as she left the bathroom, Paulina took her purse from her wallet and flipped a twenty at Myron. The crumpled bill landed sadly on the pillow. Myron stood there staring at it. He was topless in his jeans, searching around for his shirt. He looked at the money, confused, then looked up and down at Paulina as if she were hanging in a freezer.

"You have the most beautiful tits," he said, a sultry grin on his face that made Paulina feel like retching.

"Please," she said. "Save it for the women who give a shit."

"What, one party and you get all cold on me? It wasn't good for you, beautiful?"

"Ugh, don't call me that. I'm sure Muffy or Tiffani or whatever rich bitch you're going to bang tomorrow night will love that ooey-gooey shit. You're a good lay, Myron. I appreciate it. But enough of the honeydoll, baby stuff. I'm a grown woman, you're a grown man, now help me find my shirt."

"It's under the bed, doll." He smiled at Paulina's grimace. She glanced under the bed, came up with a wrinkled blue shirt. She nodded toward the twenty on the bed.

"Take it."

"What's that for?"

"Whatever you want. A taxi. A beer. Doesn't matter."

He looked at the money. "Really, you don't have to."

"Listen, I spent the better part of an entire day talking to you and listening to the most boring shit on earth. I listened to you whine about your mean parents, your crummy job, how nobody will hire you as a model anymore. And I know you have less money in the bank than you have brains up in that head of yours. I don't think you'll say no to cab fare. So just say thank-you and go home."

He watched her for a moment, looked at the money. "Thank you," he said. "But you don't have to be a bitch about it."

Paulina's mouth dropped, a startled laugh escaping her lips. "Bitch? You call me a bitch because, what, I just repeated what you've been blabbing about all night? If you don't like hearing the whole, cold, hard, clean truth, just continue to delude yourself. Facts are facts. Nobody wants to hire a forty-year-old has-been when twenty years old can be bought for less, and without the baggage. And if you didn't fuck Mitsy for a decade, you'd keep that irrelevant streak of yours going. So you don't want to believe the truth? Then, buddy, don't read the newspaper. But if you want a reality check, you little baby, what I say shouldn't hurt you any more than your life hurts you."

"See," Myron said. "That's what I mean. Most women, when you give them an orgasm, they don't treat you like you're a piece of, a, a dust ball or a termite or something. Something they can pick up and throw in the trash like it didn't exist."

"Listen, Myron. You're a sweet guy. But sweet guys get as much out of life as a little teacup puppy that someone carries around in their purse. You get fed when your master wants to feed you, but pretty soon you're a nuisance and not quite as much fun to look at. If you want more out of life than that, you have to take it. If that means being a bitch, well, I'd rather be a bitch than a pussy."

Myron stared at her. "I'm looking forward to reading the article."

Paulina nodded. "It'll be a good one, I promise you that much. I'll make sure a copy of the *Dispatch* is delivered to you first thing Sunday morning." Then she strode across the room until she was nearly mouth to mouth with Myron. "And if you so much as mention this night to anyone, I'll run a correction on Monday about your chronic herpes outbreaks."

"My what?"

"Exactly."

"Even you wouldn't stoop so low," Myron said, though he looked unconvinced.

"Try me," Paulina replied. "I love it when people think they're calling my bluff."

Myron nodded, put his shirt on, found his shoes. He thanked Paulina, grabbed the twenty and left. Paulina stood there in a room full of rumpled sheets, the air stinking of sweat and sex. Then she gathered up her belongings, went outside and caught a cab home.

21

By three o'clock, my legs were growing stiff. We'd watched countless people arrive and leave Yardley since that morning, with no sign of Dmitri Petrovsky. We'd taken turns going in to the cafeteria for cups of coffee and bathroom breaks, doing everything we could to stay alert without going insane, but I was growing impatient. And even worse, worried.

Doctors came and went, but nobody who looked like Petrovsky.

At four o'clock, Amanda asked, "Do you think we might have missed him?"

I shook my head. "I hope not. Let's make sure."

I took out my cell phone, called the Yardley switchboard, asked to be connected to Pediatrics. When a woman's voice picked up, I asked if Dr. Petrovsky would be available for any more appointments today.

"I'm sorry, sir, he's got two more patients scheduled for this afternoon, then he'll be out again until Monday."

"Do you have any idea what time he'll be finished with his patients?"

"No, sir, I'm sorry, but if you want to come in next week I'd be happy to schedule you for an appointment."

"No, thanks, I'll call back later." I hung up. "He's still there, but probably not for much longer."

Amanda nodded. She began to rub her shoulders.

"You okay?" I asked.

"Just a little stiff."

"Can I do anything to help?"

"Nah, thanks, though."

For a moment I had an ache to reach out, put my arm around her and rub her shoulders myself. Not too long ago it wouldn't have been a big deal at all, just something else that happened over the normal day of a relationship. Small gestures like that in the end meant so much, and it was only when they ended that I realized their significance.

"Henry, look," Amanda suddenly said, pointing in the direction of the entrance. "There he is."

Sure enough, Dmitri Petrovsky was leaving Yardley. He was easily identifiable with his bushy beard, ambling gait. He'd changed out of his hospital whites and was wearing a bulky overcoat, carrying a stuffed briefcase. He trudged through the parking lot as our eyes followed him. He stopped for a moment to yell at another motorist whose Saab edged a little too close, and for a moment I worried that the argument would escalate and our whole plan would be shot. Thankfully, after a heated exchange and a middle-finger gesture that left the driver steaming, Petrovsky continued walking, eventually stopping at a dark blue Nissan.

"Do me a favor," I said. "Take my tape recorder out of my bag." She did so. "Now turn it on."

She clicked the record button.

I said, "I want to record the directions. Just in case."

"Smart," Amanda said.

I started the engine, waited until I saw the brake lights

on Petrovsky's car turn red before I edged out of the parking space. I turned the corner of our row just as Petrovsky finished backing out. I allowed another car to move in front of us as all three vehicles headed for the exit.

"What if he sees us?" Amanda said.

"I don't know," I said truthfully. "Let's just hope he doesn't."

Petrovsky pulled up to the exit and put his right-turn signal on. He made the right, and the car in front of us turned left. I put my right blinker on, waited until Petrovsky's Nissan was about thirty yards away, then I pulled onto the exit ramp and began to follow the doctor.

Petrovsky kept an even speed as he circled the exit ramp that led away from Yardley. I stayed far enough behind that it would be tricky for him to see me in his rearview mirror. Neither Amanda nor I spoke. We were both focused on the road, the car and what would happen next.

When the ramp came to an end, Petrovsky kept on straight and merged onto the freeway. He pulled into the left lane; I took the middle, kept pace three cars behind. There was still light in the sky, sundown not yet for another hour, so I was able to make out his car pretty clearly. The hum of our engine seemed as loud as a bullhorn as we kept pace, threatening to give us away.

After a few miles, Petrovsky drifted over to the middle lane, then turned on his right-turn signal and headed toward a sign that read Exit 62. I relayed this to the tape recorder. When he pulled into the right lane, I allowed a silver Mercedes to do the same and I pulled in behind it. I took the exit ramp behind both cars, watching Petrovsky closely. I could make out the man hunched over the steering wheel, felt lead in my stomach as I prayed we were being cautious, keeping out of sight.

I followed his car down a one-lane highway, our speeds decreasing as the road became more residential. The doctor was steadfastly observing the thirty-five-mile-an-hour speed limit. The silver Mercedes was only a buffer for a few minutes, as it peeled into a strip mall soon after, leaving our car as the only one behind Petrovsky.

We followed him down this road for some time. Eventually the sun began to set. The sky grew darker. Soon all I could make out of Petrovsky's car were the taillights. The faint hum of the tape recorder was the only noise in the car. My pulse was quickening. I had no idea how this night would end.

About twenty minutes later, Petrovsky turned on his left blinker and pulled off onto a narrow street. I had to follow, had to hope it was too dark for him to recognize our car or see me behind the wheel. I was still about thirty yards behind him, but when his Nissan made another right and then a left within seconds of each other, I had to speed up before losing him among the turns.

"There's no way he doesn't know we're following him," Amanda said, her voice quiet, fearful. "No way."

I said nothing. Just spoke the directions into the recorder and kept driving.

We passed through streets lined with houses, lamps illuminating rows of homes. Most of them were in disrepair, casting an aura of poverty, carelessness, hopelessness. I tried not to look at them, focused on the car in front of us, felt cold sweat beading down my back. Fear and adrenaline coursed through me, and I wondered how much longer this chase would last.

Then Petrovsky made a right onto another road, this one dimly lit. I couldn't see any houses on either side. There were no lamps. It was just him and us.

I glimpsed the street sign, stated into the recorder, "Turned right onto Huntley Terrace."

Huntley Terrace was a narrow road. Once we'd driven a few miles, we passed by a few houses spaced sporadically apart, driveways hidden behind thick brush and wooden fences. There were no streetlights, no road signs. We were still twenty yards behind Petrovsky, but we were the only cars traveling this road. By this point, the gig was up.

"Henry," Amanda said. "What is that?"

I squinted my eyes, felt my stomach lurch as I saw that we were approaching a pair of metal double gates up ahead. The were bracketed by a brick wall that encircled the property within. The woods were thick on either side. I couldn't see anything beyond them.

"Oh, fuck," I said. Petrovsky had slowed down as he approached.

"What now?" Amanda asked.

"I don't know."

"I'm scared," she said. She turned to me. In her eyes I could tell she knew what I was thinking. We had to keep going.

I slowed the car down, pulled to a stop and put the car in Park. I waited to see what Petrovsky would do next. His car stopped at the gates. It stayed there for close to a minute, then I heard the sound of metal screeching as the gates swung inward. They did not look like they enclosed a residential area. They were protecting a single home. Was this where Petrovsky lived?

When the gates were open, the doctor pulled onto a gravel road and then disappeared out of sight. I waited, unsure of what to do.

And after a minute of waiting, I realized something strange.

The gates hadn't closed.

They were wide open.

Whoever was inside those gates was waiting for us.

"Too late to turn back," I said.

I put the car into Drive and slowly approached the gates. I still couldn't see anything beyond them, but as I got closer I could make out a red hue around the bend. Definitely Petrovsky's brake lights.

I drove through the gates, half expecting a Sonny Corleone sneak attack. But we passed through without anything out of the ordinary. I made the turn, then jumped as I heard the metal sounds again.

The gates were closing behind us.

"We shouldn't be here," Amanda said. "We should go."

"We can't now," I said. "Let's just see what's what."

As I continued down the path, Petrovsky's Nissan came into view. It was parked at the end of a driveway. The driveway was next to a house. It was shrouded in darkness, but there was just enough light from the moon to illuminate the seven-foot-high brick wall surrounding the entire property. It confused me. The wall wasn't high enough that an adult would have a problem climbing over it. I also noticed that every tree on the property was at least ten or twenty feet from the fence. There were no limbs that could reach the fence. It had been clearly built to keep someone smaller from getting out.

Down the driveway, I could see Petrovsky. He was standing next to his car. Hands in his pockets. He was waiting for us.

I pulled up close until I was directly behind the Nissan, then put the car into Park and shut the engine off.

"Stay here," I said to Amanda.

"The hell with that," she said, unbuckling her seat belt.

We both stepped out of the car. Petrovsky was standing in the middle of the driveway. He did not move as we approached. He did not seem surprised to see us.

As we got closer, I could see that the doctor was trembling slightly. His hands were in his pockets, his body too rigid. As I got closer, a wave of fear coursed through me. I saw that Petrovsky was shaking. The man was afraid.

"Dr. Petrovsky," I said. "It's Henry Parker. I know you saw us following you. I'm sorry to approach you under these circumstances, but I have more questions."

"Yes, Mr. Parker," the doctor said, his voice low, remorseful. "I am very sorry, too."

I heard a faint rustle come from behind us, then there was a sharp pain in my leg. Before I could shout, the gravel of the driveway came hurtling up to meet me, and then everything swam away.

22

I woke up groggy, with pain in my head and my leg. It took a moment for my eyes to adjust to the faint crack of light coming from a doorway on the far side of the room that was otherwise pitch-black. I was standing up. I was shirtless, my bare torso cold against a metal pole behind me. My head pounded, and when I tried to move I realized my hands were bound above me, my legs bound below. My arms were bound and tied to what felt like a metal pipe. I groped around, felt that the pipe went straight back into the brick wall behind me. My feet were bound behind the same pipe. I wriggled but it did no good.

Suddenly my eyes flew open. Amanda. Oh, God, where was she?

I struggled against the bonds, but I couldn't see anything, couldn't reach the rope that bound my hands.

Then a voice spoke out from the darkness, and I stopped moving.

"Don't worry, she's fine. I'm sorry my associate had to restrain you, but I promise it's for your own good." The voice was gruff, older, slightly raspy. A smoker's voice.

"Who are you?" I said. "Come over here so I can see you, asshole."

"Listen to you, talking as though you're holding all the cards. When your hand was folded before you even woke up."

I heard a spark, like a match striking flint, and then a small orange flame lit up the darkness. The flame rose until I heard a sucking sound. The flame lit the end of a cigarette, and with a puff was blown out.

I could see the cigarette about ten feet from me, and with each inhalation I caught the outline of a man's face. I couldn't see much detail, but he looked to be in his late fifties. Harsh light to go with the harsh line. He just sat there, sucked his cigarette and said nothing.

"Come on!" I shouted. "What do you want?"

"What do I want," the man said. He flicked away the cigarette and stood up. He must have turned on a light switch, because suddenly an overhead lamp cast a soft glow over the room. I made out what I could. I was in what looked to be some sort of basement. Bare cement walls and a tiled floor. There were no windows I could see. The room wasn't dingy, though, and in fact I was surprised that it appeared to be rather well maintained. A plush leather sofa rested in front of a television set, and a long-forgotten treadmill sat adorned with boxes and discarded clothes. If this was a prison or interrogation room, it wasn't the most intimidating one. The man approached me, took another cigarette from his pocket, lit it and took a deep drag.

Then he approached me, plucked the cigarette from his lips and held it out.

"Want a puff?"

"Yeah, nothing satisfies me more than sucking on a butt that was just in some strange asshole's mouth."

"You sure? It's a Chesterfield."

"Gee, now, that makes a difference. Go screw yourself."

The man shrugged, took another puff.

"I haven't smoked another brand in over thirty years. You know, you can enjoy the pleasures of so many things in life without knowing where it came from. Who made it. Thirty years ago, I would have taken a beating before I smoked. Now I can't get enough of 'em. Ironic, 'swhat it is. That delicious burn inside your lungs, just makes me want to close my eyes, savor the feeling. My ex-wife always asked why I spent so much time reading about crap like that and never listened to her. I'd say, baby, because one's interesting, and one ain't."

I stayed silent. The longer he talked, the longer I stayed alive.

"Chesterfields started to become popular back in the day when Arthur Godfrey ended his radio program by saying, 'This is Arthur buy-'em-by-the-carton Godfrey!' Since the program was sponsored by Chesterfield, pretty soon that's all anyone wanted to smoke. The nonfiltered Chesterfields were popular during Vietnam, allegedly the strongest nonnarcotic stimulant in the country. The government dropped Chesterfields into the jungle by the thousands. And the common man, he figured whatever was good enough for the fighting men and women of this country was good enough for him."

The man stepped into the light, and I finally got a better look at him.

His graying hair was full, skin worn and weatherbeaten. The crow's-feet at his eyes actually made him look handsome, like one of those blue-jeaned cowboys who spent their days on oil rigs, the kind that actually needed a Chevy flatbed. He was lean, about five foot eleven, wearing a dark green T-shirt and jeans. There was a thin scar about an inch long that ran down his right cheek. It was a faint line, slightly jagged, as though it hadn't been stitched up right. He took another pull, let the ash hang on the end for a long while smoldering before tapping it onto the floor.

My heart hammered in my chest. My wrists ached, and the pins and needles in my feet let me know they wouldn't be much help.

"Where is she?" I said.

"You need to be more trusting," the man said. "I told you she's fine. So you should believe that she is fine. I'm not gonna lie to you, Henry. You do me the same courtesy, and things are gonna work out just splendid for Ms. Davies. But let's just focus on the here and now. You and me. Got it?"

"Who are you?" I said.

"Who I am isn't as important as what I have to offer," he said.

"I don't want anything from you," I spat. "People know I'm here. That door's gonna get busted in any second and I'm gonna laugh as they haul your ass away."

"Really…they're coming for you, huh? Who, the CIA? FBI? Batman? Guess you wouldn't mind then if I leave your girl alone for a few weeks. She won't need food or water since, you know, they're *coming* for her."

"You're making a mistake," I said. "She doesn't belong here."

"Well, she's here. No changing that now. Anyway, back to what I was saying. I have something to offer you, Henry, and if you're as smart as I think you are you'll take this offer."

"What is it?" I said.

"It's simple, really," the man said, taking another puff. "I need you to tell me everything the good doctor told you

and everything you know about the kids. Spare no detail.
It's very important you lay all your cards on the table. And
if you do just that, and I believe you, behind door number
one will be your girlfriend's life. You spill, she lives. You
don't spill, her blood does. Simple as that."

"I'll take the offer," I said, "because we don't know
anything. Petrovsky didn't say a word to us. Now, let us
go."

"Oh, come on, Henry, you think it's that easy? You
think that's it? Nah, we can get some more out of you."

He took the cigarette from his mouth. Looked at the
filtered end.

"Chesterfields," he said. "Just about heaven. Can't find
the unfiltered bastards anywhere nowadays, but smoke
enough of these and they do the trick."

"Hope that lung cancer acts mighty quick," I said.

"If it gets me, it gets me," he said. "But I'll go out
with a smile."

A spark fell off the end of the butt. I watched it flutter
to the ground. I moved my wrists around, tried to feel the
pipe where my hands were tied, sliding my fingers back
and forth out of view until my thumb caught on something.
A piece of metal. Something jutting out from the pipe.

The man reached into his pocket, brought out his wallet.
He pulled out a one-dollar bill. Held it up in front of me.
Then he took the lit cigarette between his thumb and forefinger. Slowly he brought the cigarette to the bill. There
was a crackling sound as the lit end burned a perfect circle
through the paper.

When the cigarette had passed through, he held up the bill,
looked at me through the hole, smiled. "Peekaboo, I see
you."

He walked toward me, still holding the lit cigarette. As

he got closer, the light illuminated the man more. I began to shiver, my bare torso shaking. Then I noticed something that nearly made me gag. Covering the man's arms were a road map of small, white marks. Scars. Perfectly round. They were cigarette burns. And there were dozens of them.

"So what did Petrovsky tell you?" he said, his voice frighteningly calm.

"I told you, nothing. Leave us alone."

He scratched his chin, looked at me. "Hmm…no."

He took another step forward, leaned down and pressed the lit end of the cigarette against my chest.

I screamed as I heard the sound of burning, waves of pain shooting through me as I bucked and tried to kick to no avail. The pain was horrific. I hoped I would pass out.

Finally the man removed the cigarette from my skin. Then he leaned over and blew gently on the spot where he'd just burned me.

"That's gonna leave a mark," he said.

I was panting. I could felt sweat pouring down my body, getting into my eyes. I felt around where my hands were bound, found that piece of metal I'd felt before. I rubbed it with my thumb. It was a screw attached to a bolt. The end of the screw jutted out from the metal about half an inch. Just maybe…

I slowly moved my wrists until the half-inch screw was fitted snugly inside one of the loops of knot that bound my wrists. I moved it slowly up and down, back and forth, trying to loosen the knot, to create some slack.

The man tossed his cigarette onto the floor, stubbed it out with his shoe. "I hate to waste one, but I don't think you taste quite as good on the end of a butt as tobacco does."

My breath was ragged, but I tried to focus. I gently

tugged down on my wrist bonds, felt the reassuring pull that the screw was fastened inside the knot. I began to work it more, continuously pressing my wrists against the metal to wedge it in even farther. I nearly gasped when I realized the screw was in as far as it would go. I'd created a hole in the knot. Now all I had to do was make it bigger.

"Do you smoke?" the man asked.

"Fuck you," I said.

"That's a brand I'm unfamiliar with. But since you seem to be full of answers now, I'll ask again. What did Petrovsky tell you?"

"He told me your mother's a whore and your father liked to dress up like Raggedy Ann for Christmas."

The man sighed deeply. I didn't care. The longer we played this game the more time I had. I felt the knot begin to loosen, and soon I was able to slip my index finger inside the knot hole. I pulled down on the screw, worked the loop with my finger, felt it began to slip more. I couldn't let him notice, so I did it slowly. Methodically.

My chest hurt like hell, but I blocked it out. Amanda was somewhere in this house, and even if I did talk, there was no way I trusted this guy to let her live. Rule number one, when a sociopath makes a promise, believe the opposite.

"First time I got burned by one of these," the man said, "I was serving time up in Attica. The guards, *hoo,* man, the guards. They sure liked to have their fun with us. One of the prisoners got out of line, talked back, caused a ruckus at the mess hall, they'd take a lit butt to the guy's armpit. Maybe the bottom of his feet. Something sweet like that. Something that wouldn't go away so fast. At least it would smell sweet after they got done with you. I guess you can see they did a little number on my arms here. Fifty-two, if I counted right, and I won't even get into the rest of my body. 'Course, one time they burnt my arches so bad I couldn't walk for a week. So first thing I did when we got a hold of that place? When us boys took over that prison back in '71? I took a cig, lit the mother up, and stuck it in that same man's eye until it started smoking."

I heard the strike of another match, and he lit another cigarette. Another Chesterfield.

"Did you know," he said, taking a long drag, "that the human hand alone has more than nine thousand nerve endings and six hundred pain sensors? And most of that is concentrated in the fingertips?"

"Yeah, I learned that back in health class."

"What do you think it would feel like to experience mind-numbing pain in the most sensitive area of your body? Do you think you'd enjoy that? Better yet, do you think Ms. Davies would enjoy that?"

I couldn't help but think about the scars already on my hand, from when a madman played butcher shop with it a while back. I certainly wasn't aching for more.

I tugged harder, felt my finger slip through one of the rope's cords. Soon I was able to fit two, then three fingers inside, and I slowly unraveled the rope. I grabbed the end gently before it could fall, but my hands were free. My feet, though, were another matter, and there was no way I could get to them without Chesterfield man noticing. Unless...

"See, if you don't answer my question, we're going to find out just how loud you and your friend can scream. And trust me, nobody will be able to hear you."

"It can't be any louder than you scream when your 'associate' sticks his finger up your ass."

The man frowned, again sucked down the cig, leaving a long ash dangling from the tip.

"Come on, dickhead," I said. "Let's see what you got."

The man looked at me, pissed off and confused. "Let's see if you're this much fun in a minute."

He placed the cigarette between his thumb and forefinger, then reached up with his free hand to steady mine before he burned off my fingertips. As he raised the cigarette, I took a deep breath and blew the long piece of ash directly into his face.

It erupted in a cloud of gray smoke, and the man hacked and coughed and clawed at his eyes.

Before he could take a step back, I pulled off the bonds around my wrists, wound up and backhanded him across the face. He went sprawling across the floor. The cigarette skittered away and went out.

Frantically I bent over and began undoing the bonds at my feet. They were tight, but soon I was able to loosen them. Just then the man stood up, blood leaking from a cut across his cheek. He had fire in his eyes as he ran straight toward me. At that moment I pulled the bonds away from my feet, sidestepped the man and shoved his head against the metal pipe. There was a sickening thud as he bounced off it, then crumpled to the floor in a heap.

I was wobbly standing up. I heard a grunt, saw the man begin to push himself up. There was hatred in his eyes. I didn't hesitate.

I ran forward and kicked him in the head as hard as I could. The breath left him as he lay there, motionless.

As I tried to get the blood flowing back to my feet, I noticed the glint of metal coming from a key ring in his pocket. There were three keys on it. I picked it up, ran for the door. Unsurprisingly, it was locked. I took turns inserting each key inside, and on the third one it clicked home. I twisted the knob, opened the door and prayed Amanda was all right. I glanced back, saw the man unmoving but still breathing steadily. Then I braced myself for whatever horrors awaited in the rest of this house.

But when I ran up the stairs to the main floor, I was shocked to see that I wasn't being held in some dungeon. Instead, I was standing in the middle of what looked like the foyer of a typical suburban house.

"What the hell...?" I whispered.

The hardwood floors had been recently sanded and polished, and the carpeting on the stairs was white and clean. Several framed paintings hung from the walls. A crystal chandelier hung above me, and a family room with a large-screen television branched off to the left. There was a doll with braided hair lying on the floor, next to what looked like a scattered set of a child's building blocks. Everything was clean. I didn't know what to make of it.

"Amanda!" I yelled. There was no response.

I sprinted to the other end of the hall, then took the stairs two at a time to the upper floor.

I ran down a narrow hall. There were three doors, both closed. I opened the first one. It was a bathroom. Hand soaps. Clean towels. No window. No Amanda.

I approached the other door. Pushed it. It opened into what looked like a master bedroom. A king-size bed sat in the center, with a floral comforter cleanly tucked in. Oddly there were no photos anywhere, as though the place had been disinfected of humanity.

I looked around. Didn't see anything.

Then I went to the other door. Stopped in front of it. This one was different. It was painted white like the others, but the paint seemed duller. I touched the surface, immediately recoiled. The other doors were wooden. This one was metal. And I knew right away that one of the keys on my chain would open the dead bolt.

I thrust the key inside, got it on the first twist, but then froze when I heard someone coming up the stairs.

The lock unlatched and I pushed the door open.

And then I was standing in what looked like the dream room of any young girl. There were toys everywhere. Coloring books. A large dollhouse filled with tiny furniture. Tapes and CDs and games were stacked high in a corner. Pink wallpaper, and every book a child could ever want to read. And there, sitting on a made bed, her face a mess of fright and relief, was Amanda.

She jumped up and threw her arms around my chest. I winced as she pressed on the cigarette burn, then took her arm and said, "We need to go. Right now."

Then I noticed something. On the floor. A small scrap of paper. I picked it up, unfolded it. It was a receipt. It was from a store called Toyz 4 Fun. I clenched my jaw. At that moment I knew where we were. I knew what this house was.

Panic welled inside me as I shoved the receipt into my pocket, grabbed Amanda's hand as we went for the door, still slightly ajar. I heard someone running down the hall, shouting, "Ray, where the hell are you, buddy?"

I waited until the footsteps were right outside, then I slammed the heavy metal door closed as hard as I could. There was an audible *oomph* as whoever was on the other side was knocked flat off his feet.

I flung open the door and ran past, my heart hammering when I saw that the man I'd just knocked down had a gun in his right hand.

We sprinted downstairs and toward the front door. Turned the knob. It was locked. One more key left.

I inserted the last key in the lock, let out a breath when it caught, then turned the handle and opened the door to the outside.

As soon as we stepped onto the front porch, Amanda let out a bloodcurdling scream. There was a body in the driveway. It was lying in a pool of blood. The beard gave it away. It was Dmitri Petrovsky, and he was very dead.

"Run!" I shouted.

We ran down the driveway, and I recognized that we were in the exact same place that we'd cornered Petrovsky. The high brick walls and trees obscured the view beyond the house. There was nobody to hear us scream.

We sprinted around the bend, wind whistling past us, and saw the metal gates up ahead.

They were closed. And I had no keys left.

When we reached the brick wall, I knelt down, cupped my hands and said, "Climb on."

Amanda stepped onto my hands.

"One, two, *three.*"

I heaved up as she jumped. Her hands caught the rim of the wall. I pushed from below as Amanda pulled herself up, managing to straddle her legs across the wall.

"Come on!" she shouted.

Just as I got ready to jump, I heard a loud bang and a chunk of brick exploded right beside me.

"Come on, Henry, they're shooting at us!"

I jumped up, managed to get hold of the wall. Amanda gripped my wrists and began to pull. I got a small foothold in the chunk of wall that'd been blown out, then pushed off and hoisted myself up. Another shot rang out, and brick flew apart right where my foot had been.

We toppled over the wall, landed on the other side in a tangled mess. I leaped to my feet, helped Amanda up. Then we ran as fast as we could, until the woods swallowed us.

We arrived panting at the road we'd turned off of when we followed Petrovsky. Huntley Terrace. It was dark out. I had no idea where we were or what day it was.

"Come on," I said, taking Amanda's hand again. I thought back to the last time this happened, the last time we were both running for our lives. Back then Amanda was fleeing with a man she didn't know. This time, for better or worse, she knew what she'd gotten into.

We jogged down the dark road, continually looking over our shoulders to see if we were being followed. I heard nothing, saw nothing. My body felt numb. I was still shirtless, and my side ached. Amanda suddenly stopped, put her hand on my chest.

"Is that a burn mark?" she said.

"We don't have time," I panted.

Then out of the darkness a pair of headlights appeared. My eyes widened, and I ran forward waving my hands like a crazy person. I was in the middle of the road, and I only prayed the driver could see well enough not to run me over.

It was a gray Cadillac. It pulled to a stop a yard in front of me. I ran to the driver's-side window, gasping for air. The driver was a woman of about forty, a DVD from Blockbuster on her front dashboard.

"Don't...don't hurt me," she said. Her eyes were frightened. I could only imagine the sight in front of her.

"Please," I said, "my friend and I were attacked. If you could just take us away from here and call the police... Please, they're trying to kill us."

She reached for the shift, prepared to drive away, then saw Amanda huddled next to me, shivering in the lights of her car.

A minute later we were in the backseat of the Cadillac, heading away from one nightmare.

Then I felt the receipt in my pocket, and knew that another nightmare had just begun.

23

The police station was cold. Nobody had gone out of their way to offer Amanda or me a blanket or a drink or anything else to settle our nerves. I was wearing a blue workshirt with the name "Bill" stitched across the front. One of the detectives had given it to me. I didn't want to know where it came from, but didn't get the feeling Bill was looking too hard for it.

Ironically the only hospital within driving distance was Yardley. After the kind Vanessa Milne picked us up on the side of the road in her Cadillac, she took us right to the emergency room. The docs smeared the burn with something called Silvadene, then dressed it, told me to change the dressing every two hours and reapply the cream. It was just a first-degree burn. Would go away in a week, and hopefully wouldn't leave a scar. Amanda didn't have a scratch on her. But she was pissed off beyond belief.

A pair of detectives met us at Yardley, but they made us wait a good two hours before arriving. And even when they did, they didn't seem too keen to help. I found this odd, that two people had escaped from men who wanted to either torture or kill them, and they seemed about as interested as they would be in macroeconomics.

They asked several questions. First, why had we decided to follow Dmitri Petrovsky in the first place, and what we planned to ask him. I told them the truth. That Dmitri Petrovsky was linked to two children born in Hobbs County who'd disappeared, only to reappear several years later. I told them that we had a feeling based on his behavior at the pediatric clinic that he'd been withholding something. They asked for proof of misconduct. I told them we didn't have proof. That was the point of following him.

After we were released, the cops took us back to the Hobbs PD station. We were led through a cubicle farm of desks and eventually seated in a nondescript gray room with a metal table and chairs that were bolted to the floor. A pitcher of water sat in front of us, along with two glasses.

The same two cops joined us and sat down. They poured themselves two cups of water, drank them loudly. I had a strange feeling that we were being treated like the criminals here.

"Can we get some of that?" Amanda asked. The cops just stared at us. They had identical mustaches that rode straight across their upper lips, then down the sides of their mouths at a right angle. I got a gross mental image of them standing over a sink with a razor, shaving those 'staches in neat lines.

"You have any idea what this town is like now?" the fatter one asked. He had a crew cut and a neck full of angry jowls, like he'd recently graduated from the Mike Ditka finishing school. The one next to him was slightly trimmer, yet had the same scornful look in his eye. Between these two and the runaround I'd received from Lensicki earlier, it was tiresome and frustrating to see the lack of support from this department. "What's done is done, and now here you two come, harassing an upstanding member of our community. You should be ashamed of yourselves."

"Damn ashamed," the other cop agreed.

"You've got it all wrong," I said. "I just want to know why there's a doctor working at your hospital who knows two children that were kidnapped, and who ends up dead the same night we're held captive in some house in the middle of Hobbs County. The fact that all of this went down in your neck of the woods should, I don't know, make you just the least bit interested, I'd think."

"About this…captive thing," the fat one said. "I find it hard to believe that you followed this Russian doctor, as you claim, and then *you* end up being taken by some guy with a cigarette fetish? You're a reporter, right?"

"That's right," I said.

"Sure you're not looking to add a little spice to your story?"

"Go to that house and you'll see if I'm adding anything," I said angrily.

The thin one chimed in. "So you followed the doctor to his home, is that right? You waited in the hospital parking lot?"

"I don't know if it was his home," I said. "We just followed his car. In fact, I don't think he lived there at all. I think he knew we were following him, and probably did for a while. Wherever he led us wasn't his home, but he set us up."

The fat one, whom I would guess was playing bad cop, only the lines weren't really that clear, said, "You followed him into, let me go over your statement again, a gated residence off Huntley Terrace?"

"That's right," I said.

"You followed him into a gated community."

"No, it wasn't a gated community, just a home with a gate out front."

"And a brick wall surrounding the property."

"That's right."

"And *you* want us to investigate *him*." He paused, a scowl coming over his face. "Sounds to me like you two are the ones should be reprimanded."

"The gates *were* open," Amanda added. "And Petrovsky spoke to us when we got out of the car."

"That's when," the thin one said, "everything went, ahem, black. Right?"

"Right," I said. "They must have knocked us out or drugged us. I don't remember."

"And why did you follow Petrovsky to begin with?" Fatty said.

"We think he has knowledge about the kidnappings that took place over the past few years. He was the attending physician for the births of both Daniel Linwood and Michelle Oliveira. Both children disappeared and reappeared years later with no memory of their time gone missing."

"And why did you decide to follow the good doctor?" thin man said.

"When we first spoke to him at his office, he claimed to not know anything. It was a blatant lie." I paused, then added, "And I think there's been another kidnapping. In addition to Danny Linwood and Michelle."

"You fucking reporters," Ditka said. "Another kidnapping? You find two pieces of information got no connection, you put 'em together and make up some story 'bout how there's some big conspiracy. All just to sell a few newspapers, make a name for yourself. Do you have any proof of another kidnapping?"

"Proof? Not hard evidence, but…"

"Listen, fuckhead. Hobbs County is a nice town. I've lived here near twenty years. Now, ten years ago I might have said, yeah, we got some problems, not exactly the kind of place I'd want my kids growing up. But all that's different now. Things have changed. It's not right for you to go bringing up the bad times, because we're past that."

"Tell that to Dmitri Petrovsky."

"We will when we find him," the other cop said.

"Let's go right now," I said, standing up. "I'm pretty sure I remember how to get there. Us four, right now."

"Calm your horses, tough guy," Ditka said again. "We're not going anywhere."

We sat there in silence watching the cops drink water for ten minutes. Then right as I was about to grab the thing and douse Amanda and me with it, Wallace Langston entered, followed by Curt Sheffield. I'd never been happier to see anyone in my life.

"I got your message," Wallace said. "And I figured you could use a little backup."

The cops eyed Wallace with skepticism, but when they saw Curt standing there, all six foot three, two hundred sculpted pounds of him, they went right into bully mode once the bullies had been called on their bluff.

Wallace, happy to be good cop to Curt's badass one, passed out his business card to the cops.

"Gentlemen," he said. "My name is Wallace Langston, and Henry Parker is under my employ at the *New York Gazette.* Our legal counsel is on the way, but I do have some familiarity with legal rights, and unless you're holding Mr. Parker or Miss Davies for a crime, I'm going to ask you leave the room so we can speak in private. And then we plan to leave your care posthaste."

The cops conferred in a lame attempt at whispering, but we all heard every word. Since it was primarily lots of cursing under their breath, we didn't learn anything new, but they didn't seem particularly keen to grant Wallace's request. Yet when Curt stepped forward with his hands folded across his chest, they got up right quick and left the room.

As soon as Ditka and his buddy closed the door, I grabbed the pitcher and poured two glasses. We gulped them down in less time than it took Wallace to say, "Thirsty?"

Water dribbling down my chin, I said, "Yeah, thanks. Hope those assholes are better detectives than they are hosts."

"I don't think they're any worse detectives than you'll find in most departments," Curt said. "I get the feeling they're slacking off for a reason that doesn't involve apathy."

Wallace walked around to the other side of the table, pulled a chair out and sat down. He looked tired as he ran his hands through his thinning hair. Curt sat down, as well, much more at ease now that he didn't have to play bodyguard.

"Damn, it's fun to scare assholes," he said. "How you holding up, Henry?"

"My chest hurts like hell and other than getting hand-cuffed to a pipe and seeing the dead body of the doctor I planned to investigate for his involvement in several kid-nappings, I'm doing just peachy."

"Amanda?" he said.

She said, "Hey, Curt. I'm okay." Her words betrayed her. Her eyes gave away the terror we'd just escaped.

"Bullshit, but you're one hell of a trouper, Amanda. You're lucky it's my day off, no way Carruthers would let me come up here to help your ass out on my normal shift. I expect major reciprocation. I mean *major* reciprocation."

"No problem," I said. "I can pull a few strings, get you in the gossip pages at the *Dispatch* for having a thirteen-inch prick or something."

"Friends like these," Curt said.

Amanda was still silent. I could tell she was upset, but there was a lot to choose from. If she was still scared or in shock from what happened last night, or from the fact our leads seemed to have shrunk, I couldn't tell. At some point I'd need time to talk to her.

Wallace said. "Henry, tell me, what the hell were you thinking?"

I was taken aback, said stupidly, "Sir?"

"I can't think of any reason for you to be up here. I spoke to the watch commander. He told me you claimed to be pursuing a Dr. Dmitri Petrovsky about his involvement or knowledge about the disappearances of Daniel Linwood and some girl named Michelle Oliveira. Last I recall, I didn't give you permission to be working this story. In fact, I distinctly remember telling you to stay the hell away from it."

"Sir, I know," I said. "But there is more to this case than we think. Michelle Oliveira disappeared and reappeared in the exact same way as Daniel Linwood. And we were able to confirm that Petrovsky was the attending pediatrician for both children. He's involved. We can be sure about that now. He set us up last night."

"And now, what, you go on stakeouts? You put on a surveillance detail? Who are you, Kojak?"

"No, sir."

"So did you not hear me the other day, Parker? Did you not understand me when I told you to work another story?"

I mumbled under my breath. Loud enough so that everyone at the table could hear me.

"I'm sorry, what was that, Henry?" Wallace said, folding his ear forward mockingly.

"I said nobody else gives a shit. That's why I do."

"I must have missed something," Wallace said. "Where do you get off saying nobody cares?"

"Look at this!" I yelled. "You want me off the story because Gray Talbot sticks his manicured nails into things. He wants the community to heal. And I'm getting the runaround worse in Hobbs County than I did from my dad, and that's saying something. These cops either don't give a shit, or just want to sweep everything under the carpet. And meanwhile, the parents of these poor kids have to deal with the fact that there are five years missing from their children's lives and everyone else is sitting around with their thumbs up their asses like it's a source of protein."

Wallace sat back, stunned for a moment. I caught my breath. Half expected him to fire me on the spot.

"You're wrong, Parker," he said. "We do care. But what's done is done. Those kids are never getting those years back. These kind of wounds need time to heal, and the longer we leave them open, the more gangrene sets in, both for the families and their communities. Hobbs County won't win any 'best place to raise your family' awards, but it's a long way from what it used to be. People in Meriden regrouped after Michelle Oliveira came back. They banded together. Made the town safer. A better place to live. I hate to say this, but that girl disappearing was the best thing that ever happened to that town. I think you can understand why folks aren't keen to reopen old wounds."

"Maybe these wounds are deeper than anyone knows," I said.

"And why do you think that?"

I dug into my pocket. Took out the receipt I found on

the floor in the room Amanda was kept in. Put it on the table, where it sat like a rancid piece of meat.

"What is that?" Wallace asked.

"See for yourself."

He reached across the table, picked it up, unfolded it, smoothed out the crinkles, read it. Then he dropped it back on the table.

"It's a receipt from a toy store for dollhouse accessories. So what?"

"It's from the Toyz 4 Fun store in White Plains," I said. "White Plains is about fifteen minutes from Hobbs County."

"So?"

"Look at the date," I said. Wallace picked the receipt up again, read it. His eyes squinted. I could tell he was starting to follow.

"This receipt was printed less than a week ago. Then it turns up in the house where Amanda and I follow Dr. Petrovsky to, the same house where we're held and nearly killed. This wasn't some ramshackle, broken-down tenement we're talking about. This place was in good condition."

"And there was a large dollhouse in one room," Amanda said. "A girl's room. Every toy you could ever want." Wallace's eyes jerked to her. She locked him dead-on. He turned away. Knew that whatever he thought of me, Amanda wouldn't bullshit him.

"That house was being used as some sort of detainment center," I said. "That brick wall, that gate, they weren't used to keep people from getting in. They were to keep people from getting out."

"Who?" Curt asked.

"Kids," I said. "The family that lived there was holding a child captive. And recently, too. Which is why I think there's been another kidnapping. Just like Daniel Linwood and Michelle Oliveira. Somebody just bought toys for a child that was being held in that very house. And they bought them recently."

"Jesus Christ," Wallace said. "You're sure you found this in that house?"

"Sure as the day is twenty-four hours."

Amanda said, "You could just say yes, you know."

"Yes," I said. "I'm sure."

"And I saw Henry take it," she added. "And I can vouch for what we saw there."

"We need to find out whose name that house is registered under," Wallace said. "We need to get the cops there to search the place. My goodness, if this is all true…"

"Does this mean I'm back on the story?" I asked.

"One step at a time, Parker," he said. I knew this was as good as a yes. "Right now, all we need to do is…"

Just then a loud commotion began outside the conference room. We turned around, could see cops running, grabbing equipment, heading out the door. They looked panicked.

"What the hell…?" Curt said.

We got up simultaneously and headed outside. Half a dozen cops jogged by us.

"What's going on?" Amanda asked nobody in particular. We saw the fat cop from earlier rushing past. Wallace managed to get his attention.

"Officer, what's going on?"

"Four-alarm blaze," he said. "Possible survivors trapped inside the building."

"Oh, God," Amanda said.

"Where?" Wallace asked.

"Not sure exactly," the cop said. "Somewhere off Huntley Terrace."

"Huntley Terrace," Amanda said. "Isn't that…?"

I nodded, a chill running through my blood. "That's the street where we followed Petrovsky."

Wallace stood rigid. "Come on," he said. There was urgency in his voice, but something else as well. Something scared.

We ran outside. Wallace led us to a brown Volvo. We piled in; he and Curt in the front, Amanda and I in the back. He pulled out of the lot and followed the caravan of HCPD police cars as they peeled out, sirens blaring.

The silence in the car was deafening. Nobody wanting to state what was clearly on all our minds. What we were all praying wouldn't be true.

After several miles the caravan made a right onto Huntley Terrace. Amanda nudged me. I nodded back to her.

I felt her hand take mine. And squeeze.

"This is where we were last night," I said.

Wallace just drove.

A few miles along Huntley Terrace, we noticed the flashing lights multiply. I heard the familiar siren of a fire truck. Then the horrible stench of smoke filled the car, and we could see a thick, black cloud rising above the treeline. We parked the car outside the road the cop cars had turned onto. There was a small wooden sign outside the gravel road that read "482." It had been too dark to see any signs the other night. We got out and began to tentatively walk down the road to see what was going on. There was shouting, cursing, and there were more sirens on the way.

My heart was hammering in my chest. We all stayed close together. And then there they were. The same metal gates we'd climbed over last night. Beyond that the very house where we'd barely escaped with our lives.

Only now the house was engulfed in a horrific plumage of red flames. Burning that home right to the very ground.

24

The minivan pulled into the parking lot at a quarter to four in the afternoon. Caroline watched as Bob Reed pushed open the driver's-side door, then paused a moment to let the muscles in his arm and shoulder stretch. He gingerly stepped out one foot at a time, then threw his arms back in an exaggerated stretch, yawning at the top of his lungs.

The were outside of some sort of hotel or motel. Caroline could see other people entering and exiting. She didn't know where they were or why they were here, only that Elaine and Bob had spent nearly the whole car ride in a chilly silence.

When Bob regained his composure, Elaine was out and opening the minivan's door. Caroline watched as Elaine unbuckled Patrick's seat belt, then picked her child up and held him fast in her arms. Caroline felt a longing as she watched this intimate act, and even though both Elaine and Bob smothered her with kisses and presents, they always felt somewhat odd, forced. Last night, when Elaine entered her room with the curt instructions to get ready for a long car trip, Caroline didn't know what to think. She was too confused to be scared, and she hadn't been in that house long enough to really miss it. After placing Patrick on the ground, Elaine came around to her side. She stroked Caroline's hair, her fingers gentle, and Caroline smiled at the warmth of her fingertips. She gently kissed Caroline's forehead, then turned her attention back outside.

"Mommy?" Patrick said.

"Hey, sweetie," Elaine said. "Did you have a good nap?"

Patrick nodded, then buried his face back in her shoulder as she leaned down. Elaine stroked his hair, that strawberry-blond lock that confused Caroline. Neither Bob nor Elaine had red hair. She'd asked Elaine how they could have a boy with different color hair, and she just said, *God makes us all unique.*

Elaine turned to Bob, who was digging a pack of gum from his pocket, and said, "You want to get her?" Caroline assumed she was the "her" being referred to.

Bob looked at Elaine, then turned toward the van, in no real rush to say yes. Caroline had noticed that Bob had become more and more reluctant to spend time with her over the past few days. In the beginning he came into her room often, even helped her set up that beautiful new doll-house. But he'd withdrawn recently, and sometimes even seemed afraid to touch her.

Thankfully, the coughing fits had passed. Bob and Elaine seemed relieved at this. Bob had said something strange that Caroline remembered.

We're supposed to take care of this girl, not kill her.

Elaine had marched out of the room, slammed the door and didn't speak to him until dinner. And now they were parked at some strange building, after having left that house in a matter of minutes.

With a great sigh, Bob went around to the passenger side, climbed in and unhooked Caroline from her harness.

His fingers weren't nearly as gentle, as if he were unpacking a box rather than handling a human being.

"Ow," Caroline said as one of Bob's fingers accidentally jabbed her ribs.

"Christ, Bob, she's not a piece of meat," Elaine reprimanded. "Be careful."

"Sorry," he muttered.

"Honey, make sure to bring Boo Boo. You don't want to lose him."

Caroline picked the small brown teddy bear off the seat and held it fast to her chest. That bear was the only thing she'd come with. Elaine had thrown together a bag of clothes, but the bear was the only thing she wanted.

It had a goofy smile and button eyes, fur that was soft to the touch. Out of all the presents the Reeds had bought her over the past few weeks, this was by far her favorite.

"Boo Boo," Caroline said. "He's scared. He wants to know where we are."

"Tell Boo Boo he's safe and not to worry," Elaine said. "And make sure he tells you the same thing."

Caroline wanted to believe Elaine, but there was something in her eyes that belied the truth.

Bob reached in and picked up both the girl and Boo Boo, carried them gently out of the van. Caroline blinked sleep from her eyes, looked around.

"Where are we?" she asked.

Bob didn't say a word. Instead he looked at Elaine and shrugged. *You can answer this one.*

Elaine walked over, put her hand against the young girl's cheek.

"We're staying at another house for a little while," she said. "Our home needs a little renovation, so we'll just be staying here until it's ready."

"What about my room?" Caroline asked. Even though she was happy with Boo Boo, she'd be sad if she didn't get to play with her toys again. She couldn't believe all those brand-new toys and dolls Elaine and Bob had bought for her. She'd never had a dollhouse. It would be so sad if she never got to play with it again.

"Hopefully you'll be back in it soon," Elaine said. Then she smiled, gave Boo Boo a peck on the nose and made a funny *grr* noise. Caroline laughed.

"Come on, hon," Bob said. "We should check in."

"I never thought we'd see him again," Elaine said. "At least not until much later down the road. When it was time to, you know."

"I know," Bob said. "But he told us something might come up. Makes me wonder whether we should have ever listened to that scarred-up asshole. Sorry, kids, pardon my French."

"You know why we did," Elaine said. They both looked at Patrick, and for a moment Caroline thought Elaine might cry.

"Who are you talking about?" Caroline asked.

"Nobody," Elaine said. "Just a scary man that hopefully you'll never have to meet. Now, come on, let's get you to your *new* new room."

25

I got to work at six o'clock in the morning. I had to get out of my apartment, where all I could do was think about who burned down that house. And any moments I was able to forget about that, my thoughts turned to Amanda.

I'd spent half an hour the previous evening on the phone with Rent-a-Wreck, trying to explain how their car had disappeared from the scene of a massive fire. Thankfully I'd taken out insurance, but I wasn't looking forward to the paperwork. Still, with that car gone, the company was out, what, a buck ninety-five?

The cops had ushered us from the fire immediately. Before leaving, I saw the two cops who'd been questioning us. They were standing in the driveway, interviewing several people I presumed to be neighbors. There was fear on the cops' faces. They saw us as we left, but this time their attitude was gone. I wondered if this would finally get them to investigate.

Wallace drove us back to New York. He made it very clear that I was to stay on the Linwood investigation. I felt a swell of pride at this. Not only because I'd been right all along, but because now I wanted, *needed* to know what had happened to those children. And why someone seemed willing to kill to keep it quiet.

I spent the first part of the morning reading various newspapers from Hobbs County over the past few years. The archives of the *Hobbs County Register* were available online, and it was easy to see that this was a city on the verge of tremendous change and tremendous gentrification.

At around ten o'clock I stood up to grab a cup of coffee from the pantry, when I looked over at Jack's desk and noticed that the old man wasn't there. It was curious, since most mornings he was in the office before the sun rose, and I knew today wasn't his day off.

Walking over, I noticed that his computer wasn't on and the red message light on his phone was blinking. His caller ID read sixteen missed calls. I checked the log. He hadn't checked a single message since the previous night. That wasn't like Jack, who I knew carried his work home with him, often calling his voice mail to see if a source had gotten back, or if there was a juicy new scoop from one of his many contacts around the city.

Since my nerves were already a bit frayed from the previous few days, I half jogged over to Wallace's office to see what the deal was. He was reading, looked up expectantly.

"Parker. How you holding up?"

"Been better," I said. "Just doing some background work on Hobbs County right now. Hey, have you seen Jack recently?"

Wallace shook his head. "Not since last night. He filed his story, then left. Haven't seen him since."

"Well, it doesn't look like he came in today, and I just wanted to make sure everything's all right."

"Isn't Jack off today?"

I shook my head. "Not till Friday."

Wallace picked up a pen, twirled it as he thought. "I don't know what to tell you. I've known Jack for nearly thirty years, and I've seen him go through some of the toughest times of his life. Three or four wives, a near bankruptcy. Missing a day of work at this point in his career, at this point he's playing with the house's money, so I won't make a stink."

"Sir, if you don't mind, I just want to be sure you're right. He hasn't been himself for a few months now. I'm going to swing by his place, make sure the status quo is, well, safe and sound." *And sober.*

Wallace shrugged. "Do what you must. If he's there, tell him we'll consider it a sick day."

"And if he's not there?"

"He's a grown man. Check the nearest coffee shop or cigar lounge." *Or bar,* I longed to add, but didn't.

"I'll be back soon," I said. "Hopefully he's on the couch watching old Archie Bunker episodes or something."

As I was leaving the office, I heard Wallace say, "Henry?"

I turned around. "Yes?"

"Give me a call if you, well, find anything out of the ordinary." The look in his eyes admitted that as much as he wanted to think Jack was at home watching TV or at a cigar lounge burning through a Macanudo, we both knew that wasn't likely.

"I'll call as soon as I find him."

After grabbing my bag and cell phone, I hopped a cab to Jack's apartment. It was one of those brand-spanking-new NYC cabs with the video monitor in the divider. Some hairsprayed goon was gushing over a musical comedy set to open that week. I put it on Mute, then when I got tired of seeing the primped-and-coiffed anchor I turned the screen off.

I'd never been to Jack's place. He'd invited me over once or twice for a drink, but I always had to decline for one reason or another. He'd stopped by mine a few times, though not in a while. Though I'd considered the man an icon and a mentor, someone without whom I wouldn't have a career, my refusal to spend time with him outside of work seemed like an artificial boundary I'd recently had to create. I couldn't think of spending a night in better company, hearing Jack's thousands of stories about his career, what the news used to be like. I had to deprive myself of that, though, for his own sake.

A few months ago, Jack had told me that to become a legend in any line of work, you had to rid yourself of outside distractions. Focus on the ball, put in your time, and greatness would come. He frowned on taking long vacations, having friends and even giving yourself up to a lover. Jack was thrice divorced and had admitted to me that though he enjoyed the companionship, at least the physical aspect, he'd never allowed himself to become a real husband. He never offered the emotional companionship his lovers needed, and never desired to. To Jack, the perfect relationship was one where he could come home to a delicious meal, talk about his day, make love and fall asleep. He knew he wasn't able to give to someone else the same things he required, and that never bothered him. Most of his wives were aware of it before they met him. Yet they married him either in spite of this or with the misguided belief they could change him.

But Jack would never change. Not for anyone or anything. He was often wrong, but never in doubt. And that's what alarmed me.

Jack lived in a condominium in the Clinton area of New York at Forty-Eighth and Ninth. Floor-to-ceiling windows, he'd told me, and an unobstructed view that looked over the West Side Highway, where you could see past the Hudson River. A killer view. And since he'd bought it as a new construction, he regaled me about his brand-new appliances as though they were grandchildren. As far as I knew, Jack's brand-new Viking stove had been untouched in two years, to the glee of the numerous take-out restaurants in the neighborhood who would have a hard time paying the rent each month if Jack ever decided to take a cooking class.

A colleague once looked up Jack's purchase on streeteasy.com, and learned that he'd bought the apartment for a cool $1.5 million, while also putting down a higher-than-usual twenty percent for the place. It gave me hope that at some point in the future, continuing in this line of work might enable me to afford such luxury. For now, my crummy rental with the friendly rodent staff and unfriendly super would have to do.

We pulled up to his building and I paid the driver. I walked up to the lobby, slightly embarrassed that I was even doing this. Who the hell was I to have any doubts about Jack? The man had built a career any newsperson would die for, and here I was like the parent who thought his kid was playing hooky. That this child was in his sixties with a monthly mortgage payment likely larger than my college tuition was beside the point.

The doorman was an elderly gent with a wisp of gray hair and teeth slightly yellow and askew. He opened the door for me and smiled pleasantly.

"I'm here to see Jack O'Donnell," I said.

"Just a second." He picked up a black phone that looked to be connected to some amazingly fancy and complicated intercom system. He fiddled with the buttons for a minute, then flipped through a Rolodex. "Who may I ask is visiting?"

"Henry Parker."

"Just a moment, Mr. Parker."

He pressed a buzzer, held the phone to his ear and waited. After a minute he put the phone down. "I'm sorry, sir, nobody's answering."

"Hold on one sec," I said. I took out my cell phone, dialed Jack's home phone, then his cell phone. Both went to voice mail before anyone picked up. Odd. "Would you mind trying one more time?"

"Certainly, sir."

He pressed the buzzer again, held the phone to his ear. A few seconds later the man's brow furrowed. "Yes, yes, hello? Mr. O'Donnell?" The doorman seemed either confused or concerned. "Mr. O'Donnell, is everything all right? There's a Mr. Parker here to see you. Hello, Mr. O'Donnell?"

The doorman hung up,

"What happened?" I said, concern seeping into my voice.

"I don't know, it sounded like Mr. O'Donnell, but he sounded, well, I don't mean to judge, but how should I say, out of it?"

"Out of it? Like how?"

"I really don't know." He looked concerned, then said, "How do you know Jack?"

"I work with him at the *Gazette*." He seemed unsure of whether to let me up. "Look, Jack didn't come in to work today and that's not like him. I just want to make sure he's safe."

"Is that right," he said, not as a question. After considering this, he said, "He's on the fifth floor, the second elevator bank on your left."

I thanked the doorman and walked swiftly to the elevator. I rode it to five. Jack occupied the whole floor. Not a bad deal. I approached and rang the doorbell. Immediately I could sense something was wrong. Not from the door itself, but because the entire hallway stank of booze and some sort of rot.

I pressed the bell again, then banged on the door, my heart racing.

"Jack!" I yelled. "Jack, are you in there? Come on, buddy, open up."

I heard a shuffling, and froze. The shuffling came from behind the door, and it was getting closer. I backed up, didn't know what the hell was going on. I heard a sound come from inside the apartment, a soft moan that chilled my blood.

"Jack, goddamn it, open up!"

I heard a lock disengage, then the door opened a crack. It didn't open any farther. I approached the door, pushed it open wider.

"Jack? Where are…?"

My breath caught in my throat when I could see what was behind the door. Jack was lying in a puddle of what looked like vomit. His undershirt was covered in green chunks, and the whole apartment smelled like a rotted distillery. Flecks were stuck to the man's beard.

"Oh, Jesus, Jack."

I shoved the door open and pushed in, gathering the old man in my arms. He was heavy and essentially dead weight, but I managed to drag him over to the couch. The white leather was covered in odd stains. Empty bottles littered the floor, tossed about like they were nothing more than discarded paper clips.

"Jack, come on, talk to me." I patted his cheek, laying him on the couch. Then I rushed into the kitchen, found where he kept his dishes and poured a glass of water. I jogged back, tilted his head up. Raised the glass to his lips. When I poured, the water ran down the sides of his mouth, pooled in the folds of his pants.

"Come *on!*"

I tried again, this time opening his lips with my fingers. When the water entered his mouth, he began to sputter and cough. His eyes flickered open as he wiped the liquid from his lips. He blinked a few times, his eyes red, lids crusty.

"Henry?" he said.

"I'm here, Jack," I replied, cradling his head.

"Forgot to call in sick today," he said, before going slack in my arms.

_26_

I sat by the side of the bed, thinking about how much time I'd spent in hospitals recently. Jack had been taken to Bellevue, where he was diagnosed with acute alcohol poisoning.

I'd heard sketchy things about Bellevue, some of which were confirmed upon seeing several men clad all in inmate orange walking handcuffed through the halls. I just prayed the doctors here understood how important this patient was, and had passed their medical board exams with flying colors. Unfortunately, I was getting used to white hospital walls. The antiseptic smell. The forced, sad smiles on concerned friends and family members.

My ex-girlfriend, Mya, was finally at home after recovering from several surgeries after her body was shattered by a ruthless sociopath earlier in the year. I'd stayed by Mya's bed for weeks, comforting her mother when we didn't know if Mya would pull through, then comforting Mya when she went through the agony of rehabilitation and coping with the murder of her father by the same man who'd tried to end her life.

When you give yourself to someone, you carry the responsibility of not just being a friend or confidant, or even a lover, but giving yourself to them when they need it most. I knew Mya had desired for us to get back together, and perhaps the most difficult part of those weeks was being a friend while keeping my distance. Physical pain went away, or could be stunted through medication. It broke my heart to deny her my affection when she probably needed it most. But she would have been hurt more later knowing my heart still belonged to another woman.

Seeing Jack lying in bed made me wonder just what I could, or would, give the man. Perhaps I'd been too emotionally reserved. Or perhaps not given enough.

The doctors had measured Jack's blood alcohol level at an astonishing .19, well over double the legal limit in New York.

An IV was hooked into his right arm, tubes in his nose pumping oxygen, his breathing slow and steady. A bag dripped fluids into his veins as they attempted to flush out Jack's poisoned system. The doctors also informed me they would be testing for cirrhosis of the liver. They guessed—correctly—that this kind of drinking binge was not limited to last night.

A doctor entered the room. He was middle-aged, wore thick glasses on his thin nose. His eyes were red, tired. He flipped through the chart at the foot of Jack's bed, then checked out the readings on the monitors by the bedside. He scribbled in the folder, then placed it back.

"How is he?" I asked. "Dr...."

The doctor turned, then said with a faint smile, "Dr. Brenneman. I've seen worse."

"You didn't see him before they cleaned him up."

"There's always a worse, trust me. But he's lucky you found him when you did. The biggest danger with alcohol poisoning is aspiration and asphyxiation. He could have literally choked to death on his own vomit."

"Ordinarily, I'd say he owes me a drink for saving his life, but…"

"I don't think that's the wisest course of action," Brenneman said.

"When will he wake up?" I asked.

"Well, that's all up to him. We're going to keep him for a few days and monitor his fluid levels, make sure his liver functions are all up to par, but he's not unconscious or anything like that. Just sleeping."

"Got it. Thanks, Doc, I appreciate it. And I'm sure Jack does, too."

He waved his hand, dismissing any gratitude. "I'm actually a fan of Mr. O'Donnell's work," he said. "I followed his reportings on the mob wars a few years back. All that violence with Michael DiForio and his murder, it's all so tawdry and terrible, but I just couldn't turn away. They never did find the man who killed DiForio, did they?"

"No, they didn't."

"Scares you to think there's someone out there walking the streets dangerous enough to kill the head of a major organized-crime family, and slippery enough to get away with it."

"I know what you mean," I said. "So did you recognize Jack right away?"

Brenneman laughed. "Are you kidding? The man's a New York legend." Then his brow furrowed, as concern melted into his features. "To be honest, that's what upsets me the most. I've been around enough alcoholics not to judge, but you never expect to see such a, well, *legend* suffer like he has. To do to his body what he has. For some reason, and forgive me for saying this, but I guess I expected more from him."

"Yeah," I replied. "I guess we all did." Brenneman nodded, turned to leave. "Hey, Doc, mind if I ask you one more question?"

"Absolutely," he said, clutching his clipboard to his chest.

"What could cause a person to lose their memory? Not permanently, but, like, a chunk of it. A few years. What could punch a hole in someone's life?"

"Well, a few things. I assume you're referring to a kind of anterograde amnesia. Most of the time amnesia is the result of some traumatic damage to the brain, specifically the hippocampus and the medial temporal lobes. Anterograde, in which there is usually what's called a 'hole' or 'blackout episode,' happens as the result of a chemical imbalance. It's commonly referred to as Korsakoff syndrome."

"What happens when someone is a victim of Korsakoff?"

"Basically, it's a degenerative brain condition that's brought on by a severe lack of thiamine—or vitamin B1— in a person's brain. Thiamine helps metabolize fats and carbohydrates in the body."

"Thiamine—is this a natural substance? Does the body produce it?"

"No, it's like any other vitamin, it has to be absorbed in the system from outside. There's vitamin B1 in dozens of everyday foods, from bread to meat, vegetables, dairy. You'd almost have to go out of your way to deprive yourself of it.

"Is there any way this chemical imbalance—or Korsakoff syndrome—could be induced?"

"Absolutely. Have you heard of GHB or GBL?"

"Date-rape drugs, right?"

"That's the lay term for them, yes. In effect, what

those drugs do is induce a form of retrograde amnesia. Ironically, GHB is sometimes prescribed to help combat alcoholism." Brenneman looked at Jack. He figured I was asking these questions because of him. "GHB and Rohypnol, especially when mixed with alcohol, can be a potent and often lethal mixture."

"But aren't the effects of those drugs pretty short-term?"

"Assuming they're not ingested in lethal amounts, yes, they generally only cause memory lapses of four to ten hours. And though that's not a tremendous amount of time, in the grand scheme of things, people who use them for nefarious purposes can accomplish an awful lot of evil in that time."

"What about long-term anterograde amnesia? Are there any ways to induce Korsakoff syndrome in a way that could affect the brain for months or even years?"

"In severe cases, people either born with dangerously low levels of thiamine, or whose levels are brought down to a certain level, can experience a form of long-term anterograde amnesia. The damage is done to the medial thalamus, and if left untreated, if thiamine levels are left below a certain level, the memory loss can be long-term, or even permanent." Brenneman eyed me. "Ironically again, alcoholism is one of the most common causes of long-term anterograde amnesia."

Again he eyed Jack. And while Jack would face a tremendous struggle in his battle against the bottle, the more pressing fight was to uncover what had happened to Daniel Linwood and Michelle Oliveira. Jack was in good care. I couldn't say the same about Girl X.

Suddenly I heard a buzzing sound, and Brenneman's hand went to his coat. He took out a small pager, clicked it, then said, "I've been summoned. Nice to meet you, Mr...."

"Henry Parker," I said.

"Mr. Parker." He looked at Jack. "Please, take care of him. More important, get him to take care of himself." Then Brenneman left.

I stayed with Jack for another half an hour. I just watched him breathe, waiting for him to wake up. Half wanting to go over there, shake his drunken ass until his eyes opened, letting him have it about how he was throwing his life's reputation away. How he was in danger of throwing his legacy away. Instead I sat there, watching the tubes drip, the machines beep, thinking about how the man who single-handedly brought the *New York Gazette* to prominence had to be carted out of his house like a derelict.

After half an hour I couldn't sit there any longer, so I left and called Wallace from the street.

"How is he?" the man said.

"About what you'd expect, only worse."

"I knew Jack was drinking, more than usual, but I had no idea it was this bad."

"So you knew he was developing a problem." I was this close to screaming at my boss, and I didn't care.

"Yes, but he was still turning his stories in on time and he was still a valuable member of the team here."

"Wallace, we both know his stuff hasn't been top-notch in a while."

"So Jack's lost a little off his fastball. But he's still faster than most reporters, and he's got enough smarts, contacts and writing chops to make up for anything he's lost."

"He doesn't *have* to lose anything, it's being taken from

him, bottle by bottle. He's worked for you for what, thirty years? And you repay him by turning a blind eye?"

"Watch it, Parker," Wallace snapped. "You haven't been here long enough and you haven't known Jack long enough to judge either of us. We'll get O'Donnell the help he needs. Right now your only job is as an employee of this newspaper. Assuming you still want to be."

"Of course I do," I said. "More than ever."

"Good. Then show it."

Wallace hung up. I felt a great anger surge through me. Both at the runaround I was getting on the Linwood/Oliveira kidnappings, and now this. I'd looked up to Jack for so many years, spent so much of my childhood idolizing this pillar of a man, to see him reduced to a lump under a hospital throw rug was like seeing a baseball bat taken to fine crystal. That's one thing I'd learned in my years as a reporter. Every person, no matter the pubic perception, had demons. And the higher regard in which you held them in, the greater the disappointment when you realized their demons were as common as anyone else's. I refused to believe that Jack O'Donnell was a common alcoholic. The kind of guy who scrounged around his cabinets for that one drop of Knob Creek he knew was left. Jack had a gift that defied all of it. And once he got help, he could polish that crystal back to a shine.

I took a cab back to my apartment. Last night I couldn't wait to get to the office. Today I couldn't bear to spend another minute there. I needed a respite, if only brief.

I threw my stuff on the couch, went into the kitchen and found a Corona nestled behind a jar of pickles. The beer tasted flat, but I didn't care. It had alcohol and that's all I wanted right now. I needed a moment to feel oblivious, blissfully ignorant, to have that feeling all alcoholics must have when they pop the first top of the day and know that, pretty soon, the world outside wouldn't bother them for much longer.

Before I could get to the second sip, my phone rang. The caller ID read "Amanda." I picked it up.

"Hello?"

"Henry, everything all right? I've been trying to reach you all day."

"Not really. Jack was admitted to the hospital this morning. Alcohol poisoning. I walked in on him sitting in a pile of his own vileness."

"Oh, God. I remember a while ago you thought he was drinking too much."

"Yeah, I just never thought it would get this bad."

"I'm so sorry to hear that. I called you at the office, and got worried when I couldn't find you. After the past few days my mind's been all out of whack."

"I'm at home now. Having a beer. Feel the same way as you."

There was a pregnant pause, and then Amanda said, "Mind if I come over?"

Without waiting, I said, "No. That'd be nice."

"Be there in half an hour."

After we hung up, I got up and poured the rest of the beer into the sink. Then I sat on the couch and waited.

I wondered: Would Dmitri Petrovsky still be alive if we hadn't followed him? Possibly. But what the hell was he mixed up in?

I still didn't know exactly what his link was to Danny and Michelle. He was their pediatrician, but somehow he was connected to my friend the Chesterfield-chain-smoking sociopath. One more trail to follow. I needed to know who that man was, who lived in that house, and what Dmitri Petrovsky knew that made necessary his permanent silence. One thing was for certain, my digging had opened a can of worms someone very badly wanted kept closed.

I looked around my apartment. Humble even by humble's standards. I knew when I moved to New York that it was one of the most expensive cities in the world, but nothing prepared me for three-dollar cups of coffee or twelve-dollar movie tickets. I was paying about sixty percent of my income to a landlord I never met, who took longer to fix my air-conditioning than it would have taken me to install a hot tub into a Buick Skylark. I had no idea how long it took Jack to make a decent living, but I hoped it wasn't too long in the waiting.

Twenty-five minutes later my buzzer rang. I peeked out the window, saw Amanda standing on the street. She looked up at me, waved. I let her in.

She came upstairs and sat down across the couch from me. Hands folded under her chin. Her hair fell over her shoulders, worry lines at her eyes. Though she was still beautiful, the past few years had aged her slightly. We'd been through so much together, yet strangely I'd known this girl for less than two years. I still saw that brown hair and remembered that on the day we met, despite the circumstances, she had made everything stand still, if only for a moment. Women like Amanda, who were beautiful almost in spite of their lack of effort, beautiful without trying at all, they didn't come along too often.

We sat there in silence. It was the kind of quiet I hadn't experienced with many other women. I longed for that sense of confidence. Of comfort.

After a few minutes had passed, Amanda said, "What do you think the cops will do now?"

"You mean the dedicated men and women of the Hobbs County PD? Probably nothing. I'd bet my life savings that the same guy that mistook me for a barbecue started that fire, but I can't imagine the cops will work very hard to prove it. They want to wipe this whole mess under the bed and be done with it."

"What about Petrovsky?"

"I don't know. They claim they never found a body, either in the driveway or inside the bonfire. All they did was file a missing persons report when his secretary said he didn't show up at work. Petrovsky isn't married, no children, no real family in the States, so until enough time has gone by they won't have anything breathing down their necks. And the press won't be putting pressure on them if there are no weeping widows or no orphaned children to plaster on the front page to stir sympathies."

She looked sad. "It's like a crime was never even committed."

"It wasn't," I said. "Until a body turns up. Or we catch these assholes."

"If someone is willing to kidnap two children, kill a doctor, torture you and set a house on fire, I have a feeling they wouldn't think twice about disposing of a body."

"Tomorrow," I said. "We start from the other end. We've been looking for what happened to Michelle Oliveira and Daniel Linwood, who kidnapped them and why. And we haven't made a lot of headway on that end. So now we follow this." I took a crumpled piece of paper from my pocket. Tossed it at Amanda. She uncrumpled it, read it.

"The receipt," she said. I nodded.

"Toyz 4 Fun," I replied. "Let's see who was buying a young girl some early Christmas presents. And I'll bet whoever it is has another child. Someone who hasn't been reported missing yet. Someone who in a few years is meant to be another Danny Linwood."

27

James Keach walked down the off-white hallway, still shaking after nearly tripping over an old man and his walker, just thankful he didn't rip the old guy's IV from his arm. James's jacket was unzipped, one hand in his pocket while the other one hung loose. Just like Paulina had taught him.

Be cool, she said. *If anyone asks, you're visiting a relative. It's okay to be nervous—nobody likes being in a hospital—but nurses and orderlies are trained to sniff out anyone who doesn't belong. You belong, right, James? Just tell yourself you belong and you'll act like it. Just don't be a pussy, James, and you'll be fine.*

He still couldn't get over that word. His friends used it in casual conversation all the time, usually out at bars or while watching lumberjack competitions on Spike TV. He'd never been called one. And to be called that name by a woman, his boss, on a regular basis, was something James still hadn't come to grips with.

Once this task was complete, he was going home, getting under the covers and sleeping. Tomorrow he'd be joining his father on a golf outing with Ted Allen, and he'd need to be up for that. James knew his father had cashed in a favor in getting Ted Allen to hire him at the *Dispatch*. That didn't bother him much. Everybody had connections and used them. That was the point. Besides, wouldn't you rather get a recommendation from a close friend than have to slog through identical résumés from overachieving losers? That he got stuck working for Paulina Cole was something totally unexpected. Unlike any boss he'd ever worked for, Paulina actually scared the piss out of him.

James felt the thin camera in his pocket. Point. Click. Done.

That's it. This guy from IT, Wilmer or Wilbur or Wilfred or something, showed him how to use it. *Idiot proof* was his term. James laughed at that. Wondered who the idiots were they had to design it for.

He knew the tip was good. Paulina's tips always were. And while James was used to Paulina's volcanic temperament and mercurial attitude, James had noticed something different about her the past few weeks. Her moods had swung heavier, her demeanor more vicious, her attitudes more severe. Like she was gearing up for something big, steeling herself. Though he'd been running errands for her for going on a year now, she was never totally candid with him. He knew she was working on something big, but she refused to share the details.

In good time Jamesy, she'd said.

He counted off the doors as he walked down the hall.

703.

704.

705.

706.

He was there.

But the door was closed.

It wasn't supposed to be closed. He hadn't expected it

to be closed. He assumed it would be wide open, people coming and going, nobody noticing a thing. But opening a hospital door, man, someone would definitely notice that. If not a nurse then another patient. He couldn't see inside. A curtain was drawn. If a nurse was in there she'd sure as hell see him, and there was no way he could get it done without drawing suspicion and ruining the whole thing.

James stepped back. Took a breath. Leaned against the wall. He knew this was the very antithesis of what Paulina had advised, but fuck it, he needed a moment to regroup.

What should he do? Open the door, waltz in, pray nobody was in there? Or wait. Maybe someone would open the door and pull the curtain back. Make it easy for him.

A minute passed. Then five more. He was sweating.

He wiped his forehead with the sleeve of his jacket, saw the leather come away wet and shiny.

Time to sack up, Jim. Show the queen bitch what you're made of.

James stepped in front of the door and reached for the handle. He gripped it, closed his eyes and began to pull.

Just then the door swung outward, nearly knocking James off his feet. When he regained his balance, a pretty nurse was standing in the doorway. She was staring at James. His heart was racing. *Ohcrap, ohcrap, ohcrap, ohcrap, ohcrap, ohcrap...*

Then the nurse smiled, whispered to him.

"Are you here to see Mr. O'Donnell?"

James gulped, managed to eke out a "Yes, ma'am. I'm his nephew."

"That's sweet of you to come. He hasn't had many visitors. Mr. O'Donnell is resting right now," she said. "But if you want to sit with him, go right ahead."

"Thanks, I appreciate it."

The nurse held the door for James. Easy as pie.

When the door eased shut, he stepped around the curtain and saw the man in bed.

He was much older than his picture in the paper. Thinner, too, his face with a sickly gray pallor. He was breathing steadily, tubes in each nostril, an IV in his arm.

James quickly took the camera out of his pocket.

He whispered, "Say cheese, Jack."

28

The Toyz 4 Fun store was located at 136 Evergreen Court in White Plains, New York, about eight miles southeast of Hobbs County. Since the Rent-a-Wreck company refused to deal with us after we lost their car, I was forced to make an expensive upgrade at a regular rental company. Thankfully I was now officially working the story, so I was able to expense the ride. Not to mention how much of a relief it was to drive a car that didn't feel like it was in danger of spontaneously combusting at any moment.

The conversation on the ride up was pleasant, if a little awkward. It was hard to put Jack and the Linwood story out of my mind, and I think Amanda could tell I was distracted.

The Toyz 4 Fun store was wedged between a nail salon and a paper goods shop in a strip mall right off Woodthrush. We parked in the lot next to a beat-up Camry. It was a warm day out. I had on jeans and a white T-shirt, while Amanda had on a yellow sundress. The kind of outfit that made me wish we could forget about work and just sit down on a bench somewhere, sip lemonade or do whatever normal couples did when they weren't investigating kidnappings and disappearing murder victims.

The Toyz logo had the letters spelled out on different-colored building blocks on the awning. A play easel was set up in front of the store. Scribbled on the easel in erasable magic marker was "Deluxe Easel: Special Price $49.99!!!" It was nice to see an easel outside a store that didn't feature the soups of the day.

Each exclamation point was topped with a smiley face. It was the kind of store I loved to see walking down the street when I was a kid. Not the electronics extravaganzas and smutty Bratz dolls that passed for toys these days, but the true-to-heart toy stores, with owners that cared, knew you by name, knew exactly what you wanted. I didn't get many toys when I was a kid, but the once-a-year trip to the Leapin' Lizards toy store in Bend was worth waiting those other three-hundred-and-sixty-four days.

Amanda pushed the door open and a series of wind chimes rang. I couldn't help but smile.

In front of us were rows and rows of toys. Building blocks. Play-Doh. Action figures. Lego sets. Dollhouses. Erector sets. Everything a growing boy or girl needed to have fun and get into loads of trouble.

An elderly man sat behind the counter, thick glasses shielding kind blue eyes. His hair was sparse, combed over, but there was barely enough to do a passable job of it. He was wearing blue overalls with suspenders, like the OshKosh kid in his waning years. He smiled when we entered. His face was lined, but his cheeks were red, veiny, and his enthusiasm was genuine.

"Corolle doll, right?" the man said. "Or if it's a boy, let me see…how about My First Pirate Set?"

"Excuse me?" I said.

"Well, I'm guessing you two to be, what? Twenty-seven, twenty-eight? Thirty tops? Your kid is somewhere between three and six. Those toys are my most popular sellers for that age group. So what'll it be? Corolle or pirates?"

"I'm sorry sir," I said. "You've got us wrong. We don't have any kids."

"Bun in the oven?" he said.

"Nope," Amanda said.

"Gift-hunting then?"

"Sorry," I said. "We're actually here because we're hoping you can answer a few questions for us."

"Oh," the man said, confused. "Okay then, what can I do you for?"

I took the receipt from my pocket.

"Were you working here at around three-thirty on July 27?"

"Assume I was. I'm here every day unless I'm sick, and I haven't been sick in some time. My name's Freddie, by the way. Nobody will be addressed by 'sir' in this store."

"No problem, Freddie," I said. I handed the receipt across the desk. Freddie looked at me, unsure of what to do with it.

"That's a receipt from this store, right?"

He picked it up, glanced at it, said, "Looks like it."

"Is there any way you could look up in your computer and see who this receipt was issued to?"

"I'm sorry," he said. "It says here 'change'" He pointed to a line at the bottom. "Means whoever paid, paid in cash."

I grimaced. "I know it's a long shot, but is there any way you might know who purchased that item?"

Freddie looked at the receipt again, furrowed his brow. "This here is for accessories for a Victorian dollhouse," he said. "I don't do a lot of sales on dollhouse accessories. Sad to say they're a little old-fashioned. But I keep some in stock just in case. Probably to make me happy more than the kids." He thought for another moment, then said, "Elaine Reed."

"Excuse me?"

"Robert and Elaine Reed. Bob and Elaine. They came into my store all the time when their son, Patrick, was born. They bought that boy all sorts of toy soldiers, must have spent more money than they made on those things. I made sure they knew to keep them away from that boy's mouth. All those sharp parts, you know. But I remember Elaine suddenly buying everything under the sun for a girl, including those accessories. Little tables, chairs, even a tiny medicine chest."

"If they have a son, then why were they buying doll-house accessories?" Amanda asked.

Freddie said, "That's what I wondered. It wasn't just the accessories. The first thing they bought was an actual doll-house. I had to special-order it for them. And not a cheap one, mind you. Then they kept coming back over the next few days to buy more doodads for it. I assumed it wasn't for Patrick—don't know if you can tell a boy's, er, sexual orientation at such a young age. So I asked Elaine one day. Said, 'Elaine, what are all these doll parts for?' She told me they'd just had a baby girl."

"Baby girl," I said. "Seems like bad parenting to buy such tiny things for a baby."

"I thought the same thing, remembered what she'd done with Patrick and warned her about that. Elaine told me the girl was actually six years old. I thought, 'That's strange, I didn't remember her being pregnant.'"

"Did you ask her about it?" I said.

"Naw," Freddie said. "It's not my right to pry into my customers' business. But when I asked about it, Elaine kind of looked worried, like I'd pried or something. I figured they might have adopted, or something else was going on, but either way I was happy for the business. And happy for Elaine, because anyone who spends that much money on toys sure must love their child. Not to mention how happy that kid's going to be. But after that day I asked one question, Elaine and Bob never came back to my store. I hate to think I offended them."

"Was Elaine a good parent?" Amanda asked.

"Wonderful," Freddie said. "Some of them, parents, I mean, you can tell they just buy things 'cause they feel obligated to. Like they just want to shut the kid up or think they can buy affection. Elaine, though, she loved it. You could tell she couldn't wait to get home and see the smiles on her kids' faces."

"Did you happen to catch their daughter's name?" I asked.

"No, I didn't."

"I know we're asking a lot, Freddie," I said, "but is there any chance you might have an address for Mr. and Mrs. Reed? It's very important we speak to them."

"I'm sorry, who did you say you were again?"

"My name's Henry Parker," I said, handing Freddie a business card. "We're investigating a story and really need to speak with the Reeds."

"I hope everything's okay," he said. The man was legitimately concerned.

"I hope so, too," I said. "But there's a chance there's something wrong with one of their children and we need to find them."

Freddie nodded. "I'll do whatever I can. I just hope they're safe. I think a while ago Bob bought Patrick one of those Erector sets, only Elaine didn't have enough room in the car and asked for it to be shipped home." Freddie rummaged under the desk, pulled out a large file box. He opened the lid, began to sift through alphabetical orders. "Reed…Reed…Reed…here we go. Elaine and Bob Reed."

"Can you give us the address?"

"No problem. That package was shipped to 482 Huntley Terrace."

My jaw dropped.

Amanda said, "Henry, that's the house…"

"That burned down yesterday."

29

I needed to learn more about the house on Huntley Terrace. If Robert and Elaine Reed had bought it, there would have to be sale records. I could look them up on streeteasy.com. Even if they didn't have contact info for the Reeds, there would surely be a brokerage firm that would. It made sense. There was a dollhouse in the room Amanda was held in, and the place looked like the perfect abode for a family with young children. But what I didn't understand was how the two men who held us that night were connected to the Reeds. Or how the Reeds were connected by proxy to Dmitri Petrovsky.

We drove around the streets looking for an Internet café. I didn't want to have to go all the way back to the city to use the computers at work. We were getting close to something. Many different spools, but I couldn't figure out the common thread that attached them.

"Look, there." Amanda was pointing to a small pizza parlor. A sign posted outside read "Internet Access."

"You up for a slice and a socket?"

"I am a little hungry."

"Cool. Eat first, search later," I said.

We parked, walked in and scarfed down two slices and

a Coke apiece in less than ten minutes. When we finished, we took two seats in front of a lonely computer in the back of the restaurant. The keyboard was dusty, and I imagined it didn't get much use. The counterman eyed us suspiciously, as though we were as likely to rip the computer from the wall as use it properly.

When I clicked the computer off sleep mode, I entered in my credit card number for access. Once we were in, I directed the browser to streeteasy.com.

"What is this?" Amanda asked.

"Streeteasy.com is a pretty useful tool. It's an online database that records any property transactions, along with the buyer, seller, asking price and brokerage firm who handled the deal. I have a log-in."

I plugged in my log-in information and entered the name Robert Reed in the search field. Several listings came up, with records dating back to 1989, and in five different states.

"This can't be right," Amanda said. "How could he live in three different states at the same time?"

"It's probably not all the same Robert Reed. Hold on, I'll narrow the search."

I narrowed the parameters to Hobbs County. The search came up empty. I tried it again, only this time plugging in Elaine Reed instead. Again the search came up empty.

"Maybe someone else bought it for them? Or Elaine bought it under her maiden name?" Amanda asked.

"That's possible," I said. "We might have better luck searching for the exact house." We had enough information to narrow the search range.

According to Freddie at Toyz, the Reeds' son, Patrick, was currently somewhere between three and five years old. Which meant the Reeds had probably moved into the house on Huntley within the past seven years, either when they decided to try to start a family or when Patrick was on the way and space was essential. I entered the date range in the past eight years just to be sure.

The list came back with two thousand, seven hundred and eighty-three hits.

"I think we can narrow it down more," Amanda said. "We know there were at least three bedrooms in that house on Huntley. That should help, right?"

"Definitely, one sec."

I refined the search to only include houses that had a minimum of three bedrooms. The search came back with three hundred and sixty-seven hits. We were making progress.

"Now we just sift through these and look for anything on Huntley. Anything that looks familiar."

We scrolled through page after page of home sales and purchases through the past eight years. It was fascinating to see the range of prices at which houses had been bought, but it also gave an accurate overview of what the most expensive areas in the state were. Unsurprisingly, Hobbs County homes were ridiculously cheap. Until a few years ago at least, when I noticed they began to trend upward by a large margin.

We'd been sitting at the computer for nearly two hours. The computer had charged thirty-six bucks for the access. I hoped Wallace wouldn't spent too much time scrutinizing my expense account.

Finally on the two hundred and twenty-fourth listing, we found it.

"There we go," I said. "Four-eighty-two Huntley Terrace."

"Bingo," Amanda added.

According to the database, the house had been purchased in 2001 for three hundred and forty thousand dollars. There was a picture of the property on the Web site. I clicked to enlarge it.

The house was easily recognizable. As was the driveway and garage we'd seen the other night. We clicked through various photographs of the interior and exterior, looking for anything familiar. The rooms were different; obviously these shots had been taken before any renovations.

What was more surprising was that there was no sign of the metal gates, nor the brick wall surrounding the property. Whoever purchased the house in 2001 had built them custom-made.

"That's odd," I said, clicking onto the "buyer/seller" link. "According to this, the buyer wasn't Bob or Elaine Reed, or anyone named Reed at all."

"Who was it, then?"

"Someone named Raymond Benjamin," I said. "Does that name sound familiar at all?" Amanda shook her head. Then her eyes opened wide.

"Wait a minute," she said, pointing at the name on the screen. "When we were in that house, when you came into the room where I was held, didn't one of the guys call for a Ray?"

I thought hard, vaguely remembered hearing that, but between the cigarette burn and my state of panic I couldn't be sure. "You think this Raymond Benjamin might have been the same guy from the other night?"

"Be a heck of a coincidence, a guy who obviously knows the place well enough to set us up shares the same first name as the man on the property deed."

"Yes, that would be a mighty coincidence. It would also mean that Raymond Benjamin knows Dmitri Petrovsky." I tapped my fingers on the keyboard. "The guy who had me, he'd been in prison before. Attica. He was there during the riot, and that was in '71. If he was telling the truth, he'll have a criminal record."

"I think it's time to leave the pizza place," Amanda said.

"It sure is. Let's see what we can find out about Raymond Benjamin. It's been at least twenty-four hours since I asked Curt Sheffield for a favor. Let's give him a ring."

30

The diner smelled of cooking grease and burned coffee. A plate of eggs sat in front of him, untouched. Raymond Benjamin rubbed his aching jaw, then took another smoke from his pocket, lit it and inhaled deeply. It was all he could do to relax after the events of the past few days. Everything had been going just the way he'd planned, in that there were no disruptions, no mass hysterics. Everything cool, calm and quiet. And then all of a sudden the newshound Parker shows up at Petrovsky's office and everything goes to shit.

He hadn't wanted to torch the house. Benjamin actually had some fond memories of that place. But once Parker decided to follow Petrovsky, it was only a matter of time before somebody came knocking. Burning it down was a necessary evil. There was too much inside for him and Vince to get rid of in the little time they had, not to mention having to dispose of the doctor and that beat-up car Parker drove. Better to torch the whole thing and wipe their hands than risk one little thing turning up and screwing up the whole operation. Ray couldn't afford that. There was too much at stake.

Raymond Benjamin smoked his cigarette, eased back

into the booth and took out his wallet. He looked at the pictures inside. The first one was of a beautiful young couple. Ray barely remembered what life had been like back then. He'd been so impetuous, so violent. He was amazed a woman had actually had the temerity to marry him. The first photo had been a year or so before Ray Jr. was born. The boy had Ray's nose, but got the rest of his features from Ray's wife. Becca. Becca, who'd died while he was holed up in that shithole prison. Ray Jr., born in 1970, the year before the riots changed everything.

Every person was born with a specific skill set. Ray's son was born a technogeek, the kind of guy who could build computer systems out of thin air, could design corporate Web sites and security systems as easily as he buttered a bagel. The last Ray heard, his boy was making nearly a hundred grand a year. He was married with two kids. Ray hadn't seen them in a decade.

Ray himself was born with a different set of skills. And in a cruel irony, it was that skill set that led Ray to spend the majority of his twenties shuffling from prison to prison. He was a born criminal. Burglar, fighter. Age had sapped much of his brawn. No way that Parker kid would have had the upper hand when Ray had his juices flowing, when his fists were like unstoppable pistons. Now, in his late fifties, Ray was holding on to his fighting memories the way a jilted lover holds on to his, afraid of what would become of him when he realized the man he used to be was slipping away. Lives like Ray's didn't have second acts.

He thought about his time in Attica. Somehow the worst and best years of his life. They'd made him what he had become, but he wasn't sure if the pain and sacrifice were worth it. He thought about that day back in '71, when his fellow prisoners had finally risen up against the guards, who'd tortured them for so long. Ray remembered watching *Dog Day Afternoon* as a young man, just a few years after he got loose. He remembered the feeling of pride in his gut when Pacino delivered that electrifying speech. It was simply incredible, like a candle being lit in his stomach, working its way through him until his whole body was warm. He'd *seen* that in person. He'd *been* there. Everyone watched that flick and got that vicarious thrill of what it was like to make a stand. Ray had been there. He'd *made* that stand.

When Vince came back from the bathroom, the red welt above his eye was shining like a Christmas bulb. The younger man slid into the booth across from Ray, went right back to work on his ham, eggs and sausage links. Ray watched Vince eat for a bit, the man shoveling food into his yawning mouth like it was Thanksgiving and he didn't have a care in the world.

"Eat enough of that, it'll kill you before a bullet does."

Vince smiled as he gnawed on a link. "Best to go out having fun," he said.

"You know, as dumb as we were," Ray said, "things could have gone worse the other night. Much worse."

"Sure could have," Vince said, a forkful of dripping egg sliding back onto his plate. "What d'you think would have happened if the cops had come before we'd taken care of the place?"

Vince stopped chewing. Put the fork down. "We would have been in a world of shit. Years wasted," Ray said. Vince nodded as if he'd figured out the right answer on a multiple-choice test.

"Not really wasted. I mean, it's been fun, right? We've made money."

"You know we're not doing this for money, for our health," Ray said. "This isn't some two-bit scam we're pulling. There are lives at stake."

Vince laughed. "You mean like Petrovsky," he said with a goofy smile.

"No," Ray seethed. "Not fucking Petrovsky. Lives that matter. Petrovsky was a degenerate. He was a means to an end. And we have to protect that end, you hear me?"

"I hear you."

Ray lowered his voice. "I'll be talking to our friend later. We need to make sure everything is sealed up on our end. No doubt they'll find out that house was registered in my name. I'll play the 'woe is me' card, but let it end there. There isn't enough evidence in that house of anything. I gave it a once-through before we lit the match. Now I'm not too worried about the Hobbs police. If anything they're doing a good job protecting what we've created. But that Parker reporter, we can't give him anything more to latch onto. The New York media gets hold of this, it goes national. Nobody gives two shits about a poor kid in a poor city."

"I hear you, Ray. Geez, it's not like I don't know this already."

"Fucking Parker," Ray said. "Never been so stupid in my life. Ten years ago, no way that kid gets the jump on me. Never used to underestimate folks. All of a sudden Parker can ID me and probably you. His word against mine, and I've already spoken to our friend who's good with tools who'll claim I was working late that night. So here's what happens. If it even *looks* like this guy might throw a wrench into things, we don't wait for him to fall into our lap. We take him out. And the girl if necessary. No more cigarettes, no more nicey-nice. Quick, simple, and they disappear."

"Like those kids we nabbed," Vince said, satisfied.

"No. Not like those kids. Parker and Davies have to *stay* gone."

31

Manhattan's 19th Precinct was located on Sixty-Seventh Street between Lexington and Third Avenue. I'd only been there once, just a month or so after I'd arrived in New York. It was to report a lost or possibly stolen cell phone. I'd filled out a form with my information, handed it to the cop behind the front desk, and that was the last I ever heard about it. Probably for the best. The NYPD has more important crimes to worry about than who took my Nokia.

Curt had worked at the 19th going on three years. I knew he was well respected within the department, one of those up-and-comers that are a rare breed in that they're both clean-cut enough to stick on a recruiting poster, but hardworking and intuitive enough to gain the respect of the rank and file.

It was this respect that I was counting on as Amanda and I entered the precinct. The majority of cops had no love lost for me, and despite being vindicated many still considered me responsible for the death of one of their own. The irony was that even though the department loved Curt's image, he couldn't have cared less. That's the only reason he agreed to bring me into his precinct. It wouldn't win him any friends, but it would help uncover the truth.

The precinct was up a short flight of stairs. It had a red brick facade and an arched entryway, bracketed by two green lamps, above which hung a yellow banner that read "Thank you for your support." The banner was bookended by two images: the American flag and the badge of the NYPD.

Curt led Amanda and me through the precinct, though not nearly as fast as I would have liked. I could feel eyeballs boring holes through me as we snaked through the corridors, and knew that many of these men had worked with, probably known, John Fredrickson. A few years back, I defended two people Fredrickson was beating to death, and in the struggle the man's gun went off, killing him. I didn't know he was a cop, and his death was the result of choices made long before I came along. Yet perception was reality, and the feeling was if I hadn't stuck my nose in, he'd still be alive.

"Just this way," Curt said. We followed him down the hall into a row of cubicles, each one set up with large, likely obsolete computers. We entered a larger cubicle which was set up in a U-shape, two computers at either end. The walls were covered with crime-scene photos, mug shots, business cards. Curt pulled up a pair of chairs, then sat in a larger one. He shifted around a few times, then leaned forward and scratched his ass.

"That's lovely," Amanda said.

"Hey, if you can convince Chief Carruthers to spend an extra nickel on chairs that don't make your ass feel like it's the wrong side of a Velcro strip, you'd be spared seeing illicit activities such as these."

"Is it really that bad?" I asked.

"Man, come around here during lunchtime when the detectives are all eating at their desks. You'd think a family of porcupines must have made a nest in every seat. Like a messed-up orchestra, all scratching at the time same."

I said, "Think I'll file that under 'visual imagery I hope to file away and never see again.' So what is this here?"

"Here is where we find out about the criminal record for this guy Benjamin, the dude listed on the property deed on Huntley Terrace. You're sure this Ray Benjamin is the same cat who hung you out to dry in that tinderbox out on Huntley?"

"I can't be sure, but that's what we're here to find out."

"Now, you said this guy made a comment about serving time up at Attica, right?"

"That's right."

"Then our boy's damn sure got a record. Which means he's just a mouse click away from being ours."

Curt logged in to a database, then proceeded to enter first name "Raymond," last name "Benjamin," into the fields. He plugged the years 1968 and 1972 into another field marked "date range." He clicked a box marked "Caucasian" and pressed the search key. One of those helpful little hourglass icons appeared on the screen. On my computer, the sand fell through the hourglass at roughly the same speed as cars cruising Fifth Avenue during the Puerto Rican Day parade.

A few minutes and ass scratches later, the hourglass disappeared and a file appeared on the screen. A mug shot appeared in the top-right corner of the page. I recognized the man in the image at once.

"That's him," I said, pointing to the screen like I was picking him out of a lineup. "Holy shit, that's the guy."

"From the other night?" Curt said. "This is Raymond Benjamin."

I nodded. "No doubt."

Despite the picture being at least twenty years old, it was easy to tell this was the same man. The man in this photo had a fuller head of hair, fewer lines cutting across his face, but the look in his eye was the same. Defiance. Anger.

"There's no scar," I said. "When I saw Benjamin that night, there was a faint scar on his right cheek. There's nothing like that in this picture."

"Let's see here," Curt said. He clicked a button, then the photo enlarged. Curt highlighted a line below the photo. "Mug shot, dated 1969."

"Probably the last shot taken before he was sent to Attica," I said.

Amanda traced her finger down the man's cheek on the screen. "So if this photo was taken before he went to prison, there's certainly a chance he either got that scar in jail or afterward."

"Yeah, the scar actually did zigzag a little bit, like it had been stitched up by someone who got their medical license at the local butcher shop." I looked at Curt. "This is the only photo on record for this guy?"

"Afraid so," he said. "So what I want to know is how a dude who got busted for armed robbery in the sixties ended up buying a house that got burned down over thirty years later?"

"After he almost barbecued my balls," I added. "And if the house is owned by a three-time loser, why did the inside look fit for the Huxtables?"

"Obviously the house was in his name, but that was to hide whoever actually lived there," Amanda said.

"What I think happened," I said, "is that this guy Benjamin bought the house as a front. I'm not quite sure what the catalyst was, but a husband and wife named Robert and Elaine Reed have actually been the ones living on Huntley."

"They weren't in the fire though," Amanda said.

"No, no bodies found. Not that Russian doctor or anyone else," Curt said.

"So the papers are in this guy Benjamin's name, but he sublets it to the Reeds. Only there's no paperwork or documentation. The Reeds have a young son, Patrick, but according to receipts from a local toy store they'd been purchasing gifts for a young girl within the past month. I think very recently, the Reeds added a young girl to their family. Only I don't think they did it through conception or adoption."

"In vitro?" Curt said.

"No."

"Adopted a kid from Zaire?"

"Uh-uh. I think they kidnapped a child, and until that house burned down they'd been holding the girl just like whoever took Daniel Linwood and Michelle Oliveira had done. Amanda, you saw all the toys in the room you were held in. This wasn't some medieval torture chamber, this was a home. A place for a family to live."

Amanda reluctantly nodded. "Actually reminded me a little of my room when I went to live with Lawrence and Harriet Stein," she said. She turned to Curt. "I was adopted. My parents died when I was young, then I went from orphanage to orphanage until the Steins took me home. I remember my room feeling not really like an actual room a young girl would live in, but the kind of room parents *thought* a girl would want to live in. Too many floral patterns, too many dolls. Just overkill to the extreme."

"That's why the Reeds racked up a hefty bill at Toyz 4 Fun," I said. "They were pampering this kid like she was their own."

Curt said, "So why kidnap a kid if you're not holding her for a ransom? What, you just pamper her for a few years and then let her go? I mean, you're comparing this Girl X to Danny Linwood and Michelle Oliveira. Both those kids wound up returning home unharmed. If what you're saying is true, the Reeds planned to eventually let this kid go. Why go through all that trouble?"

"So she'd feel like a part of their family," I said. "When I interviewed Danny Linwood, he made a brief reference to his 'brothers.' I didn't think much of it at first, but combined with this, I think all three of these kids were taken with the intent of ingratiating them into their 'new' families."

"But why?" Amanda said. "If the kidnappers knew they were going to let them go, why bother?"

"I'm not sure," I said. "But what scares me is that the Reeds somehow knew Raymond Benjamin. He owned the house they used. So how did a supposedly regular family, a loving father and mother with a young son, wind up in bed with a career criminal, and end up stealing someone else's child?"

None of us had the answer.

"So what else can I do?" Curt said.

"We need to confirm that the Reeds did in fact kidnap another child. And if we do that, and we can find out who that child is, hopefully we can find the Reeds and they can answer all these questions."

"It'll be tough," Curt said. "I can submit a request for a breakdown of all children reported missing within the past two weeks, but unless we can narrow down where the child was from we're basically looking in every town in every city in the country."

I thought for a moment. Then I said to Curt, "Cross-check your records with Yardley Medical Center, the pediatrics unit. I have a feeling whatever child was taken was born in Hobbs County, and was a patient of Dr. Petrovsky's, just like Daniel Linwood and Michelle Oliveira."

"How can you be sure?" Amanda said.

"Thiamine levels," I said. "I spoke to Jack's doctor at Bellevue and asked what might cause a child to go through what Daniel and Michelle did. According to him, it's likely they both suffered from a severe case of anterograde amnesia, exacerbated by depleted thiamine levels. He said that it was technically a form of short-term brain damage, but when thiamine and vitamin B1 levels dropped in patients whose thiamine levels were low to begin with, it could cause exactly what afflicted Daniel and Michelle. I think whoever has been kidnapped was born with low thiamine levels, and Dr. Petrovsky supervised it all."

Amanda said, "That would have to mean the kids were preselected based on their medical histories. Which means Petrovsky knew which kids to look out for."

"I think there's a strong chance he did just that. So this new Girl X was chosen for the same reasons Dan and Michelle were years ago—they were susceptible to having their thiamine levels tampered with to a far greater degree than a normal child. With the right—or wrong—nutrition and care, you could almost literally give a child short-term brain damage and harm their memory receptors."

"Which would explain why Daniel and Michelle didn't remember a thing about their time missing," Amanda said. "And it means the Reeds are expecting the same thing from this kid. Girl X."

"Find her," I said to Curt. "I'm tired of this bullshit, like one lost kid doesn't matter. What, because Hobbs County and Meriden got a few extra bucks, a few of the houses got a nice coat of paint, this is all swept under the carpet? These kids are giving their lives for some awful cause I don't understand."

"I hear you, man. Give me some time," Curt said. "I'll need to get medical records from Petrovsky's office, which won't be easy, especially since the dude's disappeared."

"He's dead," I said. "There's just no body to bury."

"Either way, the guy won't be answering his phone. Give me a day. I'll get an answer."

"Thanks, Curt, every second counts. Benjamin wasn't expecting us to follow Petrovsky, and who knows if the Reeds are even still alive. There's a chance that, like Petrovsky, they 'disappeared' the Reeds so nobody could ask questions. We need to see if we can find the Reeds before Benjamin takes desperate measures. And this is a guy who seems to be redefining the term."

32

Raymond Benjamin dialed the number of the motel. He'd made the reservation for the Reeds just before he'd told them what was going to happen to their home. He'd broken it to them matter-of-factly. He'd told them they might have to leave at a moment's notice, but didn't really believe himself it would ever come to that. Elaine seemed pretty unnerved but agreed to cooperate. Like always. Bob stayed silent, nodded at his wife's approval. But now it was Ray who was unnerved.

When the receptionist picked up, he said, "Yes, can you connect me to the room of Robert and Elaine Reed?"

"Hold a moment, sir." Ray heard typing in the background. "Sir, we don't have any record of anyone by that name checking in."

"But you do have a reservation, right?"

"Yes, sir, Mr. and Mrs. Robert Reed, weekly rates, supposed to have checked in yesterday, but according to this they haven't."

"Fuck me," Ray said.

"Excuse me, sir?"

"Nothing. You're sure about that?"

"Yes, sir. Would you like me to have a message waiting for them when they do check in?"

Ray slammed the phone down on the cradle so hard the plastic receiver broke in half. It took him far too long to jimmy open the door to the pay phone booth, and finally he cracked the glass when he kicked it inward with his foot. Vince was leaning up against the car, an errant toothpick sticking out of his mouth. Either it was lodged between two teeth or the man had simply forgotten it was there. Ray had a sudden desire to smack the thing out of his mouth. But he restrained himself.

This wasn't going as he'd hoped. Things had taken a drastic turn once Parker and the girl had arrived at the house on Huntley, and that necessitated burning the place down. Of course, doing that meant relocating the Reed family, which was an ordeal in and of itself.

He'd begun to worry about Bob and Elaine from nearly the moment they took the girl home. There was something in their eyes that was different from the other families, a sense of sorrow that worried him from the start. He'd told them from the first time he met them that they'd have to be strong. Keep everything in perspective. Look at this as short-term pain for a long-term solution. They were doing it for the right reasons, and years from now they'd be happy they did it.

Now he wasn't so sure.

Bob and Elaine had a motive. There was a reason they were chosen. The same way there was a reason Ray was good at his job, he expected the Reeds to live up to their end of the deal. Looking back on that one week that shaped Raymond Benjamin into what he'd become, he knew how fast one moment could change everything.

Few people knew the truth about Raymond Benjamin.

That all of the violence, everything that had occurred during the horrific, bloody days from September 9 to September 13 was because of him. While the riots started because the Attica prisoners were tired of being treated like animals, there was one spark that started the explosion.

The week of September 2, 1971, a small metal bucket was placed inside Ray's cell. It contained about a gallon of water. The guard told him it was his weekly supply of water to shower with. On September 8, during mess hall, Ray mouthed off about the food. He didn't remember his exact words, but it boiled down to the meat loaf tasting like it had been some poor guy's meat. That got him one cigarette burn behind his knee.

The next morning, on September 9, Raymond Benjamin thought he was in for the worst day of his life. The previous night, one of the guards came by, dropping a single roll of toilet paper into Ray's cell. *Hope you got a clean ass, 'cause this is the last one you're getting until the end of the month.*

Frustrated, Ray threw the roll back at the officer, hitting him in the head. It barely stunned him, but soon all of 5 Company was laughing their ass off. The guard turned red, told Ray he'd see him in the morning and walked off. While his fellow inmates hooted and hollered at the newly christened "Officer Shithead," Ray sat in his cell, shivering as if death itself was waiting for him. And for all he assumed, it was.

The next morning, September 9, all of 5 Company's cells opened, the sign for morning roll call. All cells except for Ray Benjamin's. As his friends walked past, they saw him still in the cell, sitting on the edge of his bed, knees quaking. Ray had never been so scared in his life. He could hear the footsteps of the guards as they did morning rounds, could hear the clomps as his friends walked past, knowing their buddy was about to face the worst beating of his life. Perhaps the last beating of his life.

Ray sat there and prayed. He apologized to the Lord for what his life had become. He apologized for his sins and promised that, if he was given another chance, he would make the most of it. He would right those wrongs. Ray's eyes were squeezed shut, tears pouring out the sides. He hoped it would be quick, if anything. That would be something to be thankful for.

Then Ray heard something odd. Footsteps coming back his way. But they weren't the loud *thump-thump* of the guards', they were the soft, muffled steps of the prisoners. Then Ray heard a man yelling, and damned if it wasn't Officer Shithead himself.

"You assholes get back here, right now!"

The 5 Company prisoners didn't go back to roll call. Instead they walked right back to their cells and sat down. Possum, a big black man from Alabama, said, "Fuck you. You gonna take one man, you gonna take all the men."

Possum was talking about Ray.

Soon Officer Shithead was marching down the cell block, nightstick unsheathed.

Officer Shithead didn't live another minute.

After they'd beat him to death with his own baton, Ray's brothers in 5 Company managed to get his cell open. Several minutes later, a guard heard a commotion down A Tunnel, went to see what the hell was taking 5 Company so long, and that's when the devil unleashed hell.

Ray survived the riots with his life, his sanity, and just one small scar on his cheek obtained on September 13 when the cops finally opened fire. A glass pane shattered, carving out a chunk of Ray's face. William "Billy Buds" Moss, a surgeon in lockup for raping a patient, stitched it together with a spool and tweezers stolen from the nurse's office, moments before it went up in flames.

Raymond Benjamin would be ejected from the penal system two years later. Thirty-nine people died in those riots. Most of them were buried. Officer Shithead, Ray later learned, had been burned beyond recognition. There was barely enough of him left to bury.

Leaving Attica, Ray Benjamin was a changed man. Not so much in deeds. He was still prone to violence, still had the temper of a pissed-off Viking, but now he had a cause. Not to mention a massive nicotine addiction. He told friends that after all the pain cigarettes had caused him in prison, he might as well get a little pleasure out of them.

Several times a month Ray would wake up at night, remembering that morning sitting in his cell, praying for forgiveness. Waiting for a death that, with mercy, decided to pass him over. He never forgot that. Never took it for granted. And every act of violence, everything he did that "society" wouldn't approve of, was going toward making things right. It didn't matter if people couldn't understand it. *He* knew it was right.

The Reeds were part of that plan. They were doing the right thing.

But now they were gone, and Ray Benjamin felt concern for the first time in a long time. If the Reeds lost their will, they could give up everything. Ray would go down. So would the big man. And everything Ray had worked for over the past thirty years would be lost.

Ray thought about the Reeds. Where could they have gone? And why would they suddenly decide to disobey such simple fucking directions?

They weren't at the motel. Elaine wasn't picking up her cell phone. He'd given them the address, a newly cloned phone, and now he couldn't find them. It was like they'd looked him in the eye and lied to him.

"This isn't good," he said to Vince. "The Reeds have disappeared."

Vince snorted a laugh, managed to keep the toothpick in his mouth. "Ain't that ironic."

Ray looked at him, then said fuck it. He couldn't help himself.

He slapped Vince across the face, the toothpick doing a little spiral before landing in a puddle of sludge several feet away. That made Ray smile.

When Vince recovered, he was holding his jaw, a thin trickle of blood at the corner of his mouth.

"Ow, man, what the fuck?"

"Couldn't take that stupid toothpick anymore."

"Christ, you could have asked me to throw it out!"

"Consider this an apology. Come on, let's go."

They got into the car, Ray shaking his head as Vince started the engine.

"What is it?" Vince said, mopping up his lip with a handkerchief.

"The Reeds," he said. "I don't trust them anymore. They don't realize this thing is bigger than them. They're being selfish, not realizing they're putting years of work at risk. I thought they could be trusted, that they had their family's best interests in mind. I guess I was wrong."

"What are you saying, boss?" Vince asked.

"I think when we find them, we need to make them gone."

"Gone like the kids? Or, like, *gone* gone?"

Ray looked at him, didn't say a word. Vince nodded solemnly. Ray patted the kid on the back. That was his answer right there. Then they drove away.

33

"According to DMV records," Curt said, "the Reeds drive a 2002 silver Ford Windstar, license plate JV5 L16. I don't think it'll come as a huge surprise to anyone that their current address is listed as 482 Huntley Terrace."

We were still at the 19th Precinct, corralled in a conference room on the second floor. Curt had already had to shoo away three other officers who tried to reclaim the room. When they couldn't offer concrete reasons for needing the space—the excuses ranged from "It has the only good coffee machine in the building" to "Fuck your mother"—I quickly figured out the cops simply didn't want us there. And that was fine with me. The more roadblocks were put up in our effort to find out the circumstances surrounding these kidnappings and Petrovsky's murder, the more insolent I became. Though I didn't think Curt would go so far as to have my back if I lost control and tried to pick a fight. And I was getting pretty damn close to that.

Amanda said, "So at least we have direct legal proof that ties the Reed family to this guy Benjamin. But we still don't know why the hell they have anything to do with a criminal."

"What if," I said, "the Reeds weren't linked directly to Benjamin?"

"Not sure I follow," Curt said.

"We're forgetting about Petrovsky. He knew Daniel Linwood and Michelle Oliveira. His career was based around children. Bob and Elaine Reed have one son, Patrick, and we suspect they might have kidnapped another child, too."

"I'm still waiting for the search on that," Curt said. "I'm hoping you're wrong."

"Anyway, isn't it possible that somehow the Reeds became linked to Benjamin *through* Petrovsky?"

"Like some sort of middleman?" Amanda asked.

"Exactly. I'm willing to bet Petrovsky knew Benjamin, and Petrovsky knew the Reeds, as well. Amanda, is there any way you could get information about Patrick Reed? I have a feeling we might see Dmitri Petrovsky's signature on his delivery forms as well."

"I'm on it," Amanda said. She gathered up her coat and purse and stood up. "Good luck, guys." She spent an extra moment looking at me, then she left.

Curt waited until the door had closed, then he said, "So what's going on with you two?"

"Nothing," I said. "Absolutely nothing."

"You sound like you're as happy with that situation as I am with my mortgage."

"Just don't know what to do. I broke up with her, but not a day goes by I don't regret it. In my mind I can erase that mistake, but expecting her to… I wouldn't expect that."

"You think maybe part of the reason you're working this story so hard is to be close to her?"

"I don't know."

"That's not a no."

"No, it's not."

"Part of me don't feel right letting her do some of the dirty work on this. I mean, look at you, man. Seems like every few months you get beat up. You really want her that close to you?"

"That's why I broke it off in the first place," I said. "I took the decision out of her hands. But she's been with me every step of the way on this. Relationship or not, she wants to be here. And it's not my place to tell her not to."

"That's a selfish way to look at the world, especially if she might be in danger."

"I'd kill myself if anything happened to her, Curt," I said. "But she's a hell of a strong woman, and I know that anything I can take, she can, too. Probably more so. She works with kids every day, and she's seen some of the most terrible cases of abuse you can imagine. She doesn't talk about it much, because, well, who wants to bring that kind of work home with her? But don't be fooled into thinking she's in this for me, or for the adrenaline. This is a cause for her. And I respect that."

"So if it's a cause for her, and it's about my job for me, what's it about for you?"

I thought about that for a moment, then said, "The truth, man. It's about the truth. That's *my* job."

"So since we're both on the job," Curt said, "how the hell do we find the Reeds? They obviously jetted from Huntley before smokey the pyromaniac got his hands on the house. They're registered with Verizon, but the phone's going right to voice mail. No luck tracking it down just yet. There are no known family members for either Robert or Elaine Reed, and we're checking their phone records for friends and acquaintances."

"They won't be at a friend's house," I said. "Benjamin got them into the house on Huntley so they could keep private. That place was like a fortress. You don't go through all that trouble only to have Elaine spill the beans to someone in her knitting group. You said they have a minivan, right?"

"Yeah, a Windstar."

"Nobody buys a minivan for one kid. I'm getting more and more sure that they've kidnapped another child. Anyway, I'm betting they're staying at a motel somewhere. A place where nobody knows them, and nobody knows where they are except for Benjamin and his crony."

"There's a lot of motels in this country, man. You can't expect us to cover all of them."

"No, but if you're a parent with two bawling kids in a minivan, do you really think you're driving ten, fifteen hours for the same kind of motel you can get within a few miles? My bet is they're still in the state. Say a four-hour drive, make it an even two hundred and forty miles, and that's your radius from Huntley Terrace. They'll stay away from major cities and metropolitan areas."

"There's still a shitload of fleabag motels in that range, Henry."

"Christ, Curt, you're a cop. Don't you guys do this all the time?"

Curt smiled at me. "I'm on it. Go run some more of your magic. I'll give you a ring if we get any more info on the Reeds or other missing children."

"Thanks, Curt, appreciate it. You want to sock me in the eye once, gain a little street cred among your fellow boys in blue?"

"Tempting, but tell you what. Leave the building like I broke you down into tears, we'll call it even. Deal?"

"Deal."

I left the 19th Precinct with a sullen look on my face, as if Curt Sheffield had just ripped the head off my favorite teddy bear. Rounding the corner onto Lexington, I called the *Gazette* from my cell phone. I asked to be connected to Wallace Langston's office, and the editor-in-chief picked up immediately.

"Wallace, it's Henry."

"Henry, good to hear from you. What's the latest?"

"I'm in the middle of tracking down a family that I'm ninety-nine percent sure is part of some sort of weird kidnapping ring that involves the Linwood and Oliveira children. There's a link between the Reed family and this psycho Benjamin who mistook me for an ashtray. I'm running down the link, and when I have that I'll let you know. How's Jack doing?"

Wallace sighed. "They released him yesterday. He's got the rest of the week off for some R and R and detox. I've never seen the man like this before. It worries me."

"What do you mean?"

"Jack has been with this newspaper since he was a young man, Henry, younger than you are now. He's worked himself to the bone for his profession. He's a legend in this field, and he's paid his dues to become that. But Jack's not a young man anymore. You can't go with that same kind of drive, that kind of passion at his age, without compensation. I wonder…God, I can't believe I'm saying this…but I wonder if his career isn't beginning to wind down."

I felt like I'd been punched in the gut. But rather than a sensation of pain emanating from it, I felt anger. How could Wallace even begin to question the longevity of Jack's career? Things were looking bad now, but everyone was entitled to fall off the wagon once or twice. It was a divot in the road, not a full-blown earthquake. And it pissed me off to hear Wallace insinuate otherwise.

"He'll be just fine," I said through gritted teeth. "Give it a week or two, he'll be tracking leads and breaking stories like he's a new man."

"I sincerely hope you're right, Henry. But it worries and saddens me to think you may not be. Listen, my friend, keep pushing on this story. I've gotten three calls from Gray Talbot's office since your detainment up in Hobbs County. Our friend the senator is no doubt perturbed that we've ignored his requests. I expect a hate-o-gram to arrive any moment in the mail, but until you see me led away in handcuffs, keep pressing."

"That's what I do," I said. "Talk to you later, Wallace." I hung up.

It took a moment to register that my stomach was growling. I stopped at a deli and wolfed down a bagel with lox spread and a large coffee. When that was polished off, I had half a blueberry muffin for dessert. My natural reaction to that would be to run it off the next day, but my legs were beat. I hadn't put in for vacation time in ages. I didn't think Wallace would be all that surprised to see my paperwork cross his desk in the near future.

When I finished the meal, I took a cab back home, sat down on the couch and waited. This was the worst part of the game, and as a reporter the most frustrating part of the job. The waiting.

So much of my work was dependent on sources getting back to me, but every moment that phone didn't ring there was a fear that the story was slipping through my fingers. I worried that Curt's searches would turn up empty. That Amanda would discover Patrick Reed was born in Idaho and not Hobbs County like I suspected. Not to mention cigarette boy Benjamin wandering the streets somewhere, and I had a little more anxiety at that moment than I liked.

I had to distract myself. Music, that would do it. Calm, soothing music.

I turned my computer on, opened iTunes and started to play Dylan's "Not Dark Yet." The melody calmed me.

I thought about Daniel Linwood, Michelle Oliveira. Two children with their lives once laid out in front of them, yet forevermore they would be outcasts. They would always live with that stigma, never fitting in. The beauty of a child, the pain from a life stolen away.

And just while those lyrics had begun to burrow their way into my skull, my cell phone rang. If there was ever a time to be jostled out of morose thoughts.

The caller ID read "Amanda cell." I answered it without hesitating.

"Hey, wondering what happened to you."

"Seriously? It's been, like, fifteen minutes. What the hell do you expect?"

"Sorry, just a little antsy here. I feel like things are starting to become clearer."

"Well, your feelings might be real. Turns out that Patrick Reed, son of Robert and Elaine Reed, was born on May 29 four and a half years ago at Yardley Medical Center in Hobbs County."

"You're shitting me."

"Nope. And I'll give you three guesses at to who signed the delivery certificate."

"I'll take Dmitri Petrovsky for one thousand, Alex."

"Ding ding ding. I'm actually out of cash, so I hope you'll take your winning either in an IOU or a Sweet'n Low packet I just dug out of my jeans pocket."

"Amanda, you know what this means, right? The Reeds knew Petrovsky. Their son was born at the same hospital as Daniel Linwood and Michelle Oliveira. That's their link to Raymond Benjamin. Somehow he found out about these kids through Petrovsky."

"Wait," Amanda said. "Patrick Reed wasn't kidnapped, he's the Reeds' biological son. What gives?"

"Patrick isn't the issue, I just needed a connection so we could figure out how the Reeds came in contact with Benjamin. Petrovsky is the middleman. Benjamin the facilitator. The Reeds—I'm not quite sure what they are."

"So we have three pieces to the puzzle, but the three pieces are blank right now."

"Yeah, pretty much. We need to find the Reeds. Petrovsky is dead and Benjamin will kill us before he talks." I heard a beeping sound on my phone. I looked at the display. It read "Curt cell."

"Amanda, Curt's on the other line. I need to take this."

"Call me right back."

"Will do." I hung up. My palms were sweating. This was all coming together. The bigger picture was still invisible, but it would come. Benjamin. Petrovsky. The Reeds. What the hell were they all involved in?

"Hello?" I said, answering the call.

"Hey, man, I got a ton of info for you." It was Curt. He was talking fast. "We might have found your girl. Two weeks ago, Caroline Twomey, age nine, was taken from her parents' home in Tarrytown. She was reported missing the next day, but the Tarrytown PD haven't turned up any leads. I did a background check on Caroline's parents, a Mr. and Mrs. Harold and Phyllis Twomey. Harold works construction but hasn't made more than thirty-five grand a year in his whole life. Phyllis is a part-time schoolteacher. And by part-time, I mean she hasn't worked in nearly five years."

"Really? Why is that?"

"Five years ago, Phyllis Twomey was arrested for shoplifting. The store decided to press charges, and Phyllis was fined five hundred bucks and sentenced to fifty hours of community service. She hasn't worked a day since."

"What store did she rob?"

"A Healthwise pharmacy just three miles from their house. They caught her on the security camera, cops met her at her house fifteen minutes after it was called in."

"Curt," I said. "What did she steal?"

"Says here she tried to steal two dozen vials of insulin."

There it was. I knew the link. I knew why Benjamin had come to Petrovsky. I knew why Daniel Linwood, Michelle Oliveira and Caroline Twomey had been chosen.

"Curt," I said. "Daniel Linwood is a diabetic. So is Caroline Twomey. When I spoke to Michelle Oliveira's violin teacher, Delilah Lancaster, she mentioned noticing needle marks on the girl's skin. She thought it might have been drugs, but it was because Michelle is a diabetic. They're all diabetic."

"So Dmitri Petrovsky was feeding Raymond Benjamin information about diabetic children that were born in his pediatric ward. For what purpose?"

"Diabetics are more susceptible to lower thiamine levels," I said. "If they don't get proper nutrition, it can result in both short-term and long-term brain damage. One of the side effects of short-term brain damage is Korsakoff syndrome, which prevents the brain from processing certain compounds, and prevents the brain from retaining long-term memory."

"That would explain why Michelle and Dan Linwood had no recollection of their years missing."

"Right," I said. "But whoever took Dan and Michelle, and now this Twomey girl, knew about their conditions. And they were prepared for it. They didn't want to kill these children, they just needed to get them away from their families for a period of time."

"Why?" Curt asked.

"I don't know yet," I said. "But I'm sure the Reeds can answer that question for us."

"Well, that was my next piece of information. You owe me a steak dinner after all this, Henry."

"Come on, cough it up."

"You're lucky it's a slow day. I had a dozen cops calling every hotel and motel within a two-hundred-and-fifty-mile radius of that house on Huntley Terrace. We got an affirmative for a Mr. Robert Reed at a Sheraton in Harrisburg, Pennsylvania. About two hundred miles from Hobbs County."

"Holy shit, Curt, you're a godsend." I checked my watch. It was six o'clock. With any luck I could be in Harrisburg by nine. "Listen, I need to call Amanda. I'm driving up there right now."

"Like hell you are," Curt said. "You have no idea what's up there. Hell, that's not even my jurisdiction."

"Lucky for me I don't have to worry about jurisdiction," I said. "News is interstate. Sorry about that, bro."

"You asshole," Curt said. "All right, screw it. I'm coming with you. You got a car, right?"

"Sure do."

"Then count me in. And I call shotgun."

"Bitch, please. You think there's any chance in hell you're riding shotgun over the girl I'm still in love with?"

Curt laughed. "No, guess not, but at least you finally admitted it."

"What do you want, a cookie? Meet me here in half an hour." I hung up. Called Amanda. Set the meeting time. Wondered if somehow Robert and Elaine Reed expected some company.

34

"Hello, miss, are you still there?"

"Yes, Mr. Benjamin, I'm processing your information as we speak."

"Thanks a lot, dear. And just to be sure, you got that the car was loaned to a Mr. and Mrs. Robert Reed?"

"Yes, sir, I heard you the first three times. Now, can you give me Mr. Reed's date of birth and social security number?"

Raymond Benjamin repeated both numbers to the woman on the other line. He was standing at a pay phone at Eighty-First and Columbus in New York City. Vince was Uptown. He'd called frantically ten minutes ago, saying Parker, the girl and some black guy had gotten into the same car they'd been driving the other night and sped away. Vince said they looked like they were in a hurry. And that made Ray Benjamin nervous. He had a feeling somehow Parker had found the Reeds. And if he had, Benjamin would be in a world of trouble.

No, there was still time. But it meant Ray had to get creative.

The Ford Windstar had been bought in his name. He'd never used that stupid Pioneer system, since the last time he trusted a computer for direction he ended up somewhere with cows and silos. Not exactly what he was looking for.

The one thing he did have to be thankful for was reading the damn machine's instruction book. Just in case. He remembered reading that, in case of an emergency, you could call a Pioneer technician and receive help in either starting or locating your car.

When he signed the papers, he'd made sure to authorize Robert and Elaine Reed, as well. They'd be the ones driving it, and he didn't need them to be pulled over and have to explain their relationship. Thankfully he knew everything about Robert and Elaine Reed, from social security numbers to their son Patrick's birthday.

"Mr. Benjamin, how did you say you lost the car again?"

"Lost it?" Ray said. "Actually, we think our son took it out for a spin last night, got drunk and got a ride home from a friend. When he sobered up he couldn't remember where he left it. I'd really rather not get the police involved unless we have to. All I want is my car back."

There was a moment, and then Raymond heard the woman say, "Mr. Benjamin, according to our tracking system your car has been located in Harrisburg, Pennsylvania. On Lindle Road, right by the entrance to I-283 North. It looks like it's right off of exit 2. Sir, you're sure you don't want us to contact the police? Our caller ID shows you're phoning in from New York City. That's quite a drive."

"No worries," Raymond said. "I'm a fast driver."

35

The Harrisburg Sheraton was right off of the Interstate, about a hundred yards down Lindle Road and a few miles east of the Oberlin College campus. Though the night sky had descended on the city, I could see that the trees were full, the grass lush. The town had a wonderful, old-America feel. And we were less than ten miles from Hershey Park. Unfortunately, this wasn't the best time to check out the chocolatey goodness.

Some terrible techno music was playing on the radio, but I hadn't been paying attention for the past hour. Every minute that passed we were closer to finding the Reed family and getting to the bottom of this bizarre triangle.

Dmitri Petrovsky.

Robert and Elaine Reed.

Raymond Benjamin.

Three groups of people that would never have any sort of interaction in a normal world, yet for some reason they'd become intimately involved in one another's lives and businesses. I hoped Curt's boys had done their homework at the precinct, and I hoped that, if this was the place, that the Reeds hadn't already packed up ship.

My eyes were weary. A three-and-a-half-hour trip

doesn't sound like much, but after a full day's work in addition to the other stresses involving Jack and this story, it was all I could do to keep focus. I had to keep telling myself what the opportunity was here, both the truth to be revealed and the benefits for the *Gazette*. Things would be tough with Jack out. I liked Wallace, and the man had been almost endlessly supportive, but he was hardly a mentor. I was on my own at work. Thankfully the two people in the car were my backup.

The Harrisburg Sheraton was a fairly quaint hotel, the low-slung roof lined with hanging plants out front. Lamps in the grass lit up a trail that went from the parking lot to the entryway, and the guest rooms, about eight floors of them, were just a few yards beyond.

I parked the car, turned off the ignition.

"How you all feeling?" I said as we exited the car. Curt stretched, his long limbs raised into the sky. I noticed the gun by his hip. He'd come in plainclothes. There wouldn't be much love for an NYPD cop in PA. Amanda had on a nice purple blouse. She wrapped her arms around her chest, looked slightly worried.

"I'm good," she said. "Could use a bathroom break."

We walked into the hotel. The floors were covered in beige tiles, and half a dozen overstuffed chairs surrounded tables. A few hotel guests were seated, reading books and newspapers, sipping coffee.

Curt said, "They're not just going to give us the room number. I thought about this. We need a way to find out what room the Reeds are in without alerting them to the fact that we're here."

"Oh, man," Amanda said, sighing. "You guys are seriously like troglodytes. Does everything have to depend on me?"

She walked up to the reception desk as Curt and I

watched, curious, scared and feeling a little emasculated. We trailed behind Amanda just enough that we could hear, but far enough behind in case her ruse specifically did *not* include us.

"Hi," Amanda said, sprawling her arms across the desk. "Lissen, I need to see my boh-friend. He's staying in your ho-tel. I think he might be with his wife, so I guess this really is a ho-tel."

The receptionist, a guy with acne scars and a badge that read "Clark," who looked like his first day on the job was tomorrow, said, "I'm sorry, ma'am, what can I help you with?"

"My boh-friend," she slurred. "Robert Reed. He's in this ho-tel. I need to know what room he's staying in."

"Ma'am, we're not supposed to give out guests' information. If you'll just…"

Amanda dug into her purse, then slapped something down on the desk. Clark's eyes bugged open. Curt and I leaned in closer. When I saw what it was, I had the exact same reaction as Clark.

"M-Ma'am," Clark said, stammering now. "That's a condom."

"You're damn right. Robert promised me a good time tonight, so if you don't tell me where I can find him, I'm jus' gonna have to find someone else at this ho-tel to do what he can't." She looked around, a lascivious grin on her face. "Do you have a bar in this hotel?"

Clark gulped, then ran some digits into his computer. He looked at Amanda as though to make sure she hadn't started propositioning guests. She hadn't, though she was licking her lips. I had to close my mouth, look away.

"Mr. Reed is staying in room 602. Now, if you'll please, just go find him. We don't need anyone causing a scene."

"Much obliged," she said, leaning over. *"Clark."*

Amanda headed for the elevators. We waited a moment before following her. When the doors closed, I said, "You sure you weren't trained at Juilliard?"

"God, you guys could use a set of balls sometimes. Come on."

The door dinged open. We followed the signs toward room 602. The halls were lined with seashell-shaped lights, and the carpet was a zigzagging pattern of red-and-black squares. A few pieces of standard hotel art hung on the walls. Men fishing off piers. A windmill across a bay. I had no eye for art. For all I knew these pieces could have secretly been worth millions.

When we came to 602, we stopped in front of it. Curt and Amanda stood to either side of me.

"I'll do the talking," I said. "Curt, if we need you…"

"I have my badge on me, Henry."

As I got ready to knock, I heard the *ding* of another elevator opening onto the sixth floor.

"Hold on a second," I said. "Just make sure they're going in another direction. Nobody needs to see three people hanging around the hallway."

They didn't respond. The footsteps appeared to be heading our way. No big deal, I thought. Hotel guests going back to their hotel room. Even if they were heading this way, they'd enter their room and be done with it. We'd be talking to the Reeds before anyone had a chance to get suspicious.

I leaned back against the wall, pretended to fiddle with my cell phone. When I saw a shadow appear at the other end of the hall, I turned to look at the guests that were coming.

I nearly dropped the phone when they came into view.

I recognized the first man immediately, and I dove for Amanda just as Raymond Benjamin pulled a gun from his coat and opened fire.

I heard Amanda scream as bullets smashed into the wall above us. I thought we were safe, but then I heard another, deeper yell, turned to look, and saw Curt Sheffield on the ground, blood pouring from his leg.

"Curt!" I screamed.

I pushed Amanda toward the other end of the hall where an exit door was visible, and by that time Curt had taken the gun from his hip holster. Benjamin was reloading when Sheffield emptied three bullets into the hallway. Ray Benjamin managed to dive for cover, but two of the bullets struck his sidekick square in the chest. The younger man went toppling backward, his back smacking against the wall, where he slid down, leaving a bloody smear.

Benjamin was gone. I heard footsteps running toward the elevators. He was getting away.

I knelt down by Curt. His hand was pressing down on the wound, hard, but blood was still seeping through his fingers.

"Benjamin," Curt said, the pain evident in his voice. "Don't let the fucker get away."

Amanda appeared beside us. She'd taken off her fleece, then rolled it up and tied it around Curt's leg. He howled in pain as she pulled the loop together, trying to stem the flow of blood.

I looked at them both. Amanda had taken her cell phone out. She said, "I called 911. Make sure he doesn't hurt anybody else."

I nodded, then sprinted for the exit door. My pulse raced as I looked for the stairwell. A diagram of the floor plan was on the wall; the stairs were just to my left. I ran for them, banged the door open and hurtled down the stairs as fast as I could.

By the time I got to the first floor I was out of breath. When I shoved open the stairwell door, I could hear panic in the lobby. Several people were screaming, a rolling cart was overturned and an elderly man looked to be unconscious. I ran toward the lobby exit, but then another thunderous gunshot exploded in the night, and I dove behind a marble wall for protection. I waited a minute, unsure of what to do, then took a few quick breaths and ran for the exit.

As I ran into the warm evening air, I heard a car's ignition turn on and a pair of brake lights come on at the other end of the parking lot. I ran for it, saw a dark BMW peeling backward. It backed up into a pool of light cast by a lamp, and I read the license plate numbers, punched them into my cell phone.

I couldn't chase Benjamin's car. The fight was over. I had to see how my friends were.

Just as I ran back into the lobby, the elevator door opened and out came Curt Sheffield, hobbling, leaning on Amanda for support. The fleece was soaked through with blood. I heard sirens approaching from outside. I ran to Curt.

"Christ, man, how is it?"

"I'll live," he said through gritted teeth. Then he took one hand from Amanda's shoulder and grabbed my shirt. "The Reeds," he said. "They're gone."

"But we found this," Amanda said. She pulled a man's leather wallet from her pocket. "It was down at the other end of the hall, through a set of double doors. I thought I heard another noise, like several people running down the stairs. It's Robert Reed's. They must have been approaching the room. He was going for his room key, then dropped it when he heard the gunshots. The key is still inside."

"I saw them," Curt said, the pain evident on his face. "Damn it, if only I could run…"

Amanda helped him sit, kept pressure on his wound.

I took the wallet, opened it. The key card was nestled inside one of the slits inside. I went through the rest of it. Credit cards. Driver's license. And a small slot for photos.

I opened it up. There was a picture inside that looked awfully familiar.

The shot was of a young boy. It was taken from behind, from a close distance. There was nothing special about the shot. The boy's face was turned away and he was in mid-stride.

I slipped the photo from the wallet and turned it over. On the back of the photo was written one word.

Remember.

36

Curt had seen the Reeds approaching from the other end of the hallway. The family looked happy. Curt recognized Robert from his driver's license photo. And when he saw that Robert was with a woman and two children, he knew for sure that this was the family we'd been searching for.

I confirmed with the hotel restaurant that the Reeds had finished a late supper just a few minutes earlier. Then they'd gone upstairs. They must have seen Curt lying outside their room, blood everywhere. That's when they'd run.

On the way to the hospital, Curt said they'd likely seen the body at the other end of the hall, as well. If so, they probably recognized the dead man. If they knew Raymond Benjamin, chances were they'd met his flunky. And with all that death and blood, they must have known Ray Benjamin had come for them.

We followed Curt to the Harrisburg hospital, the primary hub for all the medical centers in the Harrisburg area. They'd taken Curt right into surgery. Amanda and I sat in the waiting room as a doctor explained that the bullet had nicked his femoral artery. Luckily the bullet had missed severing the vessel by half a centimeter, otherwise, he said, we'd be having an entirely different conversation.

I'd given the license plate number to the Harrisburg chief of police, a burly man named Hawley who had a look on his face that said as soon as they found Benjamin, the three of us would have hell to pay. An APB was put out on a dark BMW with New York plates, but an hour later the license plate was found abandoned in a gas station in Bethlehem. Raymond Benjamin was gone.

Curt would be laid up for several days. Amanda and I slept in the hospital that night, occasionally shifted positions in the waiting room. Amanda waking up on top of me, then moving; me waking up leaning on her shoulder, not wanting to move.

When morning came and the doctors confirmed that Curt was out of danger, we went in to see him.

Our friend was heavily sedated. His leg was swathed in bandages. We approached his bed, cautious, unsure if he could hear us or understand what happened.

As I got closer, I heard Curt whisper, "Henry."

"I'm here, buddy." I took Curt's hand in mine. Amanda stood beside me. I noticed her absently rubbing her hands on her jeans.

"The Reeds," he said. Curt swallowed, with some difficulty. Then he licked his lips. "The Reeds, man. They recognized Benjamin. They were scared."

I nodded, squeezed his hand.

"Find them," he said. "Now, get out of here before somebody else shoots me instead of you."

Amanda and I walked out of the hospital like two zombies who hadn't slept in weeks. Her eyes were bloodshot, her tank top caked with sweat and dirt. Her blouse was in some medical waste bin. Now she wore a gray sweatshirt, two sizes too large. The only thing that had survived the night physically and emotionally intact was our car.

We began the drive back to New York in silence. Amanda turned on the radio. Found some talk station that neither of us listened to, but it at least punctured the quiet. When we saw a rest stop, we pulled in and got a few fast-food burgers for the road. We ate without talking, arrived in New York three hours later barely having said a word.

When we pulled onto the Harlem River Drive in Manhattan, I turned to Amanda.

"Where does Darcy live again?" I asked.

Amanda shook her head. "Just take me home."

"Where do you mean..." I began to say, but when Amanda looked at me I realized what she meant.

I parked the car on the street, then walked back to my apartment, finding Amanda's arm intertwined with mine. I found an old pair of shorts that were too small for me, and a Cornell T-shirt. Amanda put both on. The T-shirt fit like a nightgown, drooping down to her knees. I turned off all the lights and climbed into bed.

Amanda lay down next to me. I could hear her breathing, could feel my heart beating next to hers.

She turned onto her side, nuzzling her head into the nook between my head and shoulder. Her arm wrapped around my waist. And there she lay, soon drifting into sleep. I watched Amanda for as long as I could, staring at that face, knowing how hard it would be to spend one more minute without it next to mine at night. I thought about Curt and prayed he'd recover completely, thanked whoever it was that watched over us that we'd escaped with his life.

I prayed that Caroline Twomey was still alive and healthy, and that we would find her soon. I thought about all of that, and then my muscles quit on me and I drifted to sleep.

37

I woke at seven-fifteen, like I did most mornings. My alarm was set every day to go off at seven-thirty on the dot, but my internal alarm had a wicked sense of humor, always screwing me out of fifteen minutes of shut-eye a day.

Blinking the sleep from my eyes, I leaned over to see Amanda rolled up in my comforter like a pig in a blanket, only if the pig were a beautiful woman and… I decided to just stop that train of thought before I accidentally said it to Amanda and wound up with my head shoved up my ass. She was still wrapped in my clothes, her eyes shut, snoring lightly. I leaned over and shut off the alarm clock, then rolled out of bed, picked some clean clothes out of my dresser, went into the living room and got dressed there so as not to wake her.

I left the apartment, picked up two Egg McMuffins and two large cups of coffee, and was setting up breakfast on my meager dining room table when Amanda appeared in the doorway.

"Morning," she said, rubbing her eyes. She looked at her finger—likely identifying a smudge of eye gunk—then flicked it away. She offered a goofy smile and noticed the setup. "You got breakfast?"

"Straight from the kitchen at Mickey D's."

"Yum. Just like Mom used to make."

"Your mom worked the fry-o-lator."

"All right, enough out of you, smart guy. What do you have?"

I unwrapped the sandwiches, opened the coffees. I had ketchup waiting for her, knowing she liked to slather her eggs with the stuff. She took a seat, her eyes still red, and began to pick at the food.

"How'd you sleep?" I asked.

"Better than you'd think after a day like yesterday," she said. "Guess your brain trumps all, tells you you're too tired to stay up all night thinking about things. Like Curt lying on the floor bleeding everywhere."

"Yeah," I said.

"That's all you can say?" Amanda said, looking at me as if I'd just committed to invading Iran by myself.

"Don't know what else to say. It's just overwhelming. You know, seeing Curt injured like that. Seeing Jack in the hospital the other day. Two of my best friends have nearly died over the past week. I'm sorry if I'm not as articulate as usual."

"I didn't mean to suggest you didn't care," Amanda said. "But…do you wonder, ever, if it's worth it? I mean I'm not a reporter, I haven't spent a lot of time in the 'field'…but unless you're in Afghanistan, I've never heard of any journalist being subjected to this much violence in such a short period of time. So either you happen to chase down these stories that inevitably lead to ruin, or…"

"Or what?" I said.

"Or you go looking for them on purpose."

"You know that's not true. Wallace assigned me to this story. He set me up to interview Daniel Linwood."

"And so you interviewed him. You wrote a terrific story about it. Then what?"

"That wasn't the end of it," I said. "Once I knew something was being hidden, I had to go deeper. It's what I do. If it leads to this, it leads to this, but I never want anybody to get hurt. Fact of the matter is, I don't want you coming along with me. I didn't want you to come last night."

Amanda looked hurt, confused. "So why did you let me come, then?"

"Because the last time I made a decision for you, it was the worst decision of my life."

Amanda took the bottle of ketchup, unscrewed the lid and peered inside.

"What are you doing?"

"Just making sure I'm comfortable with the amount of congealed tomato paste in here." She screwed it back on, squirted a dollop onto her sandwich. "Doesn't look too bad."

She took a bite, munched, then put it down. Looked me in the eye.

"So, what, you've grown over the past few months? All of a sudden things are clear?"

I didn't know how to respond to that. I felt my feelings for her were clearer than they'd ever been, and I'd been worse at hiding it than a silverback gorilla playing hide-and-seek. "Yes. Sort of. I mean, personally things are clear."

"Really," she said, in a manner that stated she didn't believe me.

"We were good together," I said.

Amanda chewed. "So that's your great introspection? As far as I know, we didn't break up because things were going badly. We broke up for other reasons. Do those not matter now?"

"They matter, but I know that this…thing…it's a two-person thing."

"Eloquent."

"What I'm saying is, I shouldn't have made the decision for you. And I understand how it would put you in a position where you'd be afraid to get hurt again."

"Hurt?" she said incredulously. "You're worried about me? Henry, you've cornered the market on that front. I'm not saying this to be funny, but when things happen like yesterday, I worry that you're not going to live to thirty. So you can worry about me being hurt emotionally, while I'm going to be the one at night wondering if you'll be coming home. Or if I'm going to get a call from Curt one day, and I'll hang up before he can say a word because I'll just know."

"I'm trying," I said. "I swear. But this Linwood story, I have to see it through. Especially now. One of my friends could have died yesterday. I have to find out what Ray Benjamin, Petrovsky and the Reed family are involved in. I need to know what Benjamin is going through all this trouble for. He strikes me as a career thug. The kind of guy you hire for muscle. Not the kind of guy who orchestrates a series of kidnappings spanning a decade."

"What's he been doing since he got out of prison?" Amanda asked.

"That's a good question."

"Ya think?" she said, taking another bite.

"I mean, he's had a massive house in his name, a minivan in his name. Where's his income coming from?" I looked at her sandwich. She had one or two bites left.

"What, you want me to leave because you have work to do?"

"No. I was just wondering if you were going to finish that."

She mocked throwing the last piece at me, then shoved it all in her mouth and swallowed.

"I'll walk out with you," she said. "You heading to the office?"

"Yeah. But I need to make a few calls and see if I can track down Raymond Benjamin's employment records. If the Reeds knew what was good for them, they'd be in Arizona by now."

"What about Benjamin?"

"If yesterday was any indication, he'll follow them into hell if he needs to. He was there to kill the Reed family. His gun was already drawn when he came into the hall at the hotel. If we don't find out what's going on, it won't just be another kidnapping to investigate, or having to deal with at least two people who have already been killed, but we'd have to live with the murder of an entire family."

38

Raymond Benjamin sat in the black Ford Escape and finished his third pack of the day. He rolled down the window and flicked the butt into the wind, where it landed among a pile of a dozen other butts that had come from the same vehicle.

Ray's heart had been racing for nearly twenty-four hours straight. Vince was dead. And though he had no love lost for the bumbling idiot, there was a huge difference between thinking someone a dolt and wishing them dead. He still couldn't figure out how Parker, the girl and the black guy with the gun had found the Reed family. It should have been quick, easy and relatively painless. At least for him and Vince. They'd both loaded their guns with dumdum rounds—hollow-point bullets. There were four targets: Robert Reed, Elaine Reed, Patrick Reed and the girl. Caroline Twomey. They didn't want to take any chances that one or more of them might have gotten away or fought back. He'd met Robert Reed before, and the man had some athletic genes.

The dumdum rounds were specially designed to expand upon impact, the bullets deforming when they entered the skin, causing a maximum of trauma. That way even if they didn't get off a kill shot, the wound would have been devastating enough to keep the target down. With four targets, you couldn't take chances.

Now Vince was dead. He'd worked with the man for going on seven years, and while Raymond never would have asked him to be on his team for Trivial Pursuit, he had developed an odd affection for him, like an owner with a three-legged dog.

When Parker began to investigate Petrovsky, Ray knew the plan had encountered serious problems. Reporters didn't just go away. If anything, resistance made them dig deeper. And especially after he looked into Parker, he realized that this guy would never quit, wouldn't back down, even when facing down the barrel of a gun. And to compound that, Bob and Elaine clearly left the house on Huntley in an effort to disappear, or at least hide out until they could figure out how to untangle themselves from the mess. Raymond had never fully trusted Elaine Reed. It took too long. Too much effort. When they ran away in that tin can of a minivan, to Raymond that's when the answer became clear. It wasn't something Raymond wanted to do, but it was necessary.

He'd run it up the flagpole. Nothing happened without the say-so of his employer. And, like Ray, his employer wasn't thrilled with the option but realized there was no choice. The Reeds had to disappear, along with Caroline Twomey.

As far as Ray knew, the Windstar was still in play. The Reeds were hardly versed in espionage. Hell, he'd be surprised if Elaine even knew how to use e-mail. Soon he'd have the car's location, and if the Reeds were there he would correct everything that had gone wrong.

He raised the window and turned on the engine. He

found a good jazz station with John Coltrane's quartet playing "Pursuance." He sat and listened to the entire song, felt the rhythm swim through his head. He reached into the glove compartment, closed his hand around the gun, and felt like everything would even out.

This time had been a mistake. It was unfortunate for Caroline Twomey. The next time, though, they would make things right.

39

I left the apartment with Amanda. We said our goodbyes outside. She hailed a taxi. I watched it pull away, for a second hoping that her window might lower, her head drifting out like in an old movie, where the cab would pull over and all sorts of romance would ensue. 'Course, that didn't happen. The cab pulled up to the light, then turned out of sight when it became green.

I trudged to the subway, feeling like the whole story had begun anew. We'd found the Reeds once, and that was almost out of blind luck. The next time, neither I, nor they, would be so lucky.

The Harrisburg police believed every word I said, and were more than happy to step up their patrol and look for this man Benjamin. It was maddening that we were facing such resistance in Meriden and Hobbs County, the cities that preferred to keep their heads stuck in the sand.

I got onto the subway, flipping through the *Gazette* to pass the time. As much as I was reading the paper for the articles, I also felt somewhat obligated to advertise our paper, make sure fellow straphangers were well aware of the newspaper of choice. Given the fact that I'd probably slept a total of five hours in the past two days and my eyes were totally bloodshot, they might have assumed the *Gazette* was a paper for strung-out junkies. Not exactly the target market for our reporting skills.

I got to the office at a quarter past nine. When I stepped off the elevator, I was greeted by a sight that cheered me up immediately.

Sitting at his usual desk was Jack O'Donnell. And he looked no worse for wear.

Hardly able to contain my excitement, I half walked, half sprinted through the newsroom and perched myself by Jack's desk. He was wearing one of his patented suit jackets with patched elbows, and pants that looked like they'd survived a horrific gardening accident. He smelled like Old Spice, and his beard was neatly trimmed. He looked exactly like what you'd expect a seasoned reporter would look like. The old newsman turned to me, a weary smile spreading across his lips.

"Hey there, if it isn't the boy who saved an old man's life."

"Come on," I said, "stop it." I felt like a schoolgirl complimented by the starting quarterback.

"Seriously, Henry, I owe you a great deal of gratitude. I've been on this earth for a long time—maybe I've outstayed my welcome considering some of the things I've done—but if not for you there's a good chance I wouldn't be here right now. So thank you."

"You don't need to thank me, Jack," I said. "You'd have done the same for me."

"Saved your life?" he said. "An old bag of bones like me can barely muster up the strength to get dressed in the morning, let alone go around saving lives. I appreciate the gesture, but you're the hero here."

"If you remember," I said, "you saved my life a few years ago. You know, that whole thing where they thought

I'd killed John Fredrickson? After Amanda, you were the only one that helped me. So get off this modesty kick, it doesn't suit you."

Jack smiled smugly. "Okay, I'll take it. But I promise, that's the last time you'll have to go picking me up off a floor. Unless I'm break-dancing, but then all bets are off. Speaking of bets, Wallace tells me you're in the middle of a pretty tense story. What's the deal?"

I recounted everything that had happened since I first interviewed Daniel Linwood. I told him about the discovery of Michelle Oliveira's disappearance, our attempt to follow Dmitri Petrovsky and the doctor's murder. About the Reeds and how I believed they'd kidnapped a girl named Caroline Twomey for reasons I still didn't know. And about Raymond Benjamin, the career thug who was somehow mixed up in all this.

Jack sat there, resting his head on his hands, his eyes betraying a sense of worry. When I was finished he stayed seated for another moment, took a breath, closed his eyes, and said, "It's not supposed to be this difficult, Henry. You can't put your life in danger on every story."

"That's not fair, Jack. I didn't choose for this to happen. I was assigned to the Linwood story, and then—"

"And then what? That should have been the end of it. Your piece on the Linwood boy was terrific. Case closed. So what happened?"

"Life happened," I said, feeling my blood pressure rise. "I can't speak for you, Jack, but I can't just let things go. As soon as I knew there was more to the Linwood story, as soon as I realized there were people who didn't want me digging, it's like…it's like someone turned on a switch inside me. And I can't stop until I know everything."

"You know what they call someone who needs to know everything?" Jack asked.

"A good reporter?" I replied.

"Dead," Jack said. "Every trail leads somewhere. Very few stories simply end. And if you keep playing Indiana Jones, at some point your luck's going to run out, and some very bad people are going to shut you up."

"Thanks for the pep talk," I said. "I'll take it under advisement." I stood up.

"Where are you going?" he asked.

"This story isn't finished," I said. "I have to go make some bad people upset at me."

I walked back to my desk, happy that Jack seemed healthy and vibrant, but annoyed that he was still questioning me. He had to know I couldn't just give this up. I needed to know why Raymond Benjamin got involved with the Reeds. And if, somehow, through all this he was connected to Daniel Linwood.

Rule number one in journalism: always start with the money.

Specifically, where did Raymond Benjamin get it?

I logged in to our LexisNexis terminal and ran a search for Raymond Benjamin. More than a thousand hits came up. I narrowed it down by adding search terms like "criminal," "jail" and several others. A few hits came up relating to the 1971 riots at Attica. Raymond Benjamin was named in several newspapers as one of the inmates involved, though none of them named him as having taken part in violence or murders. I scrolled down through several entries, and found one that piqued my interest.

It was printed in the *Buffalo News* out of Buffalo, New York. It was an in-depth article, four pages long, and incredibly detailed. It went on record about the horrific abuses suffered by the prisoners in Attica, and how the shoddy treatment was the catalyst for the riots.

One of the most damning pieces of evidence, the article stated, was the discovery by Dr. Michael Baden that all twenty-nine of the prisoners and all ten of their prison-guard hostages were killed by Attica guards themselves. This was a huge blow to the penal system, which for years had been spreading stories that the hostages had been killed by the prisoners, who had slit their throats. That the guards resorted to lethal measures so quickly and brutally was yet another blow to the system.

According to the article, a prisoner by the name of Raymond Benjamin was treated for facial lacerations, as well as severe dehydration and malnutrition. When asked about his conditions inside the prison, Benjamin stated he'd eaten only one meal a day the week before the riot, hadn't showered more than three times a month the prior year, and had repeatedly been subjected to other forms of torture and brutality. Strangely, though, Benjamin refused to blame the prisoners or the guards for his wounds. Benjamin was quoted as saying, "I got nobody to look at besides myself, where I come from. Sometimes you make your own choices, sometimes where you come from makes 'em for you. Me, my fate was set long before I had any say in it."

All of this seemed to jibe with what I remembered of Benjamin. He'd brought up Attica that night I was held in the basement on Huntley. And I distinctly remembered that long, thin scar running down his cheek.

I went through every article I could find pertaining to Raymond Benjamin and the riots. Then, in a small item in the *Journal News,* a paper that served Westchester, Putnam and Rockland counties in New York, I found a short item in which Raymond Benjamin was named. It was accompanied by a photograph, as well. I recognized Benjamin immediately.

The photo was taken at a ribbon-cutting ceremony at the opening of a new shopping mall in Chappaqua, New York. Chappaqua was a pretty tony suburb, and I wondered what Ray was doing there. In the photo he was wearing a hard hat. And he was clapping. The caption read, "Workers from Powers Construction celebrate. Raymond Benjamin of Hobbs County among those proud of this state-of-the-art development."

Right there, two things leaped out at me. Raymond Benjamin was from Hobbs County. Just like Daniel Linwood and the Reed family. Not to mention Dmitri Petrovsky. No doubt that's how Ray met the good doctor.

And second, according to the article, Benjamin was employed by a company called Powers Construction. I couldn't picture the man who pressed a lit cigarette to my skin working on a job site, holding a jackhammer under his gut. It didn't seem right. This was a guy whose job was to hurt, to kill, not to build.

Unless it was a sham.

I logged off the machine and went straight to Wallace's office. He was on the phone, but when he saw me enter he said, "I'll call you back," and hung up. He turned to me, pressed his palms on the desk.

"Henry," he said. "How's your friend Sheffield?"

"He'll pull through," I said. "A centimeter in another direction and it would have been a different story. He'll have a tough recovery, but he's a tough guy."

"I'm glad to hear that. And you saw Jack out there—the place wasn't the same without him."

"No, sure wasn't."

"And how are you holding up?"

"Can I use up my daily allotment of 'I've been better'?"

"Consider it done."

"Great," I said. "What do you know about an outfit called Powers Construction?"

Wallace shook his head. "Doesn't ring a bell. Why do you ask?"

"I've been doing some research on the man I think is behind these kidnappings, and he's named in a New York paper as working with this Powers Construction company. It just doesn't seem to make sense. The guy I saw seems to be more handy with a gun than a screwdriver."

"I'm sorry, off the top of my head I don't know."

"You think it could be a front? He's employed there for legal purposes, maybe does his wet work on the side? You know, waste-management consulting?"

Wallace chuckled. "It's possible," he said. "But then why would Powers Construction employ the man if he's got a record—which he would have to disclose—and to top that off, he's hardly a model employee?"

"Until now, he hasn't been in any trouble since the seventies. Something just feels off here."

"Do some looking into this Powers Construction," Wallace said. "Are they a legit outfit? And where are they based out of?"

"Putnam County," I said. "They've done work all over the surrounding towns. Including Hobbs County, which as it turns out is the birthplace of our very own psychopath Benjamin."

"You know, now that I think about it," Wallace said, "I remember reading somewhere that Powers Construction was responsible for some pretty major jobs. Not just commercial, but residential, too. If I remember correctly, a congressman who recently retired had a mansion built by Powers."

"I'll check it out," I said. "But if you're right, it definitely seems like these might be some big-time players in real estate development."

"Strange times for that market," Wallace said. "Millions of people's lives are being ruined by the subprime mortgage mess. Government's doing what it can to help, but it can't help everyone. You're going to have a lot of foreclosures over the next few years. And that means a lot of business for a company like Powers. People buy up those foreclosed homes, then either gut and renovate or simply tear them down and rebuild."

"Strange," I said, thinking. I felt like a piece of the puzzle might have just become clearer. "I spent a lot of time in Meriden and Hobbs County recently. And in both places it was obvious they'd seen more work than Joan Rivers. Each town was like a tale of two cities—one old and decrepit, one new and rebuilt."

"I'm sure if part of the town was rebuilt, it's only a matter of time before the rest catches up."

"Maybe," I said. "Even the Linwoods' house looked like it had been carved out of marble recently. When I read up on Daniel Linwood's kidnapping, the family received thousands of dollars in donations, public and anonymous. No idea if that went into their house, but I'll tell you, it wasn't the only one on the block that looked new. I'm wondering if Powers Construction has held the scalpel over Hobbs County. And if so, maybe they're tied into the mess somehow."

"Even if you think it's not about the money," Wallace said, "it's about the money."

Obviously there was a strong motive for Powers Construction to want to be a part of some major rebuilding projects in Hobbs County, as well as other towns and cities across the Northeast. I still felt like I was missing something. Follow the money, Wallace said. That's what I decided to do. I had to talk to Reggie Powers.

40

The home office of Powers Construction was located at Twenty-Third and Fifth in Manhattan. Before calling over, I decided to do a little research on the company. Their Web site had one of those incredibly flashy designs, and I could picture Reggie Powers grimacing as he handed over thousands of dollars to some tech geeks who'd likely never seen a working construction side. The company logo was an intersected *P* and *C*. Both letters looked like they were made out of curved steel, bolts and all.

Powers was, according to the site, one of the leading commercial and residential contractors in the entire Northeast. Their projects ranged from billion-dollar properties, from several financial institutions, to smaller homes and houses. They were credited for having essentially rebuilt several small towns, and were even one of the contractors called in to evaluate the Gulf Coast after the devastation of Hurricane Katrina. Whatever the size of the project, it looked like Powers Construction was the bidder to beat.

It was no secret that the construction industry had some shady underpinnings, since the majority of contracts were doled out to the lowest bidder. The problem therein was that the lowest bidders often miscalculated their budgets, necessitating a six-million-dollar property costing north of seven million. Yet the smarter, or shadier companies (amazing how often the two went hand in hand), worked out sweetheart deals to rig bids. The contractor would offer a bid far lower than any of his competitors, which was of course accepted. If they ran over budget, which was almost guaranteed, the bill would be settled under the table. This meant projects were bid on for far less money than they actually cost, keeping other companies out of the loop, but allowing the illegal parties to get rich based on the sheer number of developments they partnered on.

Reggie Powers himself had quite an interesting story. According to his online biography, he was the most influential black construction owner in the entire country. Born in Crown Heights in 1959, Powers had little formal education and had worked various construction jobs throughout his formative years. Then after the Crown Heights riots of 1991, Powers decided he was tired of seeing his neighborhood torn apart by violence, and was tired of seeing good men and women live in housing that was akin to inhumane treatment. Within five years, Powers had taken his own earnings, and with the help of lenders, bought out a company known as TBC—Thomas Blakeman Construction—renaming it Powers Construction. One of his first rebuilding projects was tearing down a number of projects in which drugs and violence were rampant. These buildings were replaced with low-income housing. According to Powers, it was the end of the dark days, and the beginning of a new Brooklyn.

Within a few years, Powers had become known not only as one of the wealthiest and most influential private contractors on the East Coast, but one of its biggest philanthropists. He donated time, money and manpower to numerous towns, and was credited with helping to lower crime rates across the board.

Of course, official biographies often swept more than their fair share under the carpet. Not to mention that Powers's relative inexperience made his volcanic rise even more shocking. I had to think that simply due to the sheer size of Powers Construction, it would be strange if they didn't have some sort of bid-rigging system going on.

Once I'd done some digging around regarding the company profile, I decided it was time to meet the man face-to-face. Reggie Powers. See what, if anything, he knew. And whether he was aware that one of his employees, Raymond Benjamin, was a murderer.

I called the main switchboard at Powers Construction, and a pleasant secretary picked up the phone. She sounded as if she'd been there a long time, even had a cadence nailed down.

"Po-*wers* Con-*struct-ion,* how may I direct your call?"

"Well, first I was wondering if you could give me the extension for one of your employees. The name is Raymond Benjamin. And after that I'd like to be transferred to Reggie Powers's office."

"One moment, sir," the woman said. I heard typing on the other end. Then I heard her mutter, *Hmm, that's odd.*

"Ma'am? Are you still there?"

"Yes, sir, sorry about that. According to our database, we do employ a Raymond Benjamin, but he doesn't have an office or an extension."

"Is there any contact information for him?"

"I'm sorry, sir, not that I have access to. You'd have to speak to our human resources department."

"That's all right. Can you transfer me to Mr. Powers's office?"

"Sure thing, just a moment."

She put me on hold. A minute later, a young man's voice came over the line.

"Mr. Powers's office."

"Hi, my name is Henry Parker and I'm a reporter from the *New York Gazette*. I'd like to come in and speak with Mr. Powers today. It's a pretty urgent matter."

"Mr. Powers has a very busy schedule today. He's not in the office right now, but if I can pass a message to him, I'll see if he has some free time."

"Absolutely," I said. "Tell him I want to speak to him about Raymond Benjamin and Dmitri Petrovsky."

"Can you spell those for me, sir?"

"Just remember the names."

"Um…okay. I'll call Mr. Powers right now. Is there a number where I can reach you?"

I gave the secretary my cell phone number. He said he'd get back to me ASAP. I hung up the phone and began to play the waiting game again.

I tried to think how Reggie Powers might be connected to all of this. Powers Construction employed Raymond Benjamin, though the fact that he was a ghost at the office pretty much confirmed that he was there to do dirty work, collect a W-2, and that was all. But why would Reggie Powers want anything to do with Dmitri Petrovsky? He seemed like the least likely person on earth to want to have anything to do with a kidnapping, especially given his background. The more the pieces came together, the more trouble I had making them all fit.

Ten minutes later, my cell phone rang. I picked it up.

"Mr. Parker." I recognized the voice as Powers's secretary. "Mr. Powers is at a job site all day today, but he said if you can meet him there at six o'clock, he'd be happy to speak with you."

"Where's the site?" I asked.

"He's overseeing the construction of a mall in Hobbs County, New York, today."

Hobbs County. Why was I not surprised. I checked my watch. It was three-thirty. I had plenty of time to drive up to Hobbs County.

"Give me the address," I said. I jotted down the information, thanked the secretary and hung up. I chewed on the tip of my pen. I had no idea what Reggie Powers would know. I sure as hell had a few questions he needed good answers to.

I put my tape recorder and notebook into a small backpack, stopped in to Wallace's office to tell him where I was going. He told me to check in once I was done with Powers. I got the sense Wallace understood how big this story was getting. And that scared me.

I took the subway Uptown to my apartment, got in the rental car and began the drive up to Hobbs County.

41

"Tomorrow," Paulina said. She was sitting at her desk, leaning back in her desk chair, the one the assistants commonly referred to as the "bitch throne." She'd caught James Keach referring to it as such one day, but rather than admonish the boy, she merely laughed and told him not to be shy about it. From that day on, James commonly referred to the chair with that moniker, using the slight whisper of a child who can't believe his parents permit him to curse in the house.

The copy was set. The pictures had been laid out. She'd pored over every inch of the article with greater focus than any story she could remember. She couldn't say for sure whether this piece would be her crowning moment as a journalist—in fact, she wasn't sure she'd want it to be—but in many ways it meant the most to her. It represented a clear turning point in her career, and would mark perhaps the first official shot of the war. To this day it had been the newsprint version of Russia versus the U.S. No casualties, lots of trash talk and hidden agendas everywhere they turned.

Paulina's article would change all of that. So while nobody quite knew just who fired that first shot at Lexington and Concord, in the future they could pin this one to her blouse. The Parker stories had been small potatoes. Going after a baby fish as though people would care. To this point, Henry hadn't been in the game long enough for people to truly care. Like Stephen Glass and Jayson Blair, the sting would have been worse if they had the tenure of, well… Paulina laughed.

A bottle of Dom was waiting in her fridge. Myron's phone number was on her cell phone. At first she debated calling him again—the last thing she needed tonight was another pity party—but ending the night with a good drink and a great lay would be the perfect capper. The end of the beginning, the beginning of the end.

And even though she hadn't seen him in many months, Paulina rather wished she'd be able to see the look on Henry Parker's face in the morning.

42

The sun bathed Hobbs County in a beautiful mélange of reds and golds. This could be such a breathtaking town, I hated to think so much evil had taken place here. When I parked the car in the lot by the construction site, I took a moment to take it in, to breathe it in. You didn't get many views like this in the city, one of the trade-ins you had to make to live there. I didn't mind so much. Spending my whole childhood growing up way out West, I'd seen enough sunsets to quench a lifelong thirst. Living amid the steel and bustle of New York didn't quite feel like home yet, but it was getting there.

I turned off the car and parked outside the site.

The mall was coming up well. Steel beams were exposed everywhere. Tools and wheelbarrows and mixers were scattered about. I had no idea where I was supposed to meet Reggie Powers. I figured there would be some sort of office structure set apart, or he'd just be waiting for me outside. Yet as I took a quick look around, there was no sign of him.

As I walked through the construction area, dipping under low beams, peeking around corners, I felt a queasy sensation in my stomach when I realized there wasn't a single person in sight.

Powers's secretary had told me Reggie would be at the site all day. But there were no other cars on the lot. No discarded papers or bags. No sign that any human beings had even set foot here today. Why would Reggie be here all day if nobody else was?

A terrible suspicion grew that I was alone here. Or even worse, not as alone as I thought.

"Hello?" I called out. My voice echoed through the structure. A chill ran through my body, and I held the backpack tighter. "Mr. Powers?"

Still nothing.

I exited the structure, walked around the exterior.

Several cranes were standing tall over the skeleton, long steel beams lying at their feet. The cement trucks were quiet, side elevators dark.

"Reggie Powers!" I called again. When again there was no answer, I decided it'd be best to get the hell out of there.

I began to jog back toward the car, winding my way around the side of the building. As I passed a blue van, I saw something that made me stop in my tracks. My breath caught.

Beside the van I could make out a human hand splayed out on the ground. As I crept closer, I could see the fingertips coated with blood. The hand belonged to a black man.

The body was on the ground in an awkward position. The right hand was splayed out above the man's head, the left arm at a ninety-degree angle. The legs were crumpled, one stuck beneath the man's torso. A single hole was in the center of his head, and a pool of blood had begun to dry.

I didn't need to check the wallet to know that Reggie Powers had been murdered.

I whipped around, looking for something, anything.

He'd clearly been dead a little while, so whoever had done it had either fled the scene, or was waiting for me.

I took the cell phone from my pocket. Dialed 911. I felt panicked as I waited to be connected, every second not knowing what the hell was happening. Was Powers already dead when I called his office? Or had he come here with the intent to meet with me, then was murdered by someone who knew…

Then I knew it. Powers meant to set me up. He knew nobody would be at the construction site. He must have told somebody before he arrived. And that somebody took him out. Somebody who'd begun to think Powers was better off dead. Somebody who felt he'd become a liability.

And when I heard the click of a gun safety being removed, I knew immediately that Raymond Benjamin had killed him.

"Step away from the van, Parker."

I put the cell phone in my coat pocket. Every muscle in my body was numb.

I recognized the voice. I'd heard it that night at the house on Huntley, as this man tried to torture information out of me.

I slowly turned around. Hands above my head.

Raymond Benjamin was standing ten feet away from me. He held a gun in one outstretched hand. The scar on his cheek seemed to glisten in the darkening sky. His face was a mask of anger and frustration.

"I didn't want it to come to this," he said. "Killing is an ugly, ugly thing. If you'd just let it be, Parker, this wouldn't be happening."

"Petrovsky. Powers. You killed them both, and for what? To hide your dirty secret? I know what all this is," I said. "All this by your hand."

Benjamin took a step closer. "Parker," he said. "I'm sorry you won't have a chance to know any better."

The sky exploded, a yellow blast echoing in the night, and I shut my eyes and waited to die. When after a moment I felt no pain, felt nothing at all except the wind on my face, I opened them. Raymond Benjamin was dead on the ground. Smoke wafted from a bullet hole in his back, right where his heart had beat its last breath. And standing there, smoking gun in his hand, was Senator Gray Talbot.

43

"It was you all along," I said, staring into the senator's cold eyes. "You were behind the kidnappings. Hobbs County and Meriden were your pet projects so you could look good come voting season. That way you could come off looking like some great savior, when in reality you were feeding people the same poison you claimed to be eradicating. You and Raymond Benjamin found children who were born with diabetes, whom you could subject to these sick experiments to rob them of years of their lives. You take them away, then use their disappearances as leverage to get good press, gentrify the towns. The crime rate plummets. Property values go up. In come landowners who are more willing to vote for you. You bring in Reggie Powers to rebuild the town. You steal lives for political gain, you fucking monster."

Talbot shook his head like a teacher whose student was too stupid to understand a simple equation. "That's the black-and-white version," Talbot said. "But who's really losing here? These kids lose a couple years of their lives, but when they come back their towns aren't criminal beehives anymore. Their schools aren't run-down. Drugs aren't sold on their blocks. It's a small sacrifice for a lifetime of happiness, for them and their families."

"So one life is worth shattering if it saves another, is that right? The ends justify the means?"

"They always do," Talbot said. "And if I'm reelected because of it, if this leads me to the governor's mansion or, heaven look upon me, the White House, it will be because I take steps weaker men aren't willing to take. If you can sacrifice one life to save others, don't you have to do that? As a human being?"

"I don't buy that," I said. "Reggie Powers contributed thousands and thousands of dollars a year to political campaigns. Want to bet if we looked up his history of donating to your fund, we'd find a little more than 'Good Samaritan' money?"

"Reggie had a good heart," Talbot said, and I detected a hint of real sadness. "He was a true hero. But he was compromised. Just like the Reed family, it was only a matter of time before Reggie's heart got the best of him."

"So you're tying up your loose ends," I said. "Dmitri Petrovsky. Reggie Powers. Ray Benjamin. Everyone who knew about this is dead. And if we hadn't found them first, the Reeds would be, too. All those lives, you're actually trying to say these people's deaths are worth furthering your demented cause?"

"Without a doubt, absolutely. You cannot put a value on one life, Henry. But I can tell you that a hundred lives, a thousand lives, are worth more than a simple few. The tree of liberty must be refreshed from time to time, with the blood of patriots and tyrants. Those children, these men, were our patriots. They gave their lives to prevent others from suffering in the future. Men like Raymond Benjamin are our tyrants. He represents everything wrong with our culture. And so while he was a means to an end, so, too, did his blood need to water the ground."

"And Daniel Linwood," I said. "Michelle Oliveira. Caroline Twomey. Their blood funds your campaign, too."

"If my platform must stand on a column these children have provided, so be it. I can live with that. I am sorry, Henry. Consider yourself a patriot. Your death will save lives."

"One thing before I, you know, go," I said.

"Yes, Parker?"

"The blood might choke the ground," I said, taking my still-connected cell phone from my coat pocket. "But with my plan I get a signal pretty much anywhere."

Talbot looked at me with horror, and right as he raised the gun to fire, I heard the sound of several sirens approaching. Talbot turned around to see a police cruiser pull into the construction site, followed by half a dozen more along with two ambulances.

A dozen cops leaped from their vehicles, guns raised, pointed at the silver-haired senator.

"Drop your weapon!" a cop yelled. "Drop it now or we will take you down!"

Talbot looked at me, and for a moment I saw a fear and confusion in his eyes that brought terror to my heart. He raised the gun an inch, aiming straight and true at me, and for a moment I believed the senator would end my life along with everything else.

Then he lowered the gun, his eyes dropping to the ground, and the gun clattered on the gravel.

Instantly he was pinned down by three police officers, who handcuffed him and then picked the man up. Standing by one of the cruisers were the two detectives who'd questioned Amanda and me after we'd escaped from Huntley. Their faces were blank, unbelieving, as they watched Senator Gray Talbot pushed into the back of a police car, which then pulled away.

I stood there in the waning daylight, looked up at the sky and took a long, sweet breath. There was one more task to be done. One more terrible question that needed to be answered.

44

The money trail was there. A spot-check of Gray Talbot's campaign finance reports showed a yearly influx of $50,000 dollars from a company called Shepherd Incorporated. Shepherd was owned by Reggie Powers, a shell company set up separately from Powers Construction. Yearly withdrawals from Shepherd, Inc. were being matched to Gray Talbot. And everyone knew what they would tell us.

Finally the story came together. Several of the players, I knew, had to believe the bullshit Gray Talbot was spewing. Several of them had to feel that what they were doing was right. That to destroy evil, you had to commit evil. That getting your cause noticed was justification for it all.

It was easy to be cynical. Both Amanda and I came from broken homes, where we could never believe a parent would go to such lengths to allegedly protect us.

Gray Talbot hired Raymond Benjamin to be his eyes, his ears, his gun. All orders went through Benjamin, nothing went to Gray. Benjamin was his wall of protection.

Benjamin, a Hobbs County native, approached Dmitri

Petrovsky in order to obtain hospital records of infants born with childhood diabetes. They screened children who would be most susceptible to Korsakoff syndrome. Once Petrovsky came back with a name, a plan was put in motion.

The child would be kidnapped. Petrovsky would develop a nutritional plan that would keep the child's thiamine levels at a level dangerous enough to cause minor brain damage, enough to bring an onset of Korsakoff, but not so severe that it would endanger the child's life.

When the child was gone, when the police search turned up fruitless, that's when Gray Talbot stepped in. He would trumpet his concern for the welfare of the community. Talk about how crime rates were unacceptable. That children were being snatched from their families.

Millions of dollars would be pumped into the communities through donations, federal and state funding. Police forces would be bolstered. Neighborhood watches on patrol. Broken streetlights fixed. Homes made safe again.

And real estate would slowly creep up.

That's when Talbot would enlist the help of Powers Construction. Reggie would come in with his trucks and his men, level the homes consumed by crack, rebuild houses that would attract more money than the neighborhood had ever seen.

Talbot would gain a wealthier, more affluent constituency. Powers would make millions from the sweetheart deals. And the communities would be better off.

Everybody won.

Except the children.

Amanda sat in the seat next to me, the radio turned to a soft rock station. The music they played was unthreatening, wouldn't offend any sensibilities, lyrics that couldn't harm a fly. That's all we wanted at that moment. Serenity. Emotionlessness.

The next few hours would be difficult. We didn't want it to start until it absolutely had to.

After I'd gone on record with the police, handed over my cell phone and explained everything that had happened, I called Amanda immediately. I told her what we had to do. I wasn't sure how the night was going to end, but if we didn't ask that one final question, I didn't know if I'd ever sleep again.

I steered the car, unable to help but think about Danny Linwood, how in some ways we both had lost years from our childhood. The difference was I had a choice. My memories and experiences helped mold me into what I was now. Danny would need time, years perhaps, to even know who he was.

We arrived at the house shortly past ten o'clock. The porch lights were out. The street was dim save a few lampposts. Turning the engine off, I walked up to one, felt the metal, inspected it. It was well cared for. No graffiti. No damage. It was doing its duty without any interference. Illuminating a world that was, for better or worse, now a safer place.

"You think they're asleep?" Amanda asked.

"No way. At that age I fought tooth and nail for every extra minute. I'd sneak an AM/FM radio into bed so I could listen to ball games, maybe a book and a flashlight. I hope kids haven't outgrown that."

"Not outgrown it," she said. "They just have more options now. Portable video games, iPods, televisions the size of a quarter. It's a miracle they don't spend half their time choosing which one to watch."

We stepped up to the porch. I saw the wind chimes again. In a moment they'd be ringing their tune.

I pressed the doorbell, heard a chime go off inside the house. There were footsteps, a woman's voice shouting something. Then the screen door opened, and Shelly Linwood was standing right in front of us.

She was wearing a terry-cloth bathrobe, her hair done up in rollers. I saw a child run past behind her. Tasha, if I remembered correctly.

"Henry? Henry Parker?" she said, unsure of what to make of this late-night visit.

"Mrs. Linwood," I said. "I need a minute of your time."

"I was just doing my hair," she said. She looked eager to get back to that, but the look on my face told her we weren't leaving anytime soon. Resignedly, she said, "Come on in."

She held the door open for us, and we walked inside.

"Mrs. Linwood, this is Amanda Davies. She works for the New York Legal Aid Society. She's a good friend of mine, and I just thought it would be good for her to meet Danny. Danny might have some questions she can answer. And if not, he'll make a new friend."

I saw a mop of hair peek from behind a doorway. Shelley turned around, said, "Danny, come in here. You remember Henry, right?"

Daniel Linwood tentatively stepped into the room. He'd gained a few pounds since I last saw him, his hair a little longer. His eyes seemed more frightened, his gait more awkward.

"Danny," I said. "This is Amanda."

She stepped forward, knelt down slightly so she was at his level.

"Hey there," she said. "I'm Amanda. Mind if we chat for a bit? I'd love to see your room."

"Show her your Xbox," Shelly said. Danny nodded reluctantly, led Amanda past us and up the stairs.

"Can we sit?" I said. Shelly nodded.

We went into the living room, sat on the same couch where I'd interviewed Danny not too long ago.

"How is he?" I asked.

Shelly sighed, scratched her neck.

"I get a call from his school almost every day. Kids picking on him. Giving him wedgies. Stealing his lunch money. It wasn't like this before."

"He's a different person now," I said. "It's going to take a long time for him to find himself."

"I know," she said. "God, I know."

"Mrs. Linwood," I said. "I want you to hear this from me. And only from me. I want you to know what I know."

She looked up, her eyes big and brown and watery. "Yes?"

"You knew about Daniel's kidnapping. You knew it was going to happen. You knew he would be taken. And you probably told them when they could do it. Know that I know. Because you'll have to live with that. Live with everyone knowing what you did."

Her mouth fell open. She stared at me, shaking her head, openmouthed.

"No," she said. "My Danny, I didn't—"

"Shelly," I said. "You've been lying too long. I know why you did it. I know you met Raymond Benjamin."

Shelly just sat there, her lower lip trembling.

"When I spoke to Danny, you even brought him a tray of food. Vegetables that would help replenish the thiamine levels that were so low in his brain. Food high in vitamin B1. Did Petrovsky tell you to do that?"

Shelly sat there, stone silent.

"Did he come to your house? Raymond Benjamin."

She continued to stare, then a tear streaked down her cheek as she nodded.

"Yes," she said.

"What did he say?"

"He told me," Shelly said, sucking in air and wiping her face, "that this town was tearing itself apart. That he'd grown up here, and there were only two options for boys Danny and James's age. Prison or the grave. Raymond said he'd been to prison, but that's only because he got caught."

"And he offered you a deal," I said. "Right? He would take Danny away for a few years. He would be gone, but he would be safe. And by doing that you would give your children a chance to grow up in a neighborhood where they'd be safe. Where they could make something of themselves."

Shelly nodded. Then she stood up. Went over to the mantel, and took down a framed photograph. She handed it to me.

It was an odd picture. I'd noticed it during my interview with Daniel. And now I thought about the photo I found in Robert Reed's wallet and it all made sense.

The photo was of Shelly's younger son, James. The shot had been taken from about five feet behind him. He was wearing a knapsack, baggy jeans. He was unaware of the photographer.

I turned the frame over and removed the knobs that held it in place. When the backing came off, the back of the photo was visible. One word was printed on it.

Remember.

"Raymond Benjamin gave that photo to me," she said. "He told me he'd taken it himself. He said if he could get that close to James, others could, too. People who meant him more harm than he did. He said it was a fair trade. A few years of Daniel's life would guarantee the safety of my whole family forever. Daniel would, in a way, be a hero. I never understood how my son could be a hero giving his life for a cause he didn't understand or even know about. I just wanted to believe in some way he was doing it for the future of James and Tasha. And he said that anytime I began to doubt myself or what I'd done, to look at that photo and remember what could happen to the rest of my family."

"What did you do, Shelly?" I asked.

Shelly began to weep. She held her head in her hands. I felt a modicum of remorse for this woman, but it soon went away.

"I told Benjamin the route Danny took to get home from practice," she said. "Six-thirty every night. I made him promise not to hurt my baby. He told me he wouldn't."

"What else did Benjamin say?"

"He promised me a family would take care of him. They knew about his diabetes and they would care for him," Shelly said through bloodshot eyes. "And I believed him. At least I wanted to. I needed to know my babies could grow up and lead full lives. I've seen what this town can do to people. I wanted my sons to have something better."

"Is that what Danny has now?" I asked. "Something better?"

"I don't know," she said. "But if he can get out of here and ends up in a safe office, making money, starting a family instead of rotting behind bars or in the dirt, then yes. He has something better. I know you can't possibly understand that, Henry. Wanting your child to not just survive but live a life. Maybe one day you will. But you can't right now."

"No," I said. "I can't."

45

I woke up the next morning, pleasantly surprised that sleep had come so easily. I think it was more due to the complete lack of energy in every one of my muscles, the utter exhaustion I felt, than any sort of blissful conscience.

As soon as we returned from the Linwood residence, I'd gone straight to the *Gazette* to write up my story. Amanda had given me a long, deep hug, and for the first time since we'd started speaking again, a hug was all I wanted.

The story was difficult to write. That so many people had been so deceitful, purposefully putting so many lives at risk, it was hard to fathom how any of them could have felt they were doing the right thing. I heard over the wire that the police had apprehended Robert and Elaine Reed in a suburb just outside Chicago. Caroline Twomey was in the process of being returned to her family. The police had reopened the kidnappings of both Danny Linwood and Michelle Oliveira. They still didn't know who kidnapped them, and they believed Gray Talbot had inoculated himself from that knowledge. It was Ray Benjamin who was the button man. And Gray had killed him to seal off the investigation. There was a chance those families who held the children would never be found, never be prose-cuted. We got lucky with Daniel Linwood.

The Reeds were found at a hotel outside Chicago. They'd driven halfway across the country after fleeing Harrisburg. The manager became suspicious when all of the family's credit cards were declined, and Elaine Reed attempted to use an expired driver's license as identification.

They claimed, like Shelly Linwood, that they were doing it to protect their son, Patrick. That Benjamin had threatened them, as well. And now Patrick would likely spend most of his childhood in foster care, and his parents would have to deal with the legal ramifications of what they'd done.

The children's lives would go on. But they would never be the same.

It's always the innocent who are forced to suffer.

Like Shelly said, maybe in a few years I would under-stand. When I had a family of my own, children I would do anything to protect, maybe that kind of sacrifice would feel justified.

But not right now.

I looked forward to seeing the paper, so when I rolled out of bed the first thing I did was go to the front door to get my morning delivery.

My neighbor down the hall, the lovely Ms. Berry, all eighty nightgowned years of her, must have been thrilled to see me standing there topless in my boxers. I waved hello. She retreated back inside. Maybe she wasn't so thrilled.

I took the paper inside, laid it on the table and read.

When I was through, my emotions were mixed. I was happy with the story, but not the outcome. All I could say is that Gray Talbot's operation would be shut down, and the man would certainly spend years behind bars.

Caroline Twomey was returned to her family. It remained to be seen what would happen to her parents. I assumed they were accessories, like the Linwoods. And it was only a matter of time before the Oliveira case was reopened, as well.

So many lives shattered by greed and fear. And I still wasn't quite sure who the villains were.

I took a hot shower, feeling like a year's worth of crud had built up, caked my skin an inch thick. I let the water run in and out of my mouth, felt the steam coat my face. It felt good.

When I washed up, I packed the paper, got my stuff together and headed to the newsroom. Though the story was a difficult one for me to write, I knew Wallace and the crew would be thrilled. It was a huge get, the kind of story that would not just have people talking today, but would ripple for months if not years. It made me glad that Wallace would be proud. Though I secretly hoped Jack would be, too. I still resented what he'd done to himself, resented that he might have jeopardized his legacy, but his validation meant more to me than he likely knew.

I took the train down to Rockefeller Plaza, remembering I'd have to return the rental later that day.

The plaza was already crowded by the time I walked over. Tourists were perched on the benches, taking pictures of the grandness of the area. People stood outside the shops waiting for that first door to be cracked open.

I'd never been much of a sightseer when I was younger. Wonders never really amazed me like they did most folk. I chalked it up to my profession, where everything had to come with some sense of detachment. If you got too personally involved in a story, it could come back to haunt you in more ways than you could imagine. I thought about my last few major stories, beginning with being sought for a murder charge a few years ago, to hunting William Henry Roberts after that. And now, with Gray Talbot behind bars and the lives of several families never to be the same, I wondered if I'd mistakenly forgotten all that. If I'd gotten too close, whether by chance or by choice.

Once this was over I wanted to step back, reevaluate my situation. I loved my job, and that wouldn't change until they dragged me out of the newsroom, kicking and screaming while I tried to beat off Security with a legal notepad. There was room to grow. Personally and professionally. And with all the time spent chasing murderers, liars and politicians (who managed to encompass both), it was time to take stock.

The wall clock read 9:05 when the elevator opened on to the newsroom floor. I expected some sort of jubilation, maybe a pat on the back or two. I'd cracked a huge case that would have ramifications potentially all the way to the top. A man considered a potential front-runner for the biggest job in the land would now be spending at least eight years behind bars. There was something sad about ruining a career. Ending a life. And I wondered where Hobbs County would be today if Gray Talbot had never thought of a boy named Daniel Linwood.

I walked to my desk looking for my colleagues, looking out for Wallace. The pride quickly turned to fear when I noticed all the reporters were sitting at their desks. They were silent. Their faces ashen gray. Some were at work, but it was perfunctory.

Evelyn Waterstone passed by. She gazed up at me for a moment, her mouth opening. For the first time I could remember, Evelyn Waterstone looked sad. She said two words to me, "Sorry, Parker," and walked on.

I didn't know what to do, but something had bitten the newsroom of the *New York Gazette.* I had to find out. The only person who didn't look like they were drowning in their own sorrows was Frank Rourke.

There was no love lost between Frank Rourke and me. We'd had a pretty intense falling-out over the shit bag incident last year, and since then never really attempted to patch things up. I never felt the need to gain his approval. My work would accomplish that in my stead.

Rourke was yapping away on his desk phone—something about preseason football—so I walked over when he hung up and stood over his desk, waiting to hear what he said.

Rourke didn't notice me at first. He just sat there drinking coffee out of a Thermos the size of my head. Then when he turned around and saw me standing there, the smile disappeared. My stomach dropped when I realized he had the same look on his face Evelyn had minutes earlier.

"Parker," he said. "Listen, man...I don't know what else to say. But I'm sorry. This sucks majorly."

"What does?" I said. "I just got here, *please,* everyone else looks like they have one foot in the grave."

Rourke said, "Oh, man, you didn't see it?"

"See what? Speak to me, goddamn it."

Rourke spun around, looked at the desk across from him. Then he stood up, went over and began rifling through the garbage can. I wondered what the hell he was doing, but then when I saw him take a newspaper out of the can, that queasiness returned. He handed it to me, front page out, and said, "Like I said, this sucks."

I unfolded the front page and held it up. It was a copy of this morning's *New York Dispatch.* When I read the headline, in huge bold print, I nearly threw up.

The headline read: A Lush Life: Jack O'Donnell and All the Booze That's Fit to Print.

The byline was credited to Paulina Cole.

The two *l*'s in *all* were liquor bottles. Below the headline were two pictures. And both made me sick to my stomach.

The first picture looked to have been taken in some sort of storage room. It was about the size of a walk-in closet, with three rows of shelves traversing the space.

Every single space was lined, front to back, with empty bottles. Wine. Beer. Whiskey. Bourbon. The caption below the photo read: Jack O'Donnell Downs in One Year What Most People Drink in a Lifetime!

The second photo, the one that made me clench the paper into a wad in my hands, was of Jack. Lying in the hospital. Tubes running through his veins.

I recognized the setting. It was taken after I'd brought Jack to the hospital after he nearly choked to death on his own vomit. Somebody had snuck into the hospital and photographed Jack while he was unconscious and recovering from alcohol poisoning. I couldn't imagine the kind of black heart needed to do such a thing.

I took the paper without saying another word to Frank and took it to my desk. There I read the entire article, every single word. And when I was done, I crumpled it up, took it to the incinerator on our floor and chucked it into the darkness.

Paulina Cole had done one of the worst hatchet jobs on Jack I'd ever read. Somehow she'd gotten one of the porters in Jack's building to collect the liquor bottles from the recycling bin every morning. Easy, since he occupied the entire floor himself. The bottles were then brought straight to Paulina Cole. Every single one was fingerprinted to confirm that Jack had in fact drunk them himself. No other fingerprints were found on any of the bottles. And there must have been several hundred in the photograph. And he'd drunk them all himself over the span of one year.

The article described how much alcohol must have been absorbed by Jack's bloodstream over that year. It also made mention of every correction in every story that Jack had written that same year, comparing it to his previous work. It portrayed Jack as a man whose professional life was now ruled by one of the most aggressive bouts of alcoholism ever seen in the newsroom, whose work had depreciated to the point where his stories were filled with more holes than an O. J. Simpson alibi.

Then the story took a more macro perspective, going into great detail about how the *Gazette* promoted Jack as one of the legends of New York journalism. Paulina ended her story with the following paragraph:

"It can be said that a news institution can be judged on one thing, and one thing only: the reputation of the men and women who report the news. Jack O'Donnell is a man whose reputation, built over years more through joviality and cronyism than true journalistic integrity, has opened a window into the true nature of this black-and-white beast. And what an ugly, ugly creature it is."

The next thing I knew I was going straight for Jack's desk. It was unoccupied. But worse than that, it was empty. The computer was off. There were no odds and ends on the countertop. There was nothing.

I marched to Wallace Langston's office and threw open

the doors. The editor-in-chief was on the phone. His face was ashen. I knew the feeling. He motioned for me to take a seat. I declined.

When he hung up the phone, I said, "Wallace, what the fuck is going on? Where is Jack?"

Wallace sighed and leaned back in his chair. I knew my anger was misplaced, but my mind was going a thousand miles an hour in a hundred different directions. "Jack is on leave," he said.

"On leave? What the hell does that mean?"

"I assume you saw the story in today's *Dispatch*," he said.

"I just finished it."

"Well, word came down from Harvey Hillerman himself that Jack had two choices. An extended personal leave to deal with his demons in a treatment center. Or the termination of his employment with the *Gazette*." Harvey Hillerman was the president and CEO of the *Gazette*. If it came from him, it meant Jack had no way out.

"And?"

"And as of this morning, Jack O'Donnell is no longer an employee of this newspaper."

I felt as if a cannonball had hit me square in the stomach. My knees went weak, and I fell into the chair across from Wallace.

"He can't do that," I said. "Jack *is* this newspaper."

"No, he's not, Henry. Jack has done more for this paper than any employee in its history. But we are not one and the same. You've seen Jack over the past few months. You know things have been going downhill. He was hospitalized just last week."

"Yeah, and I know that damn picture is out there for everyone to see."

"You need to think about Jack," Wallace said. "The man needs help. More than what you or I can do. If he chooses to do it on his own, so be it. My take is that he didn't want to be forced into doing anything. That doesn't surprise me. It's always been the way he's worked."

"So what now?" I said. "We just keep working like nothing ever happened?"

"That's impossible," Wallace said. "Jack's been here so long some of his blood does run through this paper's veins. But we have to move on. You've done some amazing work in your time here, Henry. Jack has put down his mantle for now. And I expect you to be one of the people to take it. To carry it with pride."

"You don't take that because it's been thrown down," I said. "You earn it. I can't just take Jack's place. Nobody can."

"That's true. So just do your job to the best of his ability. Learn from his mistakes. Don't let your problems overwhelm you. Because at the end of the day, you're remembered for the end of your career, not the beginning. And the saddest part of all this is a generation might only know the Jack O'Donnell on the cover of today's newspaper."

I couldn't listen to any more. I slammed the door to Wallace's office and left the building. Hailing a taxi, I instructed the driver to take me to Twenty-Seventh and Park. The offices of the *New York Dispatch*.

I left the cab, throwing the fare at the driver, and entered the building through the revolving door, feeling as if I could tear the walls apart with my bare hands. A security guard stopped me as I approached the turnstiles. He said "Sir, you'll need to check in and show your ID."

I went to the security post. Another guard sat there looking bored. "Who are you here to see?"

"Paulina Cole. *New York Dispatch.*"

"Do you have an appointment with Ms. Cole?"

"No."

"Does she know you're coming?"

"No."

The guard looked confused. "Sir, can you state your business with Ms. Cole?"

"That's between me and her."

The guard eyed me suspiciously. Then he said, "I'm going to have to pat you down." I let him. He found nothing. "Let me call upstairs."

He picked up the switchboard phone and dialed a few buttons. I was growing impatient. I needed to see that bitch face-to-face.

The guard put down the phone and said, "Sir, Ms. Cole is not picking up her phone. I can leave a message that you stopped by."

"I can wait for her upstairs."

"No, sir, I can't let you do that."

"Listen, asshole," I said. "I'm seeing Paulina Cole today. Whether you let me upstairs or not."

Just then I heard a commotion by the revolving door. Several voices were congratulating someone. A throng of people surrounding one person.

Then they parted and Paulina Cole continued walking toward the turnstiles.

She saw me and stopped. She was startled for a moment, then a slow smile spread across her face.

"Hi, Henry," she said. "It's been so long. Have you been keeping up with the news?"

"You fucking bitch," I said, starting toward her. I didn't take more than two steps before I felt a pair of hands grab my arms and pull me backward. The security guards were holding me. I thrashed and struggled to get free. "He was a friend to you," I spat. "How could you?"

"It was easy," she said, stepping forward. "And you know what probably angers you the most, Henry? That every word of it is true."

I tried to pull free, but then the two guards began dragging me outside. We passed by Paulina. She raised her hand, waved a sarcastic *goodbye* before the guards shoved me through the doors and out onto the street.

I tumbled onto the sidewalk, then scrambled to my feet. The guards stood there with their hands across their chests.

"Sir," one of them said, "if you don't leave the premises, we will be forced to call the authorities."

I took one step forward, hatred boiling inside me, but then I stopped. Jack had been broken. Defeated. Getting arrested would affect nobody but myself. Jack had been an idol to me for years. I owed him more than that.

I left the *Dispatch* and took the train up to Jack's apartment. The whole way I sat there shaking, not knowing what to say, what to think. After everything with Daniel Linwood, now that Amanda and I seemed to be on good terms, I'd finally felt like things were on the right track. No more days drinking at bars by myself. No more nights sleeping at the office because I couldn't face my own bed.

Then, I wondered, how many nights had Jack O'Donnell had just like that?

When I got to Jack's building, I buzzed his apartment, dying to see that grizzled face in the hopes that it would all make sense. There was no answer. I buzzed again. Still nothing.

I took out my cell phone and rang his house line. It went right to voice mail.

"Jack," I said. "This is Henry. Please call me back. I need to speak to you. Please tell me you're all right."

I clicked off the phone and took one last look at the building. Then I turned around and went back to work.

The old man stood by the window for a long time, watching the boy walk away until he'd disappeared from sight. When Henry Parker turned the corner, he stepped back into his apartment. His body was racked with convulsions, the sobs like mortar rounds. Then Jack O'Donnell slid down the wall until his frail, arthritic knees were tucked up under his chin, and he began to cry.

46

Though I hadn't been a reporter that long, I can honestly say I'd had some long days on the job. The longest weren't the ones where I was on deadline, typing page after page or sifting through an entire casebook worth of notes. The longest days were those where nothing happened. I wasn't waiting for a source to call back. I wasn't waiting for Legal to approve a story. I wasn't waiting on anyone or anything. The day just *passed*.

Today was perhaps the longest of my career. Every few minutes I would turn around to look at that empty desk, wishing upon nothing that Jack would appear magically and just start writing. There would be no story written by Jack O'Donnell in tomorrow's edition, or next week's papers, or any for the foreseeable future.

I was merely a soldier who, until today, had been following the example set by Wallace Langston and Jack O'Donnell. But our ranks had been broken. And who knew if it would ever be repaired.

I left the *Gazette* at five o'clock on the dot. The first day I could ever remember leaving on time. The train ride home was lonely. More so when I saw people reading the very paper that had changed the landscape of my world.

When I stepped off the train, the sun was already beginning to set, and any day now the summer sun would begin to fade into fall. I walked down the street, my bag heavy, not caring where I stepped, my eyes looking no more than two feet in front of me.

Rounding the corner onto my block, I was surprised to hear a voice call out, "Careful, there, I see a hydrant with your name on it."

I looked up to see Amanda standing in front of my building, her hair rippling lightly in the wind, her face golden in the orange haze. If there was one sight that could melt away a man's sorrows, it was that one.

She was wearing tight jeans and a red sweater. Walking closer, I recognized the sweater. I'd given it to her on our six-month anniversary. That seemed like ages ago.

"What are you doing here?" I said, silently chiding myself for the impatient tone in my voice.

"I thought you could use someone to talk to tonight," she said. "I saw the newspaper."

I nodded, only because there was nothing else to say. Amanda approached me, put her hand on my shoulder; the other hand tilted my chin upward.

"I'm sorry," she said. "I know what Jack meant to you."

"He'll get things together," I said softly. "He has to."

"I hope he does. I guess at some point everyone needs to take stock of their life."

"I've been doing a little of that," I said.

"Me, too."

I looked up at her. "Why you?"

"I don't know," she said, brushing a strand of brown hair from her eyes. "At this point in my life, I want to think about what I have. What I want. What I have that I don't want. What I want that I don't have."

"What do you want?" I said.

She smiled demurely. "I'm not a hundred percent sure," she said. "I didn't say it happened all in one day. But I wanted to wait for you. I thought it might be a nice way to end what must have been a pretty crappy day."

"You have no idea," I said.

"How's Curt doing?" she asked.

"He's going home this weekend. I sent a few Olsen twins movies to his apartment as a joke. Figured if Ashley and Mary Kate can't cheer him up, the guy's hopeless."

Amanda smiled. "You're a true friend."

"He's lucky to have me," I said. "So you came here because you wanted to talk about things? About us?"

"Not so much talk," she said. "I had an even better idea. I hope you're okay with it."

"Yeah? What's that?"

"I'm going to take you out tonight. Dinner and a movie. There's an Italian place on Eighty-Third that's supposed to serve the best gnocchi in the city."

"Wait," I said, "this sounds an awful lot like a date."

"I could be coy and play hard to get, but what's the point? Henry Parker, I would love to take you out on a date tonight."

My heart swelled. It was probably from the huge emotional swing, but suddenly I found myself hugging Amanda, pulling her as hard as I could into my chest. Then her hands were on me, pushing me away. Confused, I stepped back, looked at her.

"Are you kidding?" she said, smiling. "This is a first date. You don't get to hug before the movie popcorn."

"Wait, a first date?" I said. "Was I imagining, you know, our whole relationship?"

"Uh-uh. But when I thought about it, I realized we'd never really gone on an actual first date. Meeting when you were on the run for your life and all. So I thought let's go back, start where we never got the chance. Dinner and a movie, sport."

"Shouldn't I pay, then?"

"This is the twenty-first century, Henry, get real. Besides, I think I make more money than you."

"I can't say no, can I?"

Amanda smiled "Do you really want to?"

"Not in the slightest."

"Just a date," she said. "Then we'll go from there."

"Just give me one more chance," I said, "and I promise it will be worth it."

* * * * *

Coming in 2010
The next Henry Parker novel
THE FURY
by Jason Pinter

1

At nine in the morning, the offices of the *New York Gazette* were usually quiet as reporters read the morning papers, got ready to call their sources and blinked off hangovers. Today, however, it was a different kind of quiet. The "something must be wrong" kind of quiet.

I'd exited the elevators onto the ninth floor, expecting the usual quiet walk to my desk. Yet when I navigated the mess of chairs and debris and entered the cubicle farm, I noticed the other journalists who shared my row were nowhere to be seen.

I put my coffee and muffin down on the desk, debated simply pulling up the little plastic tab, sitting down and enjoying my breakfast. But to ignore the strange stillness of the office would have been going against every bone in my body. So I took a lap around the news floor to see what the hell was going on.

I didn't have to go far.

Half a dozen reporters were huddled around the desk of Evelyn Waterstone, the *Gazette*'s Metro editor. They were talking under their breaths, worried looks in their eyes. I wondered if there were going to be layoffs. If some of my colleagues—perhaps even myself—would be out of a job. That Evelyn had seemingly replaced the water cooler as the center of office scoop was itself noteworthy. Evelyn stayed as far away from gossip as those who gossiped stayed away from her. Whatever had happened had to be big. I walked up casually, inserting myself into the conversation through proximity alone.

"Morning, Parker," Evelyn said. She held a black Thermos between her fleshy hands, and took a long, drawn-out sip. "Another beautiful day at your local newspaper."

"Morning, Evelyn," I said, nodded hello to the other reporters, who offered the same. "What gives? One of the windows on the seventeenth floor fall out again?"

Jonas Levinson, the *Gazette*'s science editor, said, "As a matter of fact, something has died this morning. Something precious that needs to be mourned as long as we're employed by this godforsaken newspaper. As of today, my young Henry, good taste has kicked the bucket."

I stared at Jonas, waiting for some kind of explanation. Levinson was a tall man, balding, who wore a different bow tie to the office every day. He very seldom exaggerated his feelings, so at Jonas's remark a flock of butterflies began to flutter around in my stomach.

"I'm not following you," I said to Jonas. "Good taste? Evelyn, care to explain?"

"Just follow the eyes, Parker," Evelyn said. "Follow the eyes."

I opened my mouth to ask another question, but then I realized what she was saying. The eyes of every member of our group were focused on two individuals making their way across the *Gazette*'s floor. They were stopping at each desk, popping into each office, where it looked as if some sort of introductory ritual was taking place.

One of the two men was Wallace Langston, editor-in-chief. The other I didn't recognize.

"Is Wallace," I said, "introducing a new reporter?"

"Reporter? Hardly," Jonas replied.

Frank Rourke, the sports editor, said, "I never met a damn person until my first staff meeting. I got as much of an introduction to my colleagues as my stove has to my cooking pot."

"Same here," I said.

Wallace was still too far away to make out who he was introducing around the office or what his beat was, but I got the feeling Wallace would prefer if he didn't have to do the ritual en masse.

"I'm going back to my desk," I said. "Jonas, if you see good taste anywhere, I'll get the electric paddles and we'll resuscitate the bastard."

"Thank you for the offer, Henry, but I do believe time of death has already been established as—" he checked his watch "—8:58 a.m."

I walked back to my desk, trying not to think about what this could mean. The *Gazette* had been on a recent hiring freeze. We were in a war with our rival, the *New York Dispatch,* over circulation rates, advertising dollars and stories, and our efforts were taking a toll. If Harvey Hillerman, the president and owner of the *Gazette,* had hired a new reporter, he or she had to be a big enough name to cause a stir. Not to mention someone who would be approved of by the other reporters whose pay raises had been nixed last holiday season.

I sat down and was about to pick up the phone when I heard the sound of footsteps approaching my desk. I looked up to see Wallace Langston. And standing next to him, his mystery hire.

"Henry Parker," Wallace said, hand outstretched, "meet Tony Valentine."

Tony Valentine was six foot three, svelte to the point of gaunt, with the plastic smile of a cruise ship director. His hair was bleached blond, his teeth glistened and his cheekbones looked artificial. When he extended his hand to shake mine, I noticed that his palms were much paler than the rest of his bronze skin. The beauty of spray-on tans. Valentine wore a designer suit, a red pocket square neatly tucked into the pocket. The initials *T.V.* were embroidered in white script on the cloth.

His sleeves were held together by two gold cufflinks. Also monogrammed with *T.V.*

Clearly this man did not want his name to be forgotten.

"Henry Parker," Valentine said, gushing insincerity. "It's just such a pleasure to finally meet you. I've been following your career ever since that nasty business a few years back. All those guns and bullets, and now here I am, working with you. Sir, it is an *honor.*"

I shook Valentine's hand, then looked at Wallace. The name Tony Valentine sounded familiar, but I couldn't quite place it....

"Tony is our new gossip reporter," Wallace said enthusiastically. "We were able to pluck him from *Us Weekly.* Today is his first day."

"And not a day too soon," Tony said, pressing the back of his hand against his forehead, as though diagnosing a strange malady. "As much as I admire your paper—and, Wallace, please don't think otherwise—it's lacking a certain *pizzazz.* A certain *panache,* if you will. A certain sexiness."

"Let me guess," I said. "You're here to bring sexy back."

Tony pursed his lips and smiled. "You're a clever one,

Henry. I'm going to have to keep an eye on you. Maybe both if you misbehave. So guess the name of my new column."

"Do I have to?"

"You most certainly do." Tony waited a moment, then blurted out, "Valentine's Day. Because at the *Gazette,* Valentine's Day comes five days a week. Isn't that a riot?"

"Yeah, just like L.A. and Crown Heights."

Tony said, "Listen, Henry, it's been a pretty pleasure. We'll *have* to go out for a celebratory cocktail one of these nights. I want to hear *all* about what you're working on. Okay?"

"I'll check my calendar right away."

"Terrific. Wallace, on with the show?"

As Tony and Wallace walked away, I saw Wallace turn toward me. There was a remorseful look in his eye. Immediately I knew Tony's hire was at the behest of Harvey Hillerman. Gossip was a commodity in this town. I knew it, had been the subject of it. For the most part, the *Gazette* had kept its beak clean, relegating society and gossip stories to the weekend Leisure sections. Now, though, times were changing. I wondered how much an embroidered pocket square cost.

I left the *Gazette* thoroughly exhausted. Crossing through Rockefeller Plaza, I checked my cell phone. One message, from Amanda. We'd been seeing each other steadily over the past few months, trying to start over on a relationship that broke from the gate too fast. I didn't want to screw things up this time, so I was more than happy to take it slowly.

As I put the phone to my ear, I heard a strange voice call out, "Henry Parker?"

I turned to see a man approaching me. He was dirty and

disheveled, wearing rags that looked about to fall off his deathly skinny and pallid frame. His eyes were bloodshot, fingernails dirty. He looked to be in his early thirties. I'd never seen the man before in my life, yet for some reason he looked oddly familiar.

"Are you," he said, the words coming out through rotted teeth, "Henry Parker?"

I picked up the pace. I had no idea how this man knew my name, but from the looks of him I certainly didn't want to find out.

"I am," I said, speeding up as I walked through Rockefeller Plaza. The man kept pace. His sneakers were falling apart, and the gray overcoat he wore was tattered and soiled.

"Please, Henry, I need to talk to you. Oh, God, it's important."

"Call the *Gazette* tomorrow," I said. I gave him the switchboard number. He didn't seem to care. I walked faster, a slow trot, but my heart began to race when I saw that the man was matching my pace.

"Henry," he said, his eyes now terrified, "please stop. It'll only take a minute. I'm begging you, man!"

"Sorry, don't have time," I said. I broke into a jog, crossing the street just as the light turned red. As I reached the other side, I looked back. The man looked prepared to race through the oncoming traffic, but then thought better of it.

Our eyes met for one moment. His were pleading, scared, and for a moment I debated crossing back over to see what he wanted. Then I saw him reach into his pocket, put something to his nose and take a quick snort. That was all I needed to see.

I turned around and headed toward the subway. If he

really needed to reach me, he could call. I'd been through enough over the past few years to know there were some people you needed to turn your back on.

2

I stopped to pick up some pasta for dinner on my way home, got up my laundry and managed to check the mail before collapsing under a pile of errands when I entered the apartment. I peeled off my clothes, put the food in the fridge and stepped into a hot shower. The day seemed to rinse right off me. I thought about the man who'd confronted me, how there was a look of genuine terror in his eyes. I began to regret turning away. Maybe he would call the next day. I wondered what he needed to talk to me about that was so urgent.

When I got out of the shower, I threw on a pair of shorts and a T-shirt and put the spaghetti in the microwave. I sat down and began to eat, washing the food down with a glass of iced tea. I splayed a few newspapers in front of me and read while I ate. The *Gazette*'s pages looked naked without the familiar byline of Jack O'Donnell. I hoped wherever he was, Jack was getting the treatment he needed.

Dinner was a long affair. I made the pasta last, and savored every word in the newspapers. I was fascinated at just how many stories there were within this small city, and excited at how many were out there waiting to be uncovered.

When I finished dinner, I got up to put my dishes in the

sink and my cell phone rang. I put the plate down and picked it up. Didn't recognize the caller ID.

I clicked Send and said, "This is Parker."

"Henry Parker?" the voice on the other end said.

"Yes. Who may I ask is calling?"

"Henry, this is Detective Makhoulian with the NYPD. Are you busy tonight?"

I looked at my watch. It was nearly ten o'clock. What the hell did the cops want with me at this hour?

"Detective, can I ask what this is about?"

"Let me ask you a question, Mr. Parker. Does a man fitting this description sound familiar? About six-two, thin as a bone. Brown hair, hazel eyes, the look of a serious drug problem, among other things. That ring a bell?"

I felt my pulse quicken. "Actually, a man fitting that description was waiting for me outside my office tonight when I left. He tried to speak to me, but from the look of things he wasn't the kind of person you want to get close to."

"Interesting," Makhoulian said. "Listen, Mr. Parker, I'm going to need you to come down to the medical examiner's office right away. You know where it is?"

"Thirtieth and First. I've been there before. I'm a reporter."

"I know who you are, Mr. Parker. I'm going to need you to meet me there in one hour. Will that be a problem?"

"No, but I would like to know what all this is about."

"This man I'm speaking of, he was found an hour ago in an apartment in Alphabet City, dead from a single gunshot wound to the head. We have reason to believe you were the last person to see him alive."

"Okay," I said, my stomach beginning to turn. The last thing I wanted was to get tied up in the murder of a homeless junkie who happened to have seen my name in the newspaper. "Listen, Detective, no disrespect, but this guy probably saw one of my stories and figured a reporter might be more inclined to listen to a junkie than a cop. And now he's dead, and while it really is a shame, I don't think there's much I can offer to help your investigation."

"I disagree," Makhoulian said. "This man's name was Stephen Gaines. Does that ring a bell?"

"No, Detective, it doesn't."

"That's interesting. I'm going to need you to meet me at the ME's office right away. Because according to his medical records, Stephen Gaines was your brother."

Right as I'm about to die, I realise all the myths are fake. My life isn't flashing before my eyes. All I can think about is how much I want to live.

I moved to New York City to become the best journalist the world had seen. And now here I am, twenty-four years old and weary beyond rational thought, a bullet one trigger-pull from ending my life.

I thought I had the story all figured out. I know that both of these men – one an FBI agent, the other an assassin – want me dead, but for very different reasons.

If I die tonight, more people will die tomorrow.

www.mirabooks.co.uk

A shot rings out in the New York night. A starlet is murdered outside the city's most popular club.

This is the kind of story I was born to chase. My search leads me into a twisted world of shocking secrets. When the killer realises I'm getting too close to the truth, uncovering the past could jeopardise everything I care about.

In this world there's a fine line between good and evil, and the difference between innocence and guilt depends on who's holding the gun...

www.mirabooks.co.uk